Silent Fathoms

Silent Fathoms

Waves of Darkness Book 3

Tamara A. Lowery

Steele Rose Publishing

Silent Fathoms

By Tamara A. Lowery

Dedication

The National Geographic Society and the Smithsonian Institution for inspiration on places to take Viktor in this story.

Table of Contents

Foreword, Acknowledgements, and Warnings

For new readers of the Waves of Darkness series, welcome to Silent Fathoms, the third book in the series. Word count: 68,692. Being the third book, and seeing the opinion asserted among several readers and reviewers (first noticed on a video by Book Tuber, Petrik Leo; go watch his channel), I have decided to start including a "Here be Spoilers" synopsis section. This is a long series, and it will help keep readers up to date on the story thus far as they advance through the books. This will be in the after matter, with a link in the Table of Contents for quick access, in the ebook editions (reason being less clutter of the sample selection before the story for prospective readers).

Back in 2005, my husband and I thought about how popular pirates were becoming and of the continuing, if slightly waning at the time, popularity of vampires. To our knowledge, no one was combining the two. By 2006, I'd finished initial research on pirates and piracy (you must know the rules in order to properly break them, after all) and begun penning the first book in a hardbound journal someone had gifted my husband.

Of course, I learned later that several iterations of the combination of pirates and vampires were popping up in various formats. I will say that my take on things is sufficiently different enough from other content out there in the same vein (sorry, I had to) to avoid treading on others' toes.

Silent Fathoms originally saw publication through Gypsy Shadow Publishing in 2013. I split with them in 2018, mere months after the publication of the seventh book in the series, and all rights reverted to me.

Seeing as how I was unable to secure a new publisher, I decided to revise the books and release the second editions self-published. I plan to release the original seven books in the series, which complete the Sisters of Power story arc, at six-month intervals: namely every May and November.

Blood Curse was released November 2021 in ebook and paperback formats and is now available on Audible (and supposedly iTunes; I don't own an Apple device, so I can't check) as an audio book edition narrated by Greg D. Barnett.

Demon Bayou was released May 2022 in ebook and paperback formats. I hope to be able to bring it to audio sometime in the near future. Sales of the audio version of Blood Curse will decide that matter. Audio books are NOT cheap to make.

I have already started drafting a second seven books for the Daughters of the Dragon story arc, which will complete the series. I seriously doubt I can maintain the six-month schedule for their release dates, but I will try to get them out in one-year intervals. I managed to accomplish that with the series' first run, after all.

Now for the warnings.

My pirates are not nice. They murder and occasionally rape. This is not behavior I condone, but it is historically accurate, and I'm NOT writing YA here.

The books are set during the American Revolutionary period, so female characters are subjected to the prevailing male attitudes and treatment of the time. I DO have strong female characters throughout the story, but the ones not magically inclined are written somewhat realistically.

Vampires, by definition, are serial killers.

Viktor Brandewyne can be a massive asshole at times.

Finally, it's time for the acknowledgements. I'll keep them short.

I want to thank my husband, Derik, for helping me conceive this whole hoo-hah. Without him, there would be no Viktor, Grimm, or Belladonna. I also want to thank all my online and convention author friends for their advice and support in getting the tools and knowledge to get these books back on the market. They are too many to name in a short space.

Once Upon a Tide...

Hezekiah had to admit the boy had balls. He'd had his doubts three months ago, when he'd signed on to this crew. After all, how many fools would be willing to ship out with a nineteen-year-old captain and a fifteen-year-old first mate? If it hadn't been for the fact that Billy Black had vouched for him, he never would have considered sailing under Vik Brandee.

He still remembered the night he'd walked into the Black Flag in Savannah looking for a crew to sign on to. Though not the only man off that damned unlucky ship to head to the tavern, he still missed those who hadn't made it. A few he'd even called good friends.

He felt like an old man already, at the tender age of twenty-five, especially after that last voyage. Why had he signed on with that idiot, Kerns? How the man had gained a captaincy was beyond him.

Kerns couldn't navigate, was a piss-poor pirate, and couldn't hold his liquor. The hunters almost caught them because of that bastard's idiocy. If not for the storm the twit sailed them into only to wreck them on the shoals, Grimm would've led a mutiny and taken the ship. Just as well he hadn't. At first glance, the ship looked seaworthy enough, but it proved rotten, leaky, and ill-outfitted.

Still, when the crew finally realized they were going down and made for the boats, Hezekiah took great satisfaction in slitting his former captain's throat. He vowed then to never serve under a man so unworthy of his respect again.

"Mr. Grimm," the fat old pirate-turned-tavern-keeper acknowledged him. "Been a couple of seasons since I've seen ye in these parts. What brings you to the Black Flag?"

"Let's just say I'm between boats."

Billy squinted at him. "Word has it you were sailing with Rob Kerns. I find it hard to believe. The man's an idiot."

Hezekiah grimaced. "Yes, he *was*. But it's true. I last shipped under him."

"Notice ye said was."

"I left him with a second smile, bright and red, when we parted company."

The old pirate smirked. "About time. Someone should have slit the bastard's throat years ago. Reckon the ship wasn't worth taking?"

Grimm shook his head. "No, he ran aground, and it started breaking up. Worm-eaten anyway."

"Heh. Doesn't surprise me. Why don't you head on upstairs? Maggie should be unoccupied right now, provided that little bastard hasn't sneaked up there hoping for a free one. Told 'im if I caught him doing that again, I'd take it out of his wages."

"Thank ye, Captain Black." Hezekiah knew Margery was one of the Black flag's most talented girls.

"When ye come back down, come see me." Billy tapped him with his pipe. "I've got a business proposition for you."

Hezekiah thought his luck seemed to get better and better. He hadn't been so sure, though, when he'd heard what the proposition was. "Are you daft, man? I just came off a ship with a captain that never should have been, and now you're suggesting I sign on under a boy?"

"Don't underestimate the bastard," Billy cautioned. "He has real talent for our kind of work. Earned a berth here with me a few years ago and has learned more about our craft in that time than many do in a lifetime. Not just stories, either. I think the brat was born to piracy, but don't let him know I said that. He's got a big enough head, as it is."

Grimm thought he understood what the old pirate was doing. "He's gotten too dangerous for you to keep him around, hasn't he?"

Billy Black shrugged. "Voracious wencher has cost me money. Tired of my whores being too worn out to service the paying customers. Figure if he's out to sea, he can't cause trouble here. Told him if he could secure a ship, I'd help him assemble a crew. Damned if the bugger didn't show up two days later with a decent little sloop."

"Impressive. Very well, I'll give him a try. He'll need experienced mates."

"Aye, but don't hope for first mate. That berth's already filled."

"Who?"

"Little alley cat called Jim Rigger. Young Vik teamed up with the brat not long after he came to work for me." He pointed out a teenager lurking near a table of drunken sailors. The lad picked a few pockets even as they watched.

Tamara A. Lowery

"A child." Grimm was less than impressed.

Billy chuckled at his reaction. "They're cut from the same bolt, those two. Closer than brothers and thoroughly wicked. Jim is sneaky as a cat and more loyal than a dog, where Vik is concerned. I wouldn't suggest trying to separate them. Don't know about Jim, but I do believe Vik Brandee wouldn't hesitate to cut yer heart out and hand it to you with a smile, if you did."

"I'll keep that in mind."

Looking back, he had no regrets about his decision. Brandee truly had a talent for finding and taking fat prizes. It had been the most profitable three months he'd experienced since he'd turned pirate.

He was also impressed by Brandee's intelligence, ruthlessness, and skills. As far as he was concerned, the young captain had earned his loyalty and respect. He had even found that Rigger was tolerable as a first mate. Sometimes, it was easy to forget that the boy was ten years his junior.

It became apparent that a few of his shipmates didn't share his views, however. He'd heard grumblings. It never ceased to amaze him at the stupidity a man's pride could push him to. So, he listened, he watched, then, when he felt the time was right, he acted.

"Enter," Brandee answered from his cabin. He remained calm but alert when he saw who it was. *"So, things have finally come to a head."* He was mildly surprised to see that the bastards had picked Grimm as the one to do it. "What is it, Mr. Grimm?"

"I came to warn you, Captain. Some of the lads have been talking mutiny."

"I see. What about you, Mr. Grimm? Are you throwing your lot in with them?"

Grimm sized the lad up. By his reaction, he was willing to bet Brandee had known about the unrest for quite some time. "If you had asked me three months ago, I probably would have said yes. It did not sit well with me to have such a young captain."

Viktor steepled his fingers and leaned forward, his green eyes intense. His voice was deceptively calm with a hint of curiosity. "What has happened to change your mind?"

"Old Billy Black knew what he was talking about, when he said you were born to this life. These three months have been the most profitable I have ever seen. I also admire the intelligence behind your way of using different tactics with each prize."

"Why?"

"It'll make you harder to predict, therefore harder for the hunters to catch. Most pirates have one or two attacks at the most. Once a pirate's enemies figure it out, they can figure out where and when he is likely to strike next and lay a trap for him. That is something I would like to avoid, personally. Sticking with you would be my best bet for doing so."

Brandee smirked. "When you came in here, I half-expected you to be the one they picked to take my place." He stood and walked around the small desk to get a rum bottle, deliberately turning his back on the older man.

Grimm quickly took advantage of the situation. Cat-quick, he rushed up behind Brandee and had his blade at the young man's throat before he could put the bottle down. "If I'd wanted to take this ship, you'd already be dead, Captain."

"Then you'd have followed right behind him, Mr. Grimm," Jim Rigger whispered in his ear, his own blade pricking just below Grimm's ear. The boy had been silently lurking in the shadows behind the door the whole time.

Vik slipped easily out of the deadly position. Smiling, he picked up three glasses and said, "It's a good thing for you that you didn't come here to kill me then, isn't it, Mr. Grimm? Have a drink. You can put your knife away, Jim."

"Aye, Cap'n." The boy and the man both sheathed their weapons.

"Now then, Mr. Grimm, since you've chosen to warn me, what can you tell me about the mutineers, and what suggestions would you make on handling them?"

"There is only a handful stirring the others up. Take them out, and the mutiny will die."

Jim spoke up. "Isn't the usual punishment for mutiny marooning?"

"It is," Vik confirmed. "But I don't think that is what Mr. Grimm would suggest."

Grimm shook his head. "I would kill them; make an example. You have been a very generous, successful captain. It's my opinion that they are ungrateful fools. That point won't be lost on the rest of the lads."

Viktor looked at him without expression for several minutes. Hezekiah never flinched, even though he could see the younger man wouldn't hesitate to kill him.

"I like the way you think, Mr. Grimm. Assemble the crew on deck at first light. Be prepared to point out the ringleaders."

"Aye, Captain. Thank you for the rum."

☠

"I hear some of you aren't too happy to be sailing under my command."

A cautious murmuring was the only answer Brandee got. He pressed on after making eye contact, first with Jim and Hezekiah, then with the five men Grimm had named as the mutineers. "I make no apologies for my age. During these three months we have taken several fat prizes. Shares have been generous. Casualties have been low. We haven't been captured. What is the problem?"

More murmuring, mostly in agreement with the young captain's words, answered the question. Also, agitation spread among the mutineers. They saw their hold on the crew evaporate in those few minutes.

Viktor and his mates fully expected one of them to make a move at this point. Jim and Grimm, in anticipation, positioned themselves by the ones they felt to be most dangerous. But none of those men were the one who acted.

Grimm stood closest, as a grizzled pirate pulled a dragoon out, cocked it and aimed at Brandee's head. "Stop him!" he yelled, even as the man squeezed the trigger.

With no time to reach the would-be killer, he jumped in front of his captain, taking the mini ball in the upper arm. As he fell, he wondered why the young man was reaching to scratch the back of his neck.

Mere seconds later, the assassin lay dead on the deck with Viktor's dagger protruding from his eye.

Jim watched with morbid fascination as the sailor, the closest thing they had to a surgeon, dug the fragments out of Hezekiah's bicep. To his credit, the older man no more than grunted and gave an occasional hiss, as the man did his work. Luckily, the powder had been damp and a low charge. That meant the mini ball remained mostly intact and lodged in the muscle. The bone wasn't even fractured.

"There, that's the last of it I think," he told Grimm.

"Thank ye, Gordon. Heat that knife up red hot and sear the wound before you stitch me back up. It'll help stop the bleeding," Grimm directed.

To his satisfaction, the boy winced at the smell of burning skin and meat. Grimm grinned at the lad's reaction.

"That's going to leave a nasty scar," Jim whistled as Gordon began stitching the puckered, charred wound shut.

"Not the first; won't be the last," Grimm shrugged. "If it's too jagged, I can just cover it with a tattoo. At least I didn't lose the arm."

"You could have been killed. I knew I would kill or die for the Captain, but I never imagined anyone else would. Why?"

"Young though he is, Vik Brandee is the best captain I've ever sailed under. He deserves my respect and loyalty. Don't worry, Mr. Rigger, I'm not after your berth. Old Billy Black warned me against that, and I've seen how the two of you work together. But I'll gladly sail as one of Brandee's mates as long as he will have me."

Chapter 1

Viktor and Grimm sat in the captain's cabin sharing a couple of fine Havanas and some French cognac. Viktor had liberated the liquor from the Lord Mayor's mansion at the same time he'd relieved the man of his daughter. He doubted the Lord Mayor of New Orleans would see it that way, but he felt he'd done him a favor. The girl was a complete ninny, mediocre in bed, and would've been useless as a bargaining chip for a marriage alliance. Any man she would've been married off to would have eventually decided she wasn't worth the trade.

He wondered how long before the vampire, Jeorge, would grow tired of her and end her undead existence. He knew Jeorge only wanted her to keep an eye on his activities, but that window worked both ways. Not that Vik cared what the king vampire of New Orleans did, as long as he didn't violate their agreement concerning Celine Thibideaux and Angelique's brothel.

Melanie's kidnapping and turning also served another purpose for Viktor. It would cause trouble for Brumble and Sons Trading Company. He had both the Brumble boys as prisoners. The younger, he had used to replace one of his vampires from his small cadre and used his name as an alias to gain entrance to the mayor's household. As far as Melanie's father knew, she'd been kidnapped by Thomas Brumble. He never even knew he'd really been dealing with the notorious pirate, Viktor Brandewyne.

Vik had a personal vendetta against Tobias Brumble, Zachary and Thomas' father. The man had nearly beaten Jim Rigger to death when the lad had been his cabin boy, before meeting and befriending Vik. He really had nothing against Brumble's sons. Both had proven to be fairly decent men. They were merely tools to punish the father. He needed to decide what to do with Zachary.

A knock came at the door.

"Enter, Mr. Jon."

Grimm barely spared a glance at his captain, used to the fact of Viktor's acute awareness of everyone under his command. The practice of treating the entire crew, with the exception of Belladonna and himself, periodically to rum tainted with a few drops of the vampire's blood severely cut down on crew members getting out of line. He found this made his job much easier.

"Cap'n, the prisoner is asking to see you."

"Asking?"

Jon-Jon grinned. "Aye. After a few hours of demanding with no result, he's decided to ask. Even said 'please'."

"Well, since he was so polite, I guess I can oblige him. Bring him up," Viktor instructed.

"Aye, Cap'n."

Grimm took a sip of cognac then drew on his cigar. Blowing out a smoke ring, he asked, "Any plans for the man, Vik? By both his and his brother's admission, his sire won't pay any ransom."

Viktor puffed his own cigar for a few moments before he answered. "I've already got Thomas for information on Brumble's shipping business. Belladonna's shown an interest in him that I am not too happy about. Still, he is able-bodied, and his brother vouches for him." He smoked some more, then seemed to reach a decision mentally. "I'm feeling generous today, Hezekiah. We'll let Mr. Brumble decide his own fate."

Grimm raised an eyebrow. "This should be interesting."

A large black cat darted through the door ahead of Jon-Jon and Zachary Brumble. It bounded onto the desk then onto Viktor's shoulder. The pirate captain reached up and scratched the cat's head. "Hello, Lazarus. Good afternoon, Mr. Brumble. Would you care for a drink or a smoke?"

Zach shook his head. "No thank you, Captain. No offense, but the last time I accepted refreshments from you, I woke up a prisoner."

"Pity," he chuckled. "The cognac is excellent."

"If it's all right, I wouldn't mind trying some of that, Cap'n," Jon-Jon spoke up.

"Help yourself. About time you had something other than that rot-gut gin you're so fond of."

"Mother's milk."

"Only if your mother was a poorly built still. No, wait, I keep forgetting, she was a drunken whore."

All three pirates laughed at the old joke.

To his credit, Zachary held himself tall and straight during this exchange. It was the first time he had seen Brandee since he had been taken captive. Grimm, he had seen just a few days ago, when the first mate had interrupted some of the most amazing sex he had ever had. He fought to keep from smiling at the memory of the only female member of the pirate crew. He prayed he could fight off the erection it was trying to give him.

"Mr. Jon tells me that you wished to see me."

"Yes, sir, I have two matters to discuss with you."

The man's scent piqued Viktor's curiosity. "What are your concerns, Mr. Brumble?" He could smell both desire and fear, which was confusing. Also, there was something off about the fear scent. It wasn't terror, but more of a sort of worry. He found himself genuinely interested in what the man had to say.

"The woman, I think her name is Belladonna?" Viktor nodded to confirm the name, so Zach continued, "I need to know that she is safe and has not been harmed because of our indiscretion."

All three pirates blinked at the man. This was clearly not what any of them had expected from him.

"Why do you care what happens to her?" Viktor kept all emotion out of his voice.

"I could have refused her attentions. Had I known in advance that she did not have your permission, I would have. If anyone is to be punished, then punish me."

Grimm smirked. "I'm glad she hasn't bedded me, if she can bewitch a man that quickly."

Viktor ignored the remark. "Belle has not been harmed for that. Given her nature, such action would be pointless. She is an extremely willful creature and will do whatever she wishes, whether I say yea or nay. Be warned, though, sir, that she is the only one under my command that I will tolerate such behavior from."

Zachary relaxed a bit. "I am glad to find you have such a chivalrous demeanor toward women, sir."

That set off a round of raucous laughter, which quite confused the man. After a few moments, Viktor wiped his eyes and explained the joke. His mirthful grin made it impossible to hide his fangs.

"Belle being female has nothing to do with it. She is no more human than I am."

"I do not understand."

"You are one of the few men to have ever survived being bedded by a siren, boy. You're lucky she didn't rip you apart."

"I'll grant you she was more vigorous than I am used to, but nothing she did was painful."

"If she ever offers to go swimming with you, turn her down, Mr. Brumble. Belladonna likes to play with her food."

Zach blanched at the realization the pirate captain was deadly serious. "A siren? A real, honest-to-God siren? Does she turn into a mermaid? Can she really lure men to the death with her song?"

Viktor made a so-so motion with his hand. "You're only partially right. Her true form is half-shark, but never confuse a siren with a mermaid. Mermaids don't eat sirens. In fact, mermaid is her favorite food, man-flesh being a close second. Her song is not mesmerizing, although it is magical. Pray you never hear her scream. It can destroy a man's mind beyond repair. Death is preferable."

"If it's not too much to ask, how is her singing magical if it does not bewitch?"

"She is a weather witch. She can sing up a favorable wind to speed you on your way, or she may be-calm a ship without affecting any other vessels around it." Viktor grimaced at the memory. "And she is a vindictive bitch."

"Meh." Lazarus had to get his comment in.

"Back to business," Vik agreed with the cat. "What is your other concern, Mr. Brumble?"

Zach blinked as he refocused. His befuddlement when Belladonna was discussed, or just at the thought of her, convinced him that the nonsense about sirens might be true.

"Mr. Brumble?"

He shook himself and straightened his posture. "I want to petition to join your crew."

"Indeed." Viktor steepled his fingers, placed his elbows on the desk and leaned forward. "And what do you have to offer in skills? I've sailors enough to man this ship."

"I am a top-notch navigator. I have extensive knowledge of the trade routes, as well as the alternate routes used by my father's ships to cut down time and increase profit."

Viktor held up a hand to stop him. "A good navigator is always valuable, but I have your brother for the other information." He took a sip of cognac and waited to see if this would fluster the younger man.

Zach smiled, undeterred. "Thom has been captaining ships for only two years. I had command for nine, before you captured me. I know the names of all Father's fleet and who captains each one. I also know which ones will fight, run, or surrender, where they can be found at what time of the year, and what their probable cargo will be."

Viktor remained silent for several minutes; his facial expression gave away none of his thoughts. Zachary awaited his response patiently, refusing to fidget.

"Why?"

"Excuse me?"

"Why are you willing to give up such valuable information, Mr. Brumble? No physical threat has been made, nor have you been tortured or deprived of sustenance."

He sighed, his eyes showing sadness and resignation. "It was not an easy decision for me to reach, Captain Brandewyne. My father is not a trusting man, and I've striven for years to prove his paranoia that I would turn against him wrong."

"Why now? And why would he fear that from his own son?" Grimm asked.

"Father remembers what happened to the Chapelwaites. I've lost track of how many times he threatened or warned us not to do what old Mudstick did to his father."

Hezekiah and Viktor both grinned. "Them Buggers!" they laughed in unison.

"Any encounter with the crew of the *Braying Ass* is an interesting and unusual experience," Vik smiled, "and not for the weak of stomach."

Zach made a face. "I've heard the stories. Not sure if it's an experience I'd care to have. Anyway, the reason why now and not before is that I can't go back. By now, my father has sent a report to his backer that I betrayed him and threw in with pirates, even if he doesn't believe it to be the truth."

"Why would your da do that?" Jon-Jon asked.

Viktor gave a knowing smile and answered for his prisoner. "Because it's good business. If he were to defend Zachary, it would look to his as-yet-unnamed partner as if he and his sons had plotted to defraud him. That, given the nature of the smuggling business, could prove fatal."

Tamara A. Lowery

"Exactly, sir," Zach confirmed.

The vampire's sharp eyes caught a detail that hadn't been apparent when the prisoner had first come in.

Zach had been standing at parade rest most of the time, with his hands tucked behind his back. As he started to relax, he'd allowed his hands to hang at his sides. There, on his right hand, was a healing wound.

Faster than even Grimm could follow, Viktor darted around the desk and grasped Brumble's wrist. He held the man's hand up to examine it. "What happened to your hand, Mr. Brumble? This looks recent."

It startled Zach to find the pirate captain right next to him, when he had just been seated across the desk from him barely a moment before. It served to hammer home what his brother had told him. The man was definitely not human. "Your cat bit me."

"Why?"

"I didn't trust the food that was first brought to me, until I saw the creature eat it without harm. He bit me, when I took the plate away from him."

"I see." Vik looked at where Lazarus perched, washing his face. The cat had moved to the desktop, when Viktor rounded the piece of furniture. "It seems that this decision has been removed from my hands. What say you, Lazarus? Shall we let Mr. Brumble join the crew?"

"You're asking the cat?" Zach wondered if Brandee was mad.

Grimm cautioned, "Lazarus is more than just a cat."

The animal in question lazily stood up, walked across the desk, and sniffed at the prisoner. He turned his head sideways then blinked up at the captain. He gave one decisive nod and vocalized, "Myeh." Then he became intensely interested in chewing the fur between the toes of his left hind-foot.

"Very well, welcome aboard, Mr. Brumble."

"Thank you, Captain." He couldn't leave it alone, however. "Sir, I have to ask, why did you ask the cat?"

"You belong to him. When Lazarus bit you, he marked you as his property. As Mr. Grimm pointed out, he is more than just a cat." He smiled mischievously and ordered, "Lazarus, prepare to take flight."

At the command, the cat dissolved into smoke then reformed as a raven. With a hop and a flutter, he perched himself back on Viktor's shoulder.

"Demon," Zach whispered and blanched.

Viktor laughed. "Not quite. In all honesty, I'm no longer sure how to describe what he is now. Not quite a year ago, he was my first mate, Jim Rigger."

"The same Jim Rigger you say my father abused?"

"Aye, the same. Now, Mr. Jon take Mr. Brumble and find him a berth, then find something for him to do."

"Aye, Cap'n."

Tamara A. Lowery

Chapter 2

After nearly a week's absence, the siren returned to the ship. She'd been hunting the whole time, working to rebuild her strength and magic. Their encounter with Gloribeau, the second of the seven Sisters of Power who Viktor had to locate, had drained her power reserves enough to almost kill her — or worse, transform her into a mortal human. Belladonna could take human form, but it was not her natural state.

Her need proved great enough to lead her to kill all of her victims quickly. Under normal circumstances, she liked to play with her food.

She'd already told the Captain of the vision that came to her after consuming the sailors he'd sacrificed to save and revive her. He'd wasted no time in setting a course for Mexico, where she'd sensed the next Sister to be. But the vision had been weak and vague.

Her subsequent feeding frenzy fully restored her power and granted her a much more detailed vision. She went straight to her cabin to dress. Viktor didn't like her wandering the ship naked. Personally, she felt clothing to be a silly human custom, but it would save time on delivering her message if he wasn't angry or distracted.

A knock came at the door just as she finished dressing and prepared to leave her cabin.

Viktor sensed her the moment she came aboard. He could tell she was fully revitalized. He felt no concern, when she didn't report directly to him. He knew she had probably gone to her cabin to dress, and he appreciated her compliance.

When she still hadn't sought him out after nearly an hour, he grew a bit irked. Reaching out along the link they shared, he came up against her mental shields. That told him she was doing or had done something she didn't want him to know about.

Rather than force his way through the blocks, he set off for her cabin, raising his own shields in the process. He didn't want to give her any warning of his approach.

☠

The sight of Zach at the door surprised the siren. He had still been a prisoner, when she'd left to hunt. Scenting his lust made seeing his expression melt from joyful hope to confused disappointment almost comical.

"Was there something you wanted?" she asked, fully knowing that he wanted another go-round with her.

Zach recovered quickly. "I saw you pass through the corridor and wanted to make sure you were all right. I hadn't seen you since we were together, and even though the Captain said otherwise, I had to know that you hadn't been punished."

She smiled, both touched and amused by his concern. "That was sweet of you, but I'm sure the Captain told you it would be pointless to punish me for merely following my nature."

"So, you don't need his permission?"

"Hardly," she laughed.

He took that as an invitation. "Good because I've wanted to do this for days." He embraced her and kissed her passionately.

Though not unexpected, she didn't entirely welcome the advance, either. She endured the kiss for a few moments before pushing him away.

"What's wrong? I thought…," he began.

"And that was your first mistake," she told him. At that moment, she scented Viktor approaching. No sound or mental presence warned of him coming, which told her he was shielding from her. She felt it only fair, since her shields stood against him, as well. His distinct scent, unlike that of any other human or vampire on board, made him stand out to her. That, he couldn't hide.

Elevating her voice enough to make sure her Captain heard clearly, she quickly disillusioned Zachary. "What we did was fun, but I do not have sex except when I choose to, and with whom I choose. You were just convenient for me. Do not take that to mean that you mean anything to me. I am a Siren. I like to play with my food." To emphasize the point, she allowed her true teeth and golden eye color to show.

Zach stumbled back in shock, bumping into Viktor in the process. The Captain rested a hand on his shoulder and chuckled at the display.

Tamara A. Lowery

"I warned you, Mr. Brumble."

Belle took mercy, a rarity for her, but she had business to attend to. "Relax, human. I won't eat you, unless the Captain releases you to me."

"Best get permission from Lazarus, as well, pet, if that day ever comes. Mr. Brumble belongs to him." Vik showed her the healing bite on Zach's hand.

She raised an eyebrow then dismissed it with a snort. "Damn cat owes me a meal, anyway. I still haven't forgiven him for spraying Marle's skin and ruining it."

Viktor sensed the siren had something to discuss with him. "Mr. Brumble, go topside and help Mr. Jon with preparations for landfall. We should reach port in a few hours."

"Aye, sir."

Once he was gone, Belladonna announced, "I've had another vision. This one was much clearer."

"I suspected as much. You went on a feeding frenzy, pet."

"We are landing on the wrong coast."

"Excuse me?"

"We are landing on the wrong coast. The Sister I sensed is on the western coast of Mexico, not this coast. She is in a town called Juchitán."

"Damn. Even with your help, it would take months to sail around through the Straits of Magellan and back up the west coast. It would be quicker to trek over the mountains."

She gave him an apprehensive look at that announcement. "I was afraid of that."

Without explaining herself, she turned and went back in her cabin and curled up on her bunk, her back to him. He assumed she needed some rest.

"I'll call you, once we've made port, Belle." He closed the door softly and went in search of Grimm. There were things that had to be arranged for before they made landfall.

Grimm was on his way in search of Viktor at the same time. They met just outside the captain's cabin. "We've got a problem, Captain."

"Indeed, we do. Come on in, Mr. Grimm. I need a drink."

He almost hesitated outside the door. For a fleeting second, he wondered if Vik meant for him to provide the beverage. The second passed, and he joined his captain.

Viktor noticed the slight pause and change in his first mate's scent. Chuckling, he assured the man, "Not to worry, old friend, I haven't exhausted my special blend."

"I'm not even going to ask how you knew that was what I was wondering, Vik."

The vampire went to his cabinet and retrieved two bottles and two glasses. One bottle contained Jamaican rum; the other held a blend of fine brandy and human blood. He handed the rum and a glass to Grimm.

"We are going to need an expeditionary force, Hezekiah. The bitch is on the Pacific coast in a little village called Juchitán."

Grimm swore. "Bugger! That's going to take weeks! It makes our current problem even worse."

"And what problem is that?"

"The supplies for your vampires are getting low. I knew we'd be ashore a few days; but crossing the mountains and returning will take the better part of two months. I'm afraid we won't have a crew left to come back to."

Vik found the thought just as displeasing as Grimm. He could easily replace the crew with a few well-planned raids, but it would add even more time onto his quest with no guarantee of the quality of sailors he would get. "I suppose we could get Belle to help us thread the Straits."

Grimm shook his head. "Don't much like that idea, either. The waters around Tierra del Fuego are treacherous, and it would take even longer. We both know you have to make the best use of your time. We'll just have to figure out what to do about your cadre."

Lazarus materialized, un-summoned, and leapt up to Vik's shoulder. "Mreh?"

The vampire stroked the cat's head absently. Not for the last time, he wished the creature could communicate in more than just the images it passed along. Lazarus rubbed his cheek and rested his forehead against Vik's chin.

In an instant, rapid-fire images passed through his mind. Once he made sense of it, he thought he understood what the cat was trying to tell him.

"Brumble."

"Which one?" Grimm wasn't sure what he was planning.

"Both of them. Thomas is part of my cadre; his brother, Zachary, has petitioned to join my crew. I can put him in charge of keeping his brother and the other vampires fed."

"Do you think he can be trusted? He hasn't had any of the 'fortified' rum you give the crew from time to time. What's to keep him from turning the ship and crew over to the Navy, while we're gone? Coming back to a hangman's noose is worse than coming back to no crew."

Viktor understood his first mate's argument. Under normal circumstances, he wouldn't have considered leaving Zach in charge of his ship and crew. But his life had stopped resembling anything approaching normal ever since he'd run afoul of Mamaan Juma.

"I am counting on loyalty to his brother to keep him from betraying us. Besides, by now his own father has added him to the lists. He'd more likely swing from a gibbet himself, if he were to approach a Navy ship, especially since they'd only have his word that we would be returning in a few weeks," he countered his friend's argument.

"You raise a good point, Captain. Most pirate hunters aren't patient enough to wait around that long to see if Bloody Vik Brandee and the Grimm Reaper are going to show up or not. They'd think it was just a ploy to buy time and a chance to escape."

"Exactly."

Grimm finished his rum and stood. "I'll go find the lad and inform him of his duties."

"Hezekiah, make sure he only knows what he needs to know. Prisoners are to be bled into barrels of spirits, not given directly to the cadre. I don't need any new vampires depleting the supplies."

He nodded, "Aye, wouldn't do for him to learn how to destroy them, either."

"Good man."

Tamara A. Lowery

Chapter 3

Viktor studied the charts he owned of Mexico. Though slight variations depending on who had surveyed or copied them existed, they all indicated he would best be served by landing about a day south of Vera Cruz. That looked to be the shortest route across the isthmus to Juchitán. Once ashore, they would find a local guide to lead them through the mountain passes.

It amazed Zach that Brandee was so trusting of him. He was going to be left in a position which would enable him to use the pirates to buy himself back into his father's good graces. He found the idea tempting; but the more he thought about it, the more he deemed it a bad idea.

Even or maybe especially for a pirate crew, these men were unquestioningly loyal to their captain. If they even suspected him of trying to betray them, they'd gut him, or worse. He reasoned Brandee must use some sort of magic to keep them in line. Not even fear would hold the crew that long.

Then, there was the matter of his brother. He wasn't sure what to do with the vampire. He still thought of him as his little brother, Thomas. He'd always done what he could to protect the younger Brumble from their father. Now, his brother was dead, yet not dead. If only their father hadn't been a complete bastard of a sea captain, maybe they wouldn't have ended up in their current situation. They could have lived free and oblivious to these kinds of hardships.

No, he would abide by his word and serve his new captain faithfully. Brandee had long ago beaten the odds, outliving the average pirate who was lucky to see his 26th birthday. As hunted as he was, the man had a knack for survival. Zach wanted to learn from him.

Who knew, maybe he'd even make it long enough to avenge Jim Rigger, himself and his brother on his father for all the wrongs the elder Brumble had done to them over the years.

Belladonna fidgeted nervously in her cabin. Normally, when she was this agitated, she would swim and hunt. But she could sense Viktor wanted her to stay close by.

She felt like a trapped animal. If time wasn't of such importance, she would have argued strongly for sailing around the southern continent. After the ordeal in the Louisiana swamps, the thought of getting more than a day's walk from the sea terrified her. She couldn't help but think that the overland trek they were facing could easily kill her.

She was worked up almost to the point of panic by the time the captain knocked on her cabin door before he entered.

Viktor's instincts reacted instantly to her scent and behavior. "You smell like prey, pet. What is wrong?"

The announcement did nothing to calm her. He could see in her expression that she was calculating her chances of getting past him to the door. He shut and leaned against it.

"I've had blood recently, Belle. I am in control, not my Hunger, but your behavior is not making it easy." He made sure his tone relayed that he did not wish to harm her, but not to try his patience.

"I can't go with you." Her voice came out strained.

That one statement explained a lot. The vampire was nothing if not astute.

He smiled to reassure the frantic siren. "I didn't expect you to, pet. Well do I know that you are not a land creature. You need salt water like I need blood. I had no intention of risking your loss on this trek. You are too valuable to me."

Finally, she relaxed. Although relieved that he wasn't going to compel her to accompany him overland, she was regretful that she couldn't risk it. She was also, surprisingly, both touched and hurt that he wouldn't let her go along; hurt because he was doing so solely out of practicality but touched that he at least cared enough to not risk her life, even if it was only because she was useful to him.

Then she grew irritated with him, her mood shifting as quickly as the weather. Viktor immediately scented the change before it showed. He smiled slightly in the face of the oncoming onslaught. As far as he was concerned, the siren was back to normal. She seemed to always be irritated at him to some extent.

"If you have no intention of taking me with you, then why did you want me to stay here?" the storm burst. "I could have gone hunting! You know I want to feed when I'm this agitated over something!"

He raised an eyebrow at the tirade. "I gave no order for you to stay here with the ship, pet. In fact, I would prefer you go hunt elsewhere while I'm gone. I don't want you eating my crew when I'm not here to protect them."

"I wasn't talking about after you leave," she growled at him. "And stop looking so damn smug about all this! I clearly sensed that you wanted me to stay put for the present, and I've nearly gone mad with stress."

He blinked at her. Honestly, he had not consciously tried to restrain her. He told her as much. "I did not purposely try to keep you here, Belle. I do not know why you sensed that from me."

Rather than appease her, this information frightened her. Was she to be subject to the vampire's every whim, even when he was unaware of them? Viktor's psyche was as mercurial as hers, if not more so. She would be forced to shield constantly to protect herself from inconvenient mood swings on his part. Not for the last time, she cursed the feeding instincts which had trapped her into binding herself to his will.

"You smell like prey again, pet." He stood suddenly *there*, his arms locked in a steel grip around her, pinning her own and removing any leverage she might have had.

Her first impulse was to struggle, but she fought that instinct off. That reaction would only test his control over his Hunger even more. They both knew he could not feed on the siren's toxic blood. She forced herself to remain still, with muscles relaxed, and told him, "Release me, Viktor."

"No." He had no intention of letting her go while she remained this agitated. Also, she felt pleasantly soft and warm in his arms. He made sure that the hunger which showed in his eyes had nothing to do with blood. However, he couldn't keep the tips of his fangs from showing, as he lowered his head toward her.

Belle couldn't stop herself from struggling. "Viktor, no!" she pled.

His laugh was low and dark. "Ah, there's the struggle I was hoping for. You feel so delicious when you wriggle like that, little fish."

The kiss caught her completely off guard. Her whimper of fear changed to a moan of pleasure. She no longer minded being held prisoner by the wicked pirate. The man knew what he was doing.

Sensing her calm down, Viktor relaxed his grip. Finally, he pulled back from the kiss, savoring the effect he had on the siren. "That's better, pet."

"I hate you."

"Liar," he chuckled.

She glared at him. "No, I really hate you, Viktor Brandewyne. It is too close to port for us to finish what you just started. You still have too much preparation to do for your expedition." She pulled away from him brusquely. "You always do this to me."

"In my defense, pet, the last time we were interrupted by Jeorge."

Her eyes flashed golden at the mention of the New Orleans vampire. "Don't get me started about him."

"Peace, pet." Her ire amused him.

"You should never have had any dealings with him or his Kiss. I still worry that ill will come of it. Lone vampires are bad enough. Groups are nothing but trouble. And you left one of your fledglings with him. That gives him a way to monitor your movements."

"And I his, as you told me at the time," he reminded. "Besides, he really didn't give me much choice in the matter. Would you have had me jeopardize my quest by warring with him?"

"No." She pouted.

"Then why are you bitching?" He found himself enjoying baiting her.

She sputtered for a few minutes, too irritated to speak. "Because you always do this!" she finally managed to growl.

"Do what, pet?"

Belle glared at him, growling in frustration. She extended her talons and retracted them. He couldn't help smiling at her reaction.

That proved more than the siren could take. "Out! Get out of here now, or I will scream!" When he didn't move right away, she insisted, "I mean it, Viktor. I will scream, and it will destroy the minds of every human on this ship — even your precious first mate."

Viktor saw that she meant what she said and was not merely threatening. "Very well, pet. I will leave you alone. You are free to leave the ship whenever you wish."

He added, as he went out the door, "I am leaving Mr. Brumble in charge of the ship and my cadre. Leave him alone."

She stuck out her tongue at him.

Grimm noticed his captain's mood, when Vik came to check on the progress of their preparations. "Paid Belle a visit?"

The vampire grunted, causing his first mate to smirk. "I take it she's in a temper. It's been feeling like a storm brewing all day, but there's not a cloud in the sky. I figured it had something to do with her weather magic."

Viktor narrowed his eyes at him. "Odd that I got no such sense, yet you did."

Grimm shrugged. "I have no explanation for it."

"Hmph." He shook his head. Although something about it seemed off to him, he wasn't overly concerned about it. He trusted his first mate, something that he could not say of any other creature on this ship, save Lazarus.

Grimm filled him in on what preparations had been completed, then couldn't resist ribbing him about the siren. "So, what's she mad at you about this time?"

"You expect me to pick just one thing?" Vik laughed harshly.

"That bad." Grimm shook his head smirking. "Sometimes she acts like a wife."

Vik raised an eyebrow and crossed his arms. "How would you know what a wife acts like, Hezekiah? You've never had one."

His first mate grinned wickedly. "Not true, Vik. I've had more wives than I can count. I just wasn't married to any of them."

He couldn't help but laugh at the statement. "You are right. She acts just like a wife, and if I told her that, she'd get mad about it." He sighed. "She's still nagging me about that business with the New Orleans vampires, but the troubling thing that she said had her upset was my willing her to stay on board and the fear that I was going to force her to make the overland trek."

"She probably wouldn't survive it."

"I know, and I told her as much. I also told her that I did not use my influence to keep her on board. I don't know why she got the impression that I had." He frowned.

Grimm scratched his head, mulling that over. "Hmm. Curious, although I can see how that would upset her, given her nature."

"Aye." Silently, Vik thought that the time apart would be good for both of them.

Chapter 4

Four days later, they reached the spot Viktor wanted to go ashore at. Belladonna had left to hunt three days before. She made sure he knew she did not intend to return to the ship while he was ashore. That suited him fine. It meant he wouldn't have to worry about her eating any of the crew during his absence.

Zach had a few questions for him on things that Grimm had not covered with him.

"Is this the portage you want to be picked up from, Captain?"

"Unless my plans have to be altered, yes, it is." Vik anticipated the next question before he could ask it. "I will send Lazarus to you, when I am returning."

The elder Brumble brother glanced at the cat. He knew the creature had an uncanny intelligence, but he didn't understand how that would be possible.

Lazarus gazed back at him. Without warning or a command from Viktor, he shifted to his raven form. The action caught both men off guard. The vampire recovered first. "Are you showing him how you will return, old friend?"

Returning to feline form, Lazarus purred and smugly said, "Meh."

He rewarded the cat with a chin scratch, making him half-close his eyes and purr louder.

"I'd forgotten he could change like that," Zach admitted.

"Lazarus has an uncanny ability to guess what I'm thinking. I will warn you," he changed the subject, "it would be wise not to mention my name in Vera Cruz, if you have to put in there. I've made a few enemies there over the years. One of the town officials, in particular, would like to see me on a gibbet."

Zach blinked but adapted quickly. "Did you steal a great deal from him?"

"Well, there is that, because I did." He smirked. "But the reason he wishes me dead has more to do with my ravishing his daughter the night before her wedding to some rich old goat of a Spaniard. Word got to the groom, who called off the wedding."

"I see. So, the offended father was more injured by the loss of the rich alliance than the loss of his daughter's honor and virtue." He nodded understanding. For a fleeting moment, he wondered if his sister was fated for such a loveless union in order to line their father's pockets. He prayed not.

"Perhaps it is best that I avoid Vera Cruz all together. Since I need to take prisoners to feed my brother and the other vampires, I was thinking of heading up to the delta of the Rio Grande. Brumble & Sons usually has a couple of ships in that area this time of year. Emeralds aren't the only things my father dabbles in smuggling."

Brandee ran all the possible goods that could be smuggled out of that area through his mind. Only one really made sense as being profitable enough to take the risk.

"Silver?"

"That and turquoise," Zach confirmed. "Both of the captains he uses for that are total bastards. I have no qualms about taking their ships and leaving no survivors."

"Good. Go with your plan, then, Mr. Brumble."

"Thank you, Captain."

Viktor, Grimm, Jon-Jon and about five other pirates took a long boat ashore. A small stream came out at the spot they picked to land. It proved deep enough to row up several yards. It was only a matter of dragging the boat out of the water and camouflaging it.

"There should be a village just south of here," one of the men stated. "We should be able to find a guide there that can get us as far as the mountains."

"Are you sure of that, Mr. Neall? Grimm questioned.

"Aye. Fabric from this area is much prized by the villages on the west coast. They trade their pottery and other trinkets for it."

"In that case, we shouldn't have trouble finding someone to guide us the rest of the way, once we get to the mountain villages," Viktor surmised. "All right, lads, we aren't going to get anywhere standing here talking. Let's get moving."

After two hours walking, they found the remains of a village. Some of the buildings looked burnt out. They poked around, wondering what to do next. Their captain's laughter startled them unexpectedly.

"Care to share the joke, Captain?" Grimm asked.

"All this tells me is that I'm on the right track. This village was occupied less than a week ago."

"How do you figure that, Cap'n?" Jon-Jon looked puzzled.

Showing fangs as he grinned, Vik stated, "I can still smell people. The burned buildings were torched no more than two days past. They're still smoldering a little."

"Torched? You think these people did this to their own village?" Neall wondered.

Viktor nodded. "I know they did. It's not the first time I've heard of this happening, although this is the first I've experienced it personally. Somehow, they got word pirates were in the area. They did a quick firing of the buildings and moved further into the woods."

"I thought that was just a sea tale," Grimm grunted. "If it is the case, they might not be too willing to provide a guide."

Viktor smiled unpleasantly. "That had occurred to me. However, I believe I will be able to persuade someone to cooperate."

He lifted his head, sniffing the air. Catching a scent his crewmates could not detect, he focused on his hearing. There, an extra heartbeat. Though very quiet, their watcher could not escape the vampire's senses.

A brief confusion spread among the pirates when their captain suddenly disappeared. A startled yelp from behind the furthest smoldering hut preceded his return. He landed close to the spot he recently vacated, a frightened teenage boy in his grasp.

As soon as his feet touched solid ground again, the lad started struggling wildly. He was babbling away, his voice breaking in his fear.

"Damn, my Spanish is too rusty. Can any of you make out what the whelp is saying?" Vik grumbled.

"Near as I can tell, he thinks you're some kind of demon," Grimm told him. "His dialect has a lot of some native tongue mixed in. I'm more used to Cuban Spanish."

"Translate for me," he ordered. "Tell him I do not intend to harm him. Try to get him calmed down, so we can get some sense out of him."

Grimm complied, actually trying to not frighten the lad any further. It wasn't an easy task, given he was more accustomed to intimidating than to soothing, except when dealing with a wench.

The boy shook his head violently, yelling at the pirates.

"He says we're lying, that we're all devils and will steal his soul."

Then the boy started hollering at the top of his lungs, clearly crying out some kind of warning to his fellow villagers.

"Dammit, I don't want him scaring off the others or bringing an attack down on our heads," Vik grumbled. He grabbed the boy by the jaw with the intent of forcing eye contact. The lad managed to slip his head a little sideways and bit down into the tender flesh between thumb and forefinger of his captor's hand.

The vampire hissed, as the boy bit hard enough to draw blood and sealed his fate.

Instantly, a bond formed between their minds. Viktor found himself able to clearly understand and speak the boy's obscure dialect now, as if he had been born to it. There was the added benefit of the lad's silence.

"That's better," Vik spoke to him in his own tongue. *"I have no wish to harm you or your people."*

"You lie," the lad accused. *"Tia Rosalia sent word that devils who drink blood and eat men's flesh were coming here, seeking her out."*

The vampire wondered at that. This Sister must be very powerful to have sensed that much of his mission. Perhaps he should warn Belladonna, when he returned, to try to shield herself from the Sisters when she helped hunt them, if it were possible for her to.

"I do drink blood, that is true," he ceded, willing the lad to believe him. *"But I give you my word I will not drink from you or anyone from your village. I have brought my own supply,"* he pointed out three casks rigged for the long portage overland, *"and I wear this to keep my Hunger at bay."* He pulled out the emerald encrusted cross he wore next to a milky crystal and a small silver bottle.

The cross coupled with the vampire's will to convince the boy of his safety. Surely no evil being could bear the touch of such a holy object. He visibly calmed.

Secure in the knowledge that the boy would not run off or alert anyone, Viktor released his physical hold.

"What of your companions?" the boy asked. *"Will they drink my blood or eat my flesh? All the old tales warn about how clever you devils are and say that you will play with words to trick or trap men."*

Viktor smirked. This would indeed be a challenge. If the Sister's minions were this clever, she would be a force to be reckoned with. He had a brief regret that he wouldn't have the siren at his side to face her with, but he would not risk Belle's loss in the mountain crossing.

"They are mortal men, like you. She who devours the flesh of men I have sent away. I am their Captain. They obey me or die." This seemed to satisfy the lad.

Grimm was the only one of the pirates who understood any of the exchange, and that understanding was only partial. "Thought you said your Spanish was rusty, Captain. You sounded like you'd been speaking it all your life. I couldn't keep up."

"Our young friend made the mistake of biting me. When the bond clicked into place, I found myself able to understand him perfectly," he explained. He turned back to the boy and asked, *"What shall I call you?"*

"My name is Ferdinand."

"Can you understand what I am saying now?" he asked in English. The boy just looked at him, confused. Viktor could not sense any deceit.

Satisfied that the boy wouldn't be able to understand them, he turned to his first mate. "I am going to have Ferdinand take me to where his fellow villagers have hidden. I want you and the lads to remain here, Mr. Grimm. Hide as best you can, just in case anyone heard his yells earlier and comes to investigate."

Grimm nodded his understanding. Given the boy's reaction to them, it probably would be safer for only one of them to approach the villagers. They wouldn't feel as threatened. He shared Vik's opinion that sometimes charm got better or quicker results than brute force. He wasn't worried about his captain's ability to get himself out of any dangerous situation.

"He seemed to calm down a lot, when you showed him that cross, Captain. You might want to keep it visible," he suggested.

"I intend to," Vik said then switched back to Spanish. *"Ferdinand, we need the help of your people. My men will stay here. I will go with you alone to meet them. That way, they will know I mean them no harm."*

"Si, señor. Follow me."

☠

Viktor thought the villagers were as skittish at the sight of him as if he'd brought his entire crew with him. Mothers clutched children to them or herded them indoors quickly. Men tightened their grips on whatever tool or item they had in their hands, although none of them openly challenged him.

Ferdinand led him to the old man who served as the village elder. He told the pirate this was who he needed to deal with to get the help he sought.

"Abuelo, I have brought someone who needs your help," the boy announced.

"Bring him in, Ferdinand," the old man instructed. *"Have him come close, so that I may see him."*

Obediently, the boy led Viktor into the room and over to the old man. The pirate noticed that the old man seemed to be staring at some distant point and realized he must be blind. Without prompting, he took the old man's hand and placed it on his face. He patiently endured the feathery touch, as the old man probed his features.

"You are the fanged, blood-drinking devil she warned us of," he stated simply.

"I am. It is not my intention to harm anyone in your village or the Sister," he confirmed and assured.

"I know," the old man switched to English. "I am amazed that you can speak our dialect so well. Our village uses many words of our original language from before the Spaniards invaded and enslaved us."

"Young Ferdinand bit my hand shortly after I found him watching us. It was an accident that he swallowed some of my blood. A temporary bond was formed, and I gained knowledge of your tongue. It was not my intention to entrap the boy…," he started to explain.

"That last is a lie," the old man proclaimed. "Ferdinand bit you in an effort to keep you from enthralling him with your eyes."

Viktor narrowed his eyes at the old man. "How to you reckon that?"

He smiled and chuckled softly. "I may be blind, but I have other eyes. Ferdinand was not the only one watching you. He was not supposed to be there, but some boys are too willful and curious for their own good. Now, it may have cost him his soul." The last statement was a bit more somber.

Viktor shook his head, even though the old man couldn't see it. "His soul is safe from me. I have not bitten him, nor do I wish to. The effects of the small amount of my blood he swallowed will fade and eventually cease."

The old man peered in his direction. Although he was blind, Viktor could swear he was seeing into him. If he hadn't grown up with Mother Celie giving him a similar look, it would have been unnerving. As it was, coming from a blind man, it still felt a bit disconcerting.

Finally, the old man spoke. "You speak truth. Your hold over him will fade with time, provided you do not give him more of your blood. My fear, *señor*, is that you will seduce him, and he will not wish to leave your service."

"I am not a lover of boys, old man." The pirate's voice grew deadly low.

"I did not say you were. Perhaps I did not make myself clear. Ferdinand is going to be exposed to your ways and your men. He is young and impressionable — and restless with village life," the old man explained. "His lust for adventure brought him in contact with you to begin with."

He understood the man's meaning. "You fear that he will want to join my crew."

"*Si.*"

Vik smiled ruefully. "Under normal circumstances, I would not care if he did. But these are not normal circumstances. I made the mistake of killing a boy who was a favorite of one of the Sisters of Power. Now I am cursed and must seek out the other Sisters for help." He wasn't sure why he was explaining all this to the old man. It was not in his nature to do so. "I cannot afford to anger them, so, I will not permit him to join my crew. As for him being exposed to my crew, once I leave this village, it will no longer be an issue."

"You need provisions and a guide for the passage over the mountains, no?"

"Yes."

"Take Ferdinand with you. Leave him in the mountains or with *Tia* Rosalia, but do not leave him here," he instructed the pirate. "He is no longer safe here. Word will spread quickly that he bears your taint. He would follow you anyway."

Viktor stared at him for a few moments. Switching back to their native tongue, he asked Ferdinand, *"Do you know the way to Tia Rosalia?"*

"Si. I went with the men on the annual trading trip to the Western Sea."

"And could you lead me there?"

The boy grew eager and excited. *"Si. I remember the way well. When I wander from our village, I never get lost."*

Vik quirked an eyebrow. *"We'll see,"* he smirked. *"I am going to have to teach you some English, though. I don't want to have to translate everything during our journey."*

Only by the sanction of the village elder could Viktor and his men get any provisions or pack animals from the locals. Even then, it was made very clear that the sooner they left the village, the better.

Listening to all that the people of the village told him of how the pirates conducted themselves, the old man thought, *"She will like this one. He may find that he is the one trapped in her service. Tia Rosalia can be very persuasive."*

Chapter 5

The *Shining Star* finally approached the Bahamas. Wind and current fought the ship the entire trip from Boston. Captain Bainbridge couldn't explain it. The storm which blew them off course had come up unexpected and without warning. It forced them into the Gulf Stream and swept the ship over a hundred leagues out of their way before they could escape the current.

A knock at his cabin door alerted him that his cabin "boy" had arrived from the galley with his meal. Sam set the platter down on the table and closed the door. Bainbridge still wasn't happy about the "boy's" presence.

Samantha Brumble, the daughter of his employer, had discovered her father's plan to betray her brothers in order to save his own neck. The younger male Brumbles, formerly involved in an emerald smuggling scheme, both ran afoul of pirates. Tobias Brumble would rather implicate his sons as accomplices to the pirate, Vik Brandee, than admit their innocence. He feared the Royal Navy commander he was working for would think he had plotted to defraud him.

Sam stowed away on the *Shining Star* to thwart that plan. She also determined she would seek out the pirate and try to ransom her brothers from him.

Bainbridge had to admit she was clever and resourceful. He only discovered her presence when he caught her trying to steal the message and report her father had sent. As far as the crew knew, Sam was a boy. At her request, he was treating her as an apprentice, training her just as he had helped train her brothers in seamanship. She proved surprisingly apt at the craft, for a woman, he thought.

"The navigator said we should reach the harbor before tomorrow evening, Captain," she informed him.

"It's about time. I swear that storm cost us dearly, Sam," he groused.

"Yes sir, it did." She took her own plate off the serving platter and sat at the smaller table and stool set up for the cabin boy. This maintained the charade. No captain worth his salt permitted a cabin boy to share his table.

She took a small serving, but larger than what she ate the first few weeks on board. Adjusting to the poorer quality of shipboard food after a lifetime of fresh victuals proved quite an ordeal. Her appetite only just returned recently, and she stopped having seasickness. She hoped never to have that experience again.

After they finished eating, she cleared the dishes away and returned them to the galley. That done, she went back to the captain's cabin with the intent of studying the charts. Bainbridge was teaching her navigation, and she was supposed to chart a course from Port Royal to San Juan to show him what she had learned so far.

She arrived at the same time as the first mate. Knocking before she entered, she announced, "Mr. Warding is here, Captain."

"Very good, Sam. Go study your charts, lad," he acknowledged. "Come in, Henry. What is the report?"

"Sails have been spotted, sir. There's a ship at anchor just off one of the smaller islands." He seemed agitated. "Captain, you might want to have a look at it before we decide whether or not to approach it."

"What's wrong, Henry?"

"I swear it looks like the same ship that took Captain Brumble."

Sam froze, praying that the first mate did not look in her direction at that moment. She waited to hear Bainbridge's decision.

"I'll come look. Sam, you stay here and study. I want that course ready within the hour."

The first mate mistook the look of distress on her face. "Don't worry, lad. It's not that hard a lesson, and the Captain tells me you've been a quick study. You'll do just fine," he smiled at her.

"Th-thank you, sir," she managed to stammer, remembering herself.

Waiting for Bainbridge to return was pure torture.

"The lines are the same, all right," Bainbridge confirmed after looking through the glass. "I don't trust the flag. The bastard tricked us before with false colors and signals. Approach with caution."

"Are you sure, Captain?"

He sighed, looked toward the distant ship, and nodded. "They are at anchor with their sails furled. If they do not make any aggressive moves, signal for them to identify their commander. Let me know their answer."

He turned and went back to his cabin.

"I'm sorry I couldn't include you in that, Miss Brumble," Bainbridge apologized once he secured the door. "I do not think you want Mr. Warding to know your true identity."

"No, Captain. I agree that the fewer who know that the better," she said. "But please, tell me, is it the ship that took my brothers?"

"I'm not sure yet. The lines are almost identical, but we are approaching at the wrong angle to read the name. The ship is at anchor with furled sails," he told her. "So far, it has made no hostile move, nor flown any signal. If it is the pirate, we will have to run. The *Shining Star* is no match for them. The one advantage we have is that they will have to raise anchor, set sails and turn about to give chase. It takes a while for a ship that large to come about."

Sam had a stubborn set to her jaw. "Running away from this pirate will not achieve the freedom of my brothers. It is my intention to try to ransom them."

He shook his head. "I would advise against that plan, miss. I do not think you truly comprehend the danger, not only to you, but to them as well, if you follow that course."

"Then I ask you to enlighten me, Captain Bainbridge."

"Pirates are not civilized, miss, nor do they give a fig for the rules of polite society. I am sure that Brandee would take the ransom you would offer, but there is no guarantee that he would honor an agreement to free your brothers. Also, he has quite a reputation as a womanizer. He could very well demand the surrender of your virtue as part of his price for Thom and Zach's freedom. If he were to try to force you, your brothers could well be killed trying to defend you."

Her pallor let him know that she was beginning to grasp the danger. It was plain that rape had never occurred to her.

She was not deterred, however. "Women throughout history have had to endure that particular indignity. I would hope that it does not come to that, but if it does, I will survive. I love my brothers dearly, Captain. I am willing to do whatever I must to gain their freedom from this pirate."

"I do not like it, but I will accede to your wishes, miss. I just pray we all survive this bad business," he sighed.

"Thank you, Captain Bainbridge. This is the right thing to do."

"I know, miss. But it would be better to let those who are trained and equipped to do so be the ones to hunt Brandee down. I just hate to see you put yourself in danger," he argued.

Sam gave a bitter laugh. "I wonder, sir, if you would be cautioning me so strongly were I male. I somehow doubt it. My father made the mistake of underestimating me. Just because I am a woman does not make me less intelligent. You, of all people, should know that, Captain. Look at the tests you have been giving me. Has there been any fault in my answers?"

He shook his head. "No. In fact, you've been a quicker study than your brothers were. You have a good head for figures and navigation. But you are a woman, which means that you would be no match for a man in a fight."

Her granted him a sardonic smile. "I might surprise you there, sir. Growing up with two brothers and no living mother to intervene, I learned how to fight at a young age. I might not be a match for a man in strength, but I have skills and agility, and I know how to make a grown man cry like a baby." She grinned. "I fight dirty, Captain Bainbridge. One advantage to being a woman is that I am not held to some masculine false sense of honor and fair play. Life will always treat me unfairly because of my gender, but no one said I have to sit back and allow myself to be a victim."

Bainbridge looked at her in a new light. After some time, he finally spoke. "I don't know whether to envy the man you eventually take for a husband or to feel sorry for him."

"I will take that as a compliment."

A knock came at the door to the cabin. "Enter," Bainbridge responded.

Warding came in. "We've established contact with the ship. They claim to be the *HMS Quicksilver* under the command of one Commodore Critchfield. What are your orders, sir?"

Bainbridge and Samantha were the only ones on board who knew who they were looking for. Tobias Brumble always used outside couriers, so no one could tie him to the Commodore. That fact alone convinced them they had not stumbled on Brandee, after all. Thomas and Zachary never knew the identity of their father's backer in the emerald smuggling scheme. Therefore, they couldn't have been made to share that information with their captor.

"Signal back that we have an urgent and confidential message for the Commodore, Mr. Warding."

"Aye, sir."

Chapter 6

Commodore Critchfield received them in his cabin. He wondered at Bainbridge allowing his "cabin boy" to accompany him.

"Sam is privy to my mission, Commodore," he explained. "I am training the lad for an eventual captaincy in our company."

"Hmph, they seem to get younger and younger every year," Critchfield snorted. "The boy hasn't even started shaving."

"I've found it beneficial to start them out as young as possible, sir. By the time they're of an age, they know their craft as naturally as they know to breathe."

"Good point. I started out as a powder monkey, myself, when I was only ten. Now then, what is this message you have for me, Captain Bainbridge?"

He handed over the sealed papers. Critchfield examined the seal. Recognizing Brumble's insignia, he raised an eyebrow.

"This is highly irregular, Captain Bainbridge. Mr. Brumble had agreed to not use his own ships to contact me. We were to go through a private courier."

"I realize that, Commodore. I would not be here if the situation were not dire."

Critchfield gave him a skeptical look, then broke the seal and read the letter and reports. As he read, his color rose. By the time he finished, his face was livid.

"Are you aware of the contents of this, sir?" his voice held a fine edge of anger.

"I know that it contains my report of the incident and a missive from my employer. As to the body of the letter, I was not present when it was written, and the seal was not broken, as you can see."

Critchfield got his emotions under control. He reread the reports before speaking again.

"I would like to ask you a few questions, Captain."

"Of course, sir, I will answer to the best of my ability." He nodded.

The Commodore fixed the merchant captain with a steely gaze designed to intimidate, a stance which had served him well throughout his naval career to keep subordinates in line. To his credit, Bainbridge never flinched.

"Explain the reasoning of your rather skittish approach of this vessel. I've been a-sea for a very long time and recognize when another ship is keeping quick flight as an option."

"We did not know this was your ship at first, sir. The lines are distinctly a new design, but they are also familiar. Are there many other ships of this design?"

Critchfield blinked at him. "The *Quicksilver* is one of a kind, sir. I do not see how her lines could be familiar to you. She was launched only just over a year ago and has only been in these waters for five months."

"Nevertheless, sir, I have seen this design before. Perhaps another ship has been launched of this line?"

He shook his head. "There was another ship before this one, the *War God*, but she was lost on her maiden voyage more than three years ago now."

Bainbridge looked stunned for a moment, but the pieces started to click into place. "I have heard the stories. The fantastical, I've always dismissed as bilge, but one consistency was that no bodies or wreckage were ever recovered. I believe I know why, sir."

This peaked Critchfield's curiosity. "And why is that, Captain?"

"Because she was not lost; she was stolen. I have seen a ship almost identical to this one, but she is no longer called the *War God*. She sails as the *Incubus* and is captained by Bloody Vik Brandee. It is the ship that Captain Brumble and I encountered on our last voyage together. That is why we stayed ready for a rapid retreat. The *Shining Star* is no match for a ship of this class, and I seriously doubt Brandee would let us escape alive again."

The Commodore digested this new information. He had never thought much of the captain of the Bonnie Mae, the ship which had reported Brandee dead. Of course, it would make sense for the *War God* to remain hidden for a few years. Brandee was a clever bastard if even half the stories about him were to be believed. He could well believe the pirate would fake his own death to throw off the hunters.

"If you are correct, and Brandee is in possession of the *War God*, or *Incubus*, or whatever he's calling it now, then the situation is more dire than you know. The ship was designed to be a pirate hunter and has several special features an ordinary ship of the line does not. You were wise to be skittish approaching us. I shall have to dispatch a courier to Jamaica to restore Brandee to the lists. I also shall have Zachary and Thomas Brumble added to the lists. I shall probably sail to Boston to deal with the elder Brumble personally. You might want to seek another employer, Captain Bainbridge," Critchfield informed him.

"Sir? I do not understand."

"Don't worry, man. Although you took part in the emerald venture, I do not hold you culpable in their loss. However, old Tobias defends his sons a little too stridently. I have no choice but to believe that the three of them conspired with Brandewyne to defraud me. Personally, I think them foolish to make any alliance with that bloodthirsty bastard. The younger Brumbles may already be dead. It would explain why there has been no ransom demand," he explained. "However, if they are found alive, then the lack of a ransom demand only proves that they are in league with the pirate."

Bainbridge found himself in quite a predicament. He could not defend his employer or the younger Brumbles without drawing suspicion down on himself or revealing Samantha's identity. He didn't care so much about himself, but he would not betray her trust.

It began to look as if the only chance for saving Zach and Thom would be for the *Shining Star* to find the *Incubus* before the Commodore or any Navy ship did.

Chapter 7

The verdict was more than Sam could stand. She knew Bainbridge had to choose between protecting her and defending her brothers. She would not be the cause of their unchallenged condemnation. She now understood her father's reasoning for sacrificing them to save himself, but she still did not forgive that decision.

"My brothers are not in collusion with any pirate, sir," she protested. "And, greedy though he is, neither is the man I once called father."

Critchfield looked at her sharply. "Who the hell do you think you are, boy, to speak to me thus? And what do you mean your brothers and father? Old Brumble only has two sons that I know of, and there never was and rumor of any bastards floating around."

Holding her back straight and chin high in defiance, she announced, "I am Samantha Brumble, and I will ransom my brothers from the vile pirate who hold them."

Tamara A. Lowery

The Commodore stood dumbfounded for the moment. Bainbridge hid his face in one hand, not believing the disaster this mission just degenerated into.

Never taking his eyes from the young woman, Critchfield asked, "I take it by your reaction that you knew this female was aboard your ship, Captain?"

"I did, sir."

"Are you mad? A ship is no place for a woman."

"Commodore, with all due respect, you did not know I was a woman until I revealed my identity," Sam countered. "On both this vessel and aboard the *Shining Star* no one outside of this cabin knows my true gender."

He scoffed, "You couldn't keep up the charade for more than a couple of weeks."

Bainbridge corrected him, "Actually, sir, she has maintained her secret for almost two months. Our voyage took longer than expected. We were blown off course by a bad storm system. And, she has a natural aptitude for navigation and sailing. She has passed every test set her thus far and has demonstrated endurance and agility to match many a seasoned seaman."

"So, you are both mad," Critchfield concluded. "Just how old are you anyway, Miss Brumble?"

"I don't see how that has any bearing on the situation."

"Humor me."

"I am nineteen." She shrugged.

"Your father is a bigger fool than I thought," he sneered. "Not only is he in league with one of the most notorious pirates of our time, but he has failed to marry you off at an appropriate age. You should be at home with a husband and a whelp or two running around at your age, instead of gallivanting off to sea on some fool's errand."

Sam ignored the barbs and locked on the accusation against her father. "No one in my family is in league with any pirates, Commodore, especially not my father. I stole his seal and forged that letter," she admitted.

"And why would you do that, Miss Brumble?"

"Because I believe in my brothers' innocence. I don't know if my father does or not, but his original letter shows that he was willing to condemn them to the gallows to save his own neck." Her voice showed her fury with her sire. She held out the original letter with the broken seal still clinging to the paper.

Glaring, he snatched the missive from her and read it over. Clearing his throat, he finally ceded, "I see your point, Miss Brumble. Tobias is a bastard for betraying his sons, but he is a shrewd bastard. I will accept that there was no collusion with the pirates in the theft of the emeralds. I will not place your brothers on the lists. I shall have to give some serious thought on whether to continue doing business with him, however. It would appear from Captain Bainbridge's report that Brandewyne has targeted your family. That is bad for business."

"So, you will free my brothers if you find them?" she asked hopefully.

He stood and looked at her with a disapproving frown. "I seriously doubt they still live. Go home, Miss Brumble. Find a husband and raise lots of babies. Leave the pirate hunting to the men."

"No."

"Excuse me?"

"I will not abandon my brothers and sit at home just hoping that they are rescued and maybe never learning what happened to them. I intend to find the pirate who took them and ransom them, if they are still alive. If they are dead, then I intend to avenge them," she told him.

"Stubborn female," he grumbled. "You cannot be swayed from this suicidal course?"

"I will not."

Critchfield got a determined and cruel look on his face. Without warning, he reached over and grabbed her arms. Pulling her to him, he kissed her roughly.

Sam struggled, startled by the Commodore's behavior. She managed to pull back some and demanded, "What do you think you are doing? Release me!"

He shifted his grip on her so that one arm was around her waist, freeing his other hand to grope her breast. When Bainbridge tried to pull him off her, he elbowed him in the stomach. The merchant captain sat down hard; the wind knocked out of him.

Sam continued to struggle, scratching and clawing to no avail. Then she caught Critchfield off guard with a fist to the side of the head. He was stunned enough to let her go.

"You are no gentleman, sir," her voice held pure venom. "How dare you take such liberties?"

Rubbing the side of his face, he laughed bitterly. "Get used to it, girl. If you actually do find Brandee, he'll do far worse. If you're lucky, he'll kill you after he's raped you. If not, he'll probably sell you to a brothel somewhere."

When he moved towards her again, a leer on his face, she drew her knife and took a defensive stance. He actually laughed. "Don't tell me someone was fool enough to try to teach you to fight, girl."

"No one aboard the *Shining Star* has taught me, but I am quite adept at defending myself."

"Ha! You're just a female. You're no match for a man, let alone one with as much combat experience as I have. Put that silly knife away." Despite his taunting, he circled her cautiously.

"I grew up with two older brothers and no mother. I've known how to fight since I could walk. Even my nursemaids would tell you I was an impossible child," she retorted as he made his move.

She dodged the grab and made a feint of her own. He blocked it, as she anticipated he would. Twisting in the grasp he tried to get on her, she brought the knife in and up to slice his cheek.

"Bitch!" he brought his fist crashing into the side of her head.

Sam instantly crumpled to the deck. Critchfield loomed over her unconscious form. He retrieved the knife and moved to slice her face as she had his. The muzzle of a blunderbuss pressed against his temple stopped him short.

In his surprise and rage, he had forgotten about Bainbridge.

"Drop the blade and step away from Miss Brumble, sir. Your behavior has been unworthy of your status. You are no gentleman." Bainbridge could barely contain his outrage.

Critchfield straightened and handed the knife over, hilt first. He nodded in respect to the merchant captain. "No sir, I am not. I have been at sea for too many years to observe the niceties of polite society. Miss Brumble needs to understand the dangers she faces if she is determined to continue her masquerade. If you are truly concerned for her, sir, you will force her to return to her father. She does not belong here."

Convinced that they would be allowed to leave without further risk of attack, Bainbridge tucked his weapon back into his belt. Kneeling, but never taking his eyes off Critchfield, he lifted the unconscious woman into an easy carrying position.

He paused at the doorway and said to the Commodore, "I will take her back to the *Shining Star*, and, because I do care for her safety, I will aid her in her quest and try to protect her as best I may. If I were to take her back to her father, she would just devise a way to escape and resume her search. She would not fare as well if discovered by another captain."

Critchfield could not resist a parting shot. "Do what you feel you must, Captain Bainbridge. But if you ever pull a weapon on me again for any reason, I will have you flogged."

"Sir, I have no intention of ever crossing your path again, if I can avoid it. Good-bye."

He turned and carried Sam back to their ship.

Chapter 8

Critchfield cleaned and tended the knife wound. It stung from the gin he used to wash it but did not appear to need to be stitched. The wound was shallow and had not gotten into the muscle. Even the scar would be minimal.

He had mixed emotions about the discovery of and encounter with Samantha Brumble. She had surprised him with her spirit and fight. All the females he had encountered in his lifetime had been properly docile and submissive, save for the occasional shrew. He wasn't sure what to make of her. It was as if a man had been born in a woman's body, as best he could explain it to himself. He was simply not familiar with the concept of a female being capable of such determination and with a capacity for such intelligence. She was an anomaly to him.

He shook it off. Tobias Brumble's daughter was not his concern. He reread the reports, trying to see beyond what was written. The information about the slaughter of his agent's entire crew by some unknown female supposedly working with Brandee troubled him. He would have liked to question the two survivors himself, but who knew where they were by now. It surprised him Bainbridge hadn't retained the boy as part of his own crew, however. He should have asked him about that. It was too late now.

He wondered at Brandee working with anyone else. His reputation painted him as a lone hunter. He was more likely to pirate another pirate than work in tandem with them. He thought it more likely that this unknown had run afoul of the bastard and was looking for vengeance. The only problem with that theory was that both pirates targeting his emerald operation at both ends was too much of a coincidence.

No, he did not like it one bit.

Opening his desk drawer, he pulled out a fresh sheet of paper and his quill and ink. He composed a terse dispatch to forward to Port Royal.

In it, he put that reports of Vik Brandee's death were erroneous. Not only was the pirate still alive, but very active and possibly partnered with an as yet unknown female with a penchant for bloodshed. Privately, he had doubts about that part of the report. The "female" was more likely a male who had taken to dressing as a woman. Critchfield had encountered that a few times, and it was easier to believe than that a woman was capable of such violence.

He thought about including a footnote that Brandee may be holding a couple of hostages but decided against it. The Brumble boys were probably already dead. Even if they had not plotted with Brandee, if they were still alive, they were most likely working with him now, since no ransom had been demanded. Besides, he really didn't want to have to explain why or how he knew that the Brumbles weren't pirates. The Admiralty courts would not look kindly on the smuggling, especially since he hadn't cut any higher-ups in on the action.

Once satisfied with the message, he rang for his cabin boy.

"Yes, sir?"

"Take this to Mr. Turlington. He is to see that it gets to Port Royal as quickly as possible." He handed the sealed message over to the lad.

"Aye, sir." He left to deliver it to the officer the Commodore indicated.

"What's this then, Paul?" Turlington asked when the lad delivered Critchfield's message.

"The Commodore says this needs to be delivered to Port Royal as quickly as possible, sir," Paul answered.

"Why the urgency?"

Paul looked around to see if anyone was listening before he replied with a whisper, "I overheard talk that Bloody Vik Brandee is still alive and that he has a ship just like this one."

Turlington blanched. "Good heavens! I hope the Commodore gave advice to steer clear of him if not part of an armada. If that news is true, most of the ships-of-the-line in these waters will be no match for him. Tell Commodore Critchfield I'll leave immediately."

As Paul ran off to do so, Turlington hollered, "Mr. Hanson, make the fast launch ready to sail! I want her in the water an hour ago!"

"Aye, sir."

He turned and went to his cabin to pack a sea bag. If the winds stayed favorable, he and his small crew would reach Port Royal in just under two weeks.

Tamara A. Lowery

Chapter 9

The trek over the mountain passes tried everyone's patience. Even with the blood bonds reinforced, Viktor could sense the tension among the crewmates he'd brought with him. None of them liked being this far out of their element, especially with no promise of treasure or sport.

He and Grimm agreed it might put him on a bad footing with the Sister to allow his men to do what they did best among people under her protection. Only an iron will kept Viktor from giving in to the urge to hunt. The people of the villages they passed through would have made perfect prey.

The only relief from the tedium of the trip was teaching Ferdinand to speak English. The boy picked it up fairly quickly. He made a point to practice by translating for the group when they had to deal with locals. By the time they reached Juchitán, he was reasonably fluent and only had to pause to think about what he was saying occasionally.

Grimm fought off the tedium by teaching the boy knots. Again, Ferdinand proved a quick study. So much so, that Grimm suspected he would make a decent sailor someday.

One thing was apparent; the boy was developing a severe case of hero worship. The way he hung on every word Vik uttered and eagerly followed all orders would have been annoying if it hadn't been useful.

"Captain, can I talk to you about the boy?" Grimm used French, since Ferdinand's English had improved so much.

Taking the hint from his first mate, Viktor used the language as well. *"What is it, Mr. Grimm?"*

"He's showing quite a bit of promise. I was thinking we could find a place for him on the crew, when we get back to the ship, if you've no objection."

Vik gave an irritable sigh. He'd been thinking the same thing. *"Ordinarily, I would have no problem with it, Hezekiah, but the old village elder was his grandfather and hinted that it would displease Tia Rosalia if I kept the lad."*

"Then why did we bring him with us?"

"To give his people a chance to cool off. The old man feared the villagers might harm him for leading us to them."

"Well, there is that." Grimm switched back to English. "Ho, Ferdinand!" he called the boy over.

"Yes, Mr. Grimm?"

"How close are we to Juchitán?"

He looked around to take in the surroundings and look for landmarks. Only a few things had changed since he'd last been that way. He recognized a rock formation and answered, "We should reach the farmlands around it in about an hour's walk."

Grimm nodded. "Do you know where exactly to find *Tia Rosalia*?"

Ferdinand shook his head. "No, I did not go to visit her when I was here before. We were only here to trade, which was rare. Usually, we trade with the mountain villages, and they relay goods on to the Western Sea."

"We will ask around when we get there," Vik declared. "Someone will be able to direct us to her." Not for the last time, he wished it had been practical to bring Belladonna with them. However, just seeing how his men reacted to being away from the sea so long reinforced his belief that the trek would have proven fatal to the siren.

He hoped it wouldn't take too long to find Rosalia. His supplies were running low, and he wanted to get her permission to hunt. Normally, he wouldn't worry about permission, but he didn't want to mess up getting her cooperation and magical help. The trip was just wasted time, otherwise.

When the farmlands started giving way to more settled areas, Viktor sent Ferdinand on into the village to ask around about *Tia* Rosalia. Before an hour had passed, the lad returned to the small group of pirates.

"Captain, no one will tell me where *Tia* Rosalia is. They only tell me to go to the cantina and wait," he reported.

"Wait." Somehow, he was not surprised.

"*Si*. They say that word will be taken to her, and if she wishes to see you, she will send someone to bring you to her," he nodded.

Grimm rubbed the back of his neck. "At least she's not trying to run and hide like Dorada did."

"Yes, there is that," Vik ceded. "Very well, lead the way to the cantina. I'm sure the lads would be glad of a hot meal and fresh beer."

"*Si!* It is this way." Ferdinand motioned for them to follow him, delighted with the position of importance this afforded him with the pirates.

A few stopped and looked their way, as they passed through the village. None of the pirates were perturbed or alarmed by this, though. They were used to the reaction to their presence everywhere they went and had grown to expect the attention. Jon-Jon was the one to notice that several villagers crossed themselves after they passed by them.

"Cap'n, I think they suspect what you really are," he warned.

"As long as they don't get in my way or try to stop me," Brandee dismissed it.

The others went on alert, however, as they started gathering a crowd. No one tried to stop them; rather, they closed in behind them, following.

To Grimm, every instinct screamed this was a trap. He wanted to turn and attack. He did not like having that many people he didn't know at his back. He could see the same urge in varying degrees in the eyes of his fellow crewmates. He knew the Captain's will was the only thing holding them in line. Staying ready, he resolved to not attack unless Viktor gave the word, or the villagers made any hostile actions.

"We are here," Ferdinand finally announced, as they arrived outside a non-descript building that sort of blended in with the others around it. Only faded lettering on the worn, whitewashed stucco gave any indication that it was the cantina.

It took a few moments for their eyes to adjust to the gloom inside. Only Viktor and, to a lesser extent, Grimm could clearly see the wary looks directed at them from the few patrons in the place. By the time they were seated, almost every local had exited, except the barkeep and one serving girl. This only served to fuel Grimm's sense they had walked into a trap.

"I don't like this, Captain. It doesn't feel right."

"I'm starting to think you're right, Mr. Grimm. But I don't think they intend to attack us. Mr. Jon, check any other exits. Do not offer battle, though," he ordered.

"Aye, Cap'n." Jon-Jon moved to follow the order. It didn't take him long to determine that the building was completely surrounded.

Sitting back down, he told them, "There are locals at least three or four deep at every door and window. None of 'em look to be armed, but we'll have to fight our way out of here."

"Perhaps, perhaps not," Brandee countered. "They would be a problem, if we wanted to leave right now, but I will wait here for the Sister or for someone to bring us to her. I can't place my finger on the exact point yet, but I have the feeling this is the start of some sort of test."

Grimm nodded, "Makes sense. It was feeling like finding this Sister was almost too easy. Well, I don't know about the rest of you, but I'm hungry. We might as well get some food while we wait."

Eyeballing the serving girl, Vik agreed. "Food sounds good; of course, what I'm hungry for doesn't come from a kitchen, unless it's carrying a tray."

She came to their table, smiled and set down a tray with a large earthen jug and glasses enough for all the pirates. *"Buenos Dias, señors.* Would you like *pescado, pollo, o carne del cerdo?* I am sorry, we have had no *filete* for many months now."

On closer examination, she was not as young as any of them first thought. The dimness of the room hid the fact she was a woman in her prime rather than a girl. Her voluminous skirts hinted at a voluptuous body, her dark eyes danced with a secret laughter, and her silky black braids hung to almost mid-thigh. Her bronze skin carried the warm scent of spice and sun. Viktor ached for a taste of her.

Each of the pirates named their meat of choice. Jon-Jon was the first to uncork the jug, since obviously neither the Captain nor Grimm were interested in it. His first taste of the clear liquid nearly made him choke. What had appeared to be water turned out to be very potent liquor.

"What is this stuff, lass? I've never tasted anything like it."

"It is *mescal, señor*, from the northern deserts," she answered. "I will bring you soup and tortillas while your dinner is cooking."

"Soup?" Grimm questioned.

"*Si*. It is a local specialty. Very spicy."

As he watched her walk back to the kitchen, Vik observed, "Perhaps it is for the best that Belle couldn't come with us after all."

"As if her presence would stop you from wenching," Grimm chuckled.

"It wouldn't, but I won't have to listen to her bitch about it this way."

Before long, the woman returned pushing a cart. A small cauldron sat on it, lidded. She lifted the lid with a rag and set it aside as steam rose from the contents. The aroma of the soup stirred their hunger. As soon as she placed the filled bowls in front of them, they set to as if they were starved.

Except for Viktor, who only tasted the soup before he turned his attention back to the wench. He reached out and caught her wrist, before she could return the soup cart to the kitchen. She looked at him, puzzled but not alarmed.

"Is the soup not to your liking, *señor*?"

He gently pulled her closer. "The soup is fine, pet, but it is not what I am hungry for."

She tried to pull free, only to find his grasp unbreakable. Realizing the struggle was futile, she allowed him to pull her into his lap. She twisted away from his attempt to kiss her and presented him with a spoonful of the soup, instead.

"You should eat your soup, *señor*. You will need your strength," she teased.

Chuckling, he humored her and allowed her to feed him.

Just as she promised, the soup tasted quite spicy, indeed. He felt its warmth spread through his body. The heat seemed to concentrate around his eyes and ears and in his chest.

His vision swam, and sounds became distorted. He sensed something not right about the situation, but a strange complacency seemed to overwhelm him. He heard a lovely voice singing, causing strange visions he didn't understand to pass before his eyes — or possibly only through his mind. He almost reached the point where he would be willing to do anything to make the sensations continue, when the heat around his chest intensified sharply.

It still took a few moments for him to realize the nearly scalding heat came from the outside of his body rather than from within.

The woman gasped in surprise as he stood inhumanly fast. The painful burn from the milky crystal called the

Elder's Stone he wore next to his skin cleared his head of the spell she was casting. His eyes aglow, he glared at her where she'd been dumped on the floor. She'd already started to get to her feet.

"Who are you?" he demanded.

"I am my father's daughter." She smiled evilly. "Do not think you have escaped me so easily, Viktor Brandewyne."

With sudden clarity, he realized she was the Sister he had come here to find. Before he could deal with her, however, he found he had other problems to attend to first.

His men were in the throes of the spell. Two were huddled in on themselves just rocking back and forth. Two others stumbled around giggling maniacally and repeatedly colliding with the walls as if trying to walk through them. Jon-Jon brushed at himself in an almost panic and repeatedly said, "Get them off!" in a shrill voice. Grimm looked like he was having a seizure as he convulsed in his chair and kept a death grip on the table edge.

Viktor rounded on the witch and snarled, "Remove your spell, bitch!"

In response, she chuckled and ordered, "Take him, but do not harm him."

The five crewmen, including Jon-Jon, stopped what they were doing and focused on their captain. Slowly, they moved to circle him and began to close the circle in.

Thinking fast, he saw his options as cripple or kill his men or try to break the control she held over them. He reached out along the invisible lines connecting them to his will and found them still to be his.

Now to see whose will was stronger, hers or his.

He concentrated and ordered, "Mr. Jon, have the men stand down!"

They all grabbed their heads, apparently in pain, as the Sister and the vampire fought for control. Finally, awareness came back into their eyes with the exception of one. The man screamed and collapsed to the floor, as blood streamed from his eyes, nose, mouth and ears. His death caused Viktor to stumble a bit when the blood bond broke.

The witch frowned, irritated at the vampire's ability to break her hold on his men, even though the struggle left one dead. Then she noticed Grimm still convulsed as his will fought her spell. She realized he had no direct bond with Viktor. Free from having to concentrate on the other five pirates, she focused all of her energy on the first mate.

Grimm could not stand against the Sister's full power. His seizures ceased, and he stood to face his Captain. His mind screamed at him to stop, but his body was played like a puppet by her spell. He couldn't even voice his dissent.

Viktor growled, "Enough of your games witch. Release my first mate, now!"

"Free him yourself, if you can," she taunted.

"Curse be damned! Release him or I'll gut you where you stand!" He moved for her with lightning speed. He was surprised to find Grimm intercepting him just as quickly. He could only reason that her spell gave his first mate a speed to match the vampire's.

"Get out of the way, Hezekiah," he warned. "I don't want to hurt you, but I will not hesitate to do so, if it comes to it."

Rather than obey, Grimm grappled with him, almost matching his strength. They struggled for a few minutes, neither gaining the upper hand. Just as Viktor thought he might have to kill his friend; Grimm got a handful of his shirt and ripped the front open. The three necklaces the vampire wore spilled out: a small silver vial, an emerald encrusted gold cross, and a milky white crystal bound in silver wire.

The crystal flared to a brilliant light, intense enough to rival the full moon. As soon as the glow enveloped them, Grimm released Viktor and took a heavy breath.

Viktor's quick reflexes were all that stopped him from putting a fist through his friend's face.

"Hezekiah?"

"Aye, Captain. I'm free of her." He nodded.

"Where's Ferdinand?" Vik remembered the boy.

"The *chico* is mine, *Vampiro*," the witch answered. "I did not make my magic strong enough to hold you, it seems, but it did give him back to me. You had no right to steal him."

He narrowed his eyes at her. "Give me one good reason not to slit your throat, Rosalia." As he advanced on her, she retreated from the crystal's glow.

"You are *El Uno*, but you need my help," she replied, never taking her eyes from the crystal. "How is it you come to hold the Elder's Stone? Why does it resonate so strongly with that one?"

Hezekiah gave her an unfriendly look. He detested the way she had tried to enslave him, and it disturbed him she could sense the fragment of old Zeke's power he carried. Viktor had never suspected it, and he'd just as soon no one put the idea in his Captain's mind. Even though it wasn't, he knew Viktor would take it as a betrayal.

"The stone was given to me by Mother Celie," Vik answered tensely. "It freed me from your spell just as it freed Mr. Grimm, so I don't know what you mean about resonating with him." As an afterthought, he added, "What I did to the boy was not permanent. If you had bothered to use your magic to do so, you would have sensed he was no longer under my control when we arrived."

Her demeanor remained petulant, making him wonder if she wasn't as powerful as she would have him believe. "Then why is he still with you?"

"His grandfather asked me to bring him as a guide, to protect him from the men of his village. They were rather overly frightened of me, considering I offered them no violence and only brought a small fragment of my crew." His emotions calmed and fell under control as he spoke. He hoped he could smooth things out with the Sister, so they could attend to the business he needed to conduct with her.

Rosalia took a deep breath and composed herself. "You are right, *señor*. Sometimes my temper gets the better of me. I have been incensed ever since I sensed your power touch one of mine. I am very territorial."

"I've noticed that about all the Sisters of Power I have found so far," he nodded. "That is why I have not hunted since I came ashore."

"That was wise of you. However, you dealt honorably with Ferdinand. I cost you the life of one of your men, therefore, I owe you a life. Barring *el chico*, you may feed from one of my followers," she offered.

He felt skeptical of the generosity. "Will it be someone of your choosing or mine?" His voice remained carefully neutral.

Rosalia smiled. "You suspect another trap. To prove my good faith, you may select your victim. I only ask that you do not feed from Ferdinand. I will leave it to your judgment whether to kill or just feed on your chosen victim."

Viktor considered it for a while. He saw no way she could use this as another attempt to bind him to her service, so he nodded his acceptance. "Thank you."

Still glaring at the Sister, Grimm spoke to his captain. "Captain, if you don't mind, I don't want to spend any more time here than necessary. Can we find out what her price is, so we can get on with things?"

"You do not like me, *señor.*"

"No, I do not," he answered. "If you ever try anything like what you did on me again, I will kill you, Sister or no."

"You won't have to, Hezekiah. She'll already be dead by my hand." Viktor's expression carried cold warning. "Mr. Grimm is one of my men. I protect what is mine, and you are not the only one in this room who is territorial."

Rosalia's expression became solemn and guarded. Her black eyes gave nothing of her thoughts away. She remained silent for several minutes before she responded. "He is not truly yours, or I would not have been able to take him after you freed the others."

"I trust him enough to not feel the need to force my will or blood on him."

She gave him a sardonic half-smile. "You surprise me. You do not strike me as the trusting sort. Be careful that your trust does not betray you."

"Hezekiah knows that I wouldn't hesitate to kill him if he were to turn against me. Now, I would like to get down to business." He closed the subject on Grimm. "I need to acquire some of your magic, and we both know it will come with a price. What will this price be?"

Rosalia eyed him up and down, temptation flitting briefly over her features. The look was not lost on the vampire. "It is almost tempting to let you finish what you were starting before our little contest of wills, but that would be too easy. My magic and help are not bought so cheaply."

He gave a wicked laugh. "Trust me, in that regard, I am many things, but cheap isn't one of them."

"I have no doubt, *señor*. I may even ask you to prove it to me, when or if you return with what I want."

"And what exactly do you want?"

"I need you to bring me some devil's hoof. It can be unprepared or powdered, whichever is more convenient to transport," she told him. "I used the last of my supply in the soup. Unfortunately, I did not have as much as I needed, it seems."

Viktor and Grimm both looked skeptical about the request. The first mate especially didn't like the idea of giving her the substance she had used to try to enslave them.

Vik was doubtful about what exactly she was asking for. He had no idea of where to start searching for it, either. "I know you won't make this easy, but could you at least tell me where to start looking?"

"Ha! All I can tell you is that it is not found anywhere around here, or I would have it in plentiful supply." She snorted.

"That was oh so very helpful." His voice dripped sarcasm.

"Bueno." She smiled, deliberately ignoring the sarcasm. "Take Ferdinand with you when you leave. It is safe for him to return to his village but take him no further than that. You may go hunt now. I will see to it your man receives a proper burial." She dismissed him.

With a nod to his men to follow, he turned and strode out the door. The villagers cleared a path around them. A few local men went into the cantina, and the rest of the villagers went back to their business and errands.

Silent Fathoms

Chapter 10

Once they all stood outside, Viktor stopped and eyed the locals for potential prey. His Hunger kept growing nearly to the point where it would be difficult for him to stop at just one kill. The last thing he needed was to lapse into a feeding frenzy. He doubted it would sit well with *Tia* Rosalia and could end up costing him the rest of the men he'd brought with him.

Looking out toward the ocean, he saw a possible solution to his dilemma. A slow smile spread across his face. He pointed to the harbor and asked, "Mr. Grimm is that ship flying British colors?"

"I do believe it is," Grimm confirmed.

"Good. Take the lads. Ask around and see what you can find out about this devil's hoof that she wants. I'm going to hunt."

"Aye Captain." He blinked to find himself talking to empty air. Viktor left so quickly not even Grimm saw him move.

☠

The sailor in the crow's nest nearly jumped out of his skin when a heavy hand fell on his shoulder. He turned to find a tall, travel-worn man standing with him. The man's eyes were so green they seemed to glow.

"How did you get up here? I know I didn't fall asleep on watch," the sailor demanded as he reached for his boson's whistle. He never got it up to his lips.

"I flew up like a little bird," Viktor said with a smile seconds before he tore the man's throat out. When he finished draining the body, he ripped the head off and tossed it and the body into the bay below.

Several sailors went to investigate the splash. Viktor dropped in on one who didn't. A few others turned to look, sensing movement. They only saw a blur of motion as Viktor snapped the man's neck and vanished over the side with his victim. He hovered just above the water that lapped against the hull of the ship and fed. Once again, he beheaded the empty husk. He had no desire nor need to create anymore vampires.

He had to fight his Hunger to keep it from possessing him. Every fiber of his being screamed at him to take out the vessel's entire crew. Rather than abating, his Hunger grew with each kill.

If he allowed himself to go on a feeding frenzy, he knew he might not be able to stop himself short of destroying a large percentage of the seaside village. He started to wonder if his drastic increase in appetite was a side effect of the spell Rosalia tried to put on him.

Before he finished, he drained five more sailors off the British merchant ship. He needed to take a few more, but it was getting harder to keep what was happening quiet. Already, the disappearance of their crewmates one by one spooked several of the remaining sailors.

"Too bad Belle couldn't be here," he thought. *"She'd have enjoyed the sport."* He also considered that she might have been able to warn him about the spell on the soup, and he wouldn't have lost a man.

He finally began to feel sated for the moment, but he still intended to accept Rosalia's offer of one of her people for blood. He just wanted to make a few arrangements for the next leg of his journey first.

He returned to the village and sought out the market to look for a liquor vendor. It didn't take long to find several. He would have been surprised if there hadn't been any, Juchitán being a port town.

With a minimum of haggling, he bought a cask of brandy and an empty cask of equal size. He had the vendor divide the liquor between the two casks. The man wasn't puzzled by the request. He assumed that Viktor would be watering the liquor down to stretch out its duration.

Viktor had every intention of diluting the contents of the casks but not with water. He went in search of the largest man he could find. He reasoned that the larger the man, the more blood to be had.

It amused him slightly to see how a few of the villagers scurried off toward the cantina after answering his questions about who the largest man was. He wasn't too worried about it. Rosalia had given him leave to take anyone in her service except the boy Ferdinand. He intended to take her up on the offer.

Finally, he located a giant of a man called Rodrigo. He appeared easily the same size as Viktor's ship smith, Anvil, and dwarfed the vampire. As Viktor stood around six-foot-three, that said a lot. For a moment, he wondered if two casks would be enough.

"Perdona me, amigo," he said to get his victim's attention. "Could you give me a hand with these?" He pretended to have difficulty carrying the two casks.

"Si." Rodrigo nodded and lumbered over to pick one up.

As he stooped, Viktor tried to bespell him, only to find that he couldn't. The man wasn't particularly strong-willed, but Rosalia's magic lay heavy on him. He didn't understand why the Sister was making this difficult. She had told him he could hunt one of her people.

"Where do you want this, *señor*?" Rodrigo asked.

"Follow me."

He figured he might as well make use of the man first. He led him back to where they had left their supply wagon to save the trouble of carrying the casks back. The stable offered a hook and hoist inside for loading and unloading cargo and fodder. It would suit his needs adequately.

As soon as the giant finished setting the cask down, Viktor used his inhuman speed to knock the man unconscious. He really didn't want to deal with a struggle. It wasn't that he didn't think he could take Rodrigo in a fair fight, but rather that he didn't want to draw too much attention.

He used some rope to bind the man then hoisted him by his ankles. Positioning the first cask under him, he lowered him into the open top until his shoulders rested on the rim. He slipped one of his stilettoes out of its sheath and slit the giant's throat. The rim of the cask caught the initial arterial spray, so very little blood was lost. Viktor had done this particular operation several times before.

The wave of magic which hit him caused him to stagger back from his kill. Only then, he realized Rosalia had still been trying to ensnare him. She must have hoped he would feed directly. The trap probably would have worked for a while at least. He didn't know how long he would have been trapped in her service.

He felt fortunate for the presence of the British ship in port. He'd wondered about its business here. He'd never heard of regular English trade on this coast. Spain guarded her territories jealously. Could it be old Zeke somehow put it in his path?

He would be even more cautious around this Sister. He did not wish to give her a third opportunity to try to enslave him. If he didn't need her willing help, he would have killed her for the insolence.

To be safe, once both casks were filled, he dipped the crystal he wore in them before sealing them. Something must have worked. The blood-brandy mixture glowed briefly before the scent of her magic faded.

He felt glad he had not decided to turn Rodrigo. He already had a vampire in New Orleans spying on him through one of his making. He would not allow Rosalia such a luxury.

He grasped the body under the arms after he'd lowered it back to the ground and dragged it outside. He then flew with it to the roof of the cantina. The roof was flat, and a trap door led down into the building. When he knocked, a young man opened it and popped his head up to see what was going on.

Viktor spoke to him in Spanish to avoid the delay of translation. *"Tell Rosalia I said thank you for allowing me to hunt. I have brought her the body of my victim for her to dispose of as she sees fit."*

"Si, señor." The head went back below the roof level.

Viktor didn't wait around to see what the Sister would do. He launched from the roof and went in search of his men.

He found them back at the wagon. Grimm decided they should go ahead and get supplies built up while trying to get a lead on some devil's hoof. He had the men securing the goods when Viktor walked in.

"Any news, Mr. Grimm?"

"Aye, actually," the first mate responded. "Took me a bit to get the feel of the local dialect, but it's easier to understand than the boy's. It looks like our best place to start looking is going to be close to Vera Cruz."

"Of course," he responded sourly. "The one place in all of Mexico that I am least welcome, and that's where we have to go."

"Well, we may not have to go into the port city proper," Grimm consoled. "No one here actually knows or, if they do know, will tell what devil's hoof is. But a few said they've heard of a cave in the mountains near Vera Cruz where the Devil is rumored to dwell."

Vik raised an eyebrow at that. The expression wasn't lost on Grimm, who gave him a sardonic grin. "I know. It sounds pretty dubious to me, too."

"Well, it is a place to start, at least." Viktor shrugged. "And we have to go back to that shore to return to the ship."

"My thoughts exactly."

Ferdinand arrived at the stable with his own travel pack. He made straight for Viktor as soon as he saw him.

"*Capitan* Brandee, *Tia* Rosalia asked me to give you a message," he said.

"What is it?"

The boy spoke slowly, concentrating on the words. He wanted to continue practicing his English. "She said thank you for returning Rodrigo's body for a proper burial. It means much to his family. She said she had expected you to turn him." That last part was said with a look of confusion. "Is that the right word?"

Viktor nodded. "It is. Your English is improving every day, Ferdinand."

"*Gracias*. I have my bundle and am ready to travel when you are."

"Very well. Put your gear in the wagon, and we'll head out."

Tamara A. Lowery

Chapter 11

Belle had long since distanced herself from the ship. It both relieved and frustrated her that she wasn't accompanying Viktor on his overland trek. They both felt sure she wouldn't have survived that far away from her element, but as much as she hated to admit it to herself, she worried about him facing the Sister on his own. Her vision of Rosalia had given her a sense the witch was wily, not to be trusted, and posed a very real danger to Viktor.

Her increasingly human-like emotions where he was concerned were throwing off her hunting skills. In weeks, she'd only caught one sick, weak mako shark.

Now she was famished. It had been days since she had seen anything larger than plankton, and she didn't eat plankton.

A distant vibration in the water caught her attention. Floating and still, she strained every sense she had. After a few minutes, she had a pretty good idea of what direction it was coming from. She headed that way, but not quite at top speed. She didn't want her approach detected by the potential prey.

After a few hours of swimming, her prey finally came into sight. It was a school of tuna, a huge school of tuna. Several of them, in fact most of them, dwarfed her in size, and the school looked big enough to fill a cubic mile.

Even though starving, she slowed her approach to a lazy, almost disinterested drift. She didn't want to spook the fish. Gradually, patiently, she worked her way closer to the school. Once she was swimming alongside one of the giants, she stabbed one of her talons through its brain, killing it instantly.

She thought about letting it drift and making a second kill. There had been almost no blood, and the rest of the school hadn't yet realized there was a predator in its midst. But she decided against it. She needed to feed now. She could always track down the others later.

As soon as she started ripping her kill apart, the nearest tuna scattered. They reformed as a group about a mile away and started putting as much distanced between them and the siren as possible.

While she ate, Belladonna wondered how soon Viktor would return to his ship. She found she actually missed him. That emotion irritated hr. She vented her frustration on the tuna carcass, savaging it.

Considering the fish was probably three times her size, she made quick work of eating it. Only a few scales escaped her appetite. Other predators had arrived, drawn by the scent of blood in the water. A white tip shark was bold enough to get close. It drew her attention. The various sharks usually kept their distance from the siren, especially when she was feeding. They instinctively recognized her as one of the few creatures that would prey on them.

She emitted a low growl and darted toward the white tip. A reef materialized in front of her, and she nearly couldn't stop her forward momentum in time to avoid a collision.

She surfaced in a rage and pulled herself onto the shore of Hell's Breath Island. As soon as her legs formed, she stormed over the rise to the rocky depression where Zeke kept his fire.

"Damn you, old man! I was hunting!" she growled at him.

Completely unfazed by her tirade, Uncle Zeke pointed to a rock on the other side of the fire, a tacit command to sit. She snarled at him. He fixed her with an unreadable stare and pointed again. She stomped over to the rock, flopped down onto it, crossed her arms and stuck her tongue out at him.

Looking into the fire, the old wizard spoke to the petulant siren. "You was huntin' the wrong fish, girl."

That got her attention. She narrowed her eyes and asked, "What do you mean by that, Zeke?"

"That mermaid, Alyssa, is going to whelp any day now. It is time to find her and put her down."

"Viktor is not going to like it. He told her he would not let me harm her."

Zeke blinked, the only sign of his surprise. "He told you he said that?"

"No. Grimm did."

The old man peered closely at her. "Just how strong is the bond between you and your master?"

She wanted to argue that Vik wasn't her master, but she knew it to be a lie. "It would probably do irrevocable damage to both of us, if I were to fight him full strength."

The old man stood and paced; a completely uncharacteristic action for him. Obviously, he was bothered by this turn of events. Without warning, he kicked the edge of the fire vigorously and scattered sparks all over the startled siren.

"What the hell was that about?!" she demanded and brushed the burning flecks away from her.

"How alert do you feel now?"

"Very and quite pissed!" she snarled.

He shook his head. "Be quiet and reach out with all your senses. How clear are they?"

Obediently, she made herself relax and just be. After a few moments, she opened her eyes. She hadn't realized she'd closed them.

Zeke raised an eyebrow at her. "If your pupils were any more dilated, your eyes would be black."

"It's been so long since my senses were this sharp. I'd forgotten what it's like." Her voice resonated with awe. She felt almost drunk on the power and sensory input. Only one thing felt wrong. There was a blind spot. "Where is Viktor?"

"Don't you know?"

"No." She shook her head. "I can't sense him at all."

"Good. Then he can't sense you either. Now you are protected from him stopping you from killing the mermaid."

There was one question she had to ask. "Have you broken my bondage to him permanently?"

"Do you want me to?"

She started to say, "Yes," but stopped. Did she? "I — don't know. Part of me wants to be free of him, but part of me doesn't." She hit her thigh with her fist and growled in irritation. "What is wrong with me? I should jump at any chance to reclaim my freedom! Why am I not? I don't owe

Viktor Brandewyne any loyalty. The only reason I'm tied to him is because of an accident."

"Was it really an accident, girl? Do you really believe that?" His question implied otherwise.

She looked at him sideways. "You know something, old man. Are you saying he deliberately trapped me?"

"Not deliberately," he cackled, "at least not on his part. But I'm not saying that it was an accident either. Just like that whelp Alyssa's fixing to drop, some things are meant to be."

"Well, if this is meant to be, why do you offer the hope of freedom?"

Zeke shrugged. "Figured why not? Just because you're bound to him doesn't mean it has to be permanent. You are still needed to help him track down the Sisters, however."

"Then there is no point in severing the bond."

"You'd be free to go your way after he finished what he has to do."

"No, I wouldn't," she argued. "Viktor likes control. He may not have done it deliberately the first time, but if I were to rejoin his crew free of his influence, he would find some way of capturing me again. So, I don't see the point in it."

"Hmph," he snorted then laughed. "You're smarter than I thought. All right then. Be off with ye. You've got a mermaid to hunt. Just remember to spare the whelp and bring him back to Hell's Breath — alive."

Before she could blink, Hell's Breath and Uncle Zeke were gone, and she found herself floating in the sea again.

As soon as her tail reformed, she headed out to seek for any trace of the vampire-tainted mermaid.

Tamara A. Lowery

Chapter 12

"Sails approaching fast from the northeast!" the lookout called down.

Captain Wormsloe peered through the glass and focused on the vessel. At current speed, the approaching ship should reach them right at dusk. The flagging proclaimed it to be a courier ship.

He smiled to himself. The news they could gain from it may be valuable. It would definitely be fresh. He was really getting tired of the stale news they got, when they could get any at all. Often it was several months old.

She would be glad of this encounter, as well. He could guarantee that the unsuspecting crew of the courier would not be pleased to learn what was in store for them.

Of course, first he had to find a way to stop them short of ramming their ship.

Steps were taken to make the ship look like a harmless merchant. Wormsloe had his crew run the signal that they had mail to relay, gambling that the Navy courier wasn't under strict orders to stop for no one.

The gamble paid off. The courier pulled alongside just as the sun dipped below the horizon. By the time they were close enough to tie up, his passenger had joined him.

"Captain Wormsloe," she greeted him. "What is going on?"

"Good evening, m'lady. We're about to tie up to this Navy courier. They may have fresh news — and food," he replied.

She gave him a carefully closed-mouth smile. "That is good to hear. I could use a good feed."

"I thought as much." He turned his attention to the other ship.

"Ahoy, *Lorelei*," came the call from the other vessel. "Permission to come aboard?"

The woman raised an eyebrow. "My, they are making this interestingly easy."

"Permission granted," Wormsloe called back.

Before long, the vessel's commander and two of his crewmen crossed the gangplank. Upon seeing a female, the officer bowed and introduced himself. "Captain Turlington at your service, ma'am. Captain?"

"Wormsloe." He shook the proffered hand. He knew the Navy man would be dead before sunrise, more than likely, but he would give no indication of that knowledge."

The woman nodded her head in the approximation of a bow. "I am called Carpathia."

"Forgive my forwardness, ma'am, but you have the bearing of a noblewoman," Turlington observed.

"You are quite observant, sir. However, I am traveling incognito, and to give you my title would reveal my true identity." She smiled.

He returned the smile. He found her exotic accent mesmerizing. Her ivory pale skin and silky black hair proved quite stunning. And her eyes — a man could get lost in those eyes.

"Captain Turlington, are you alright?"

He blinked, having to physically shake himself free from her hypnotic quality. "Y-yes, ma'am. My apologies. I don't know what came over me."

"No apology is necessary, Captain," she replied. "While Captain Wormsloe has some bags of mail he hopes you could help relay, I was hoping you had some news of the goings on in these waters."

"Of course, ma'am. We would have hailed your vessel if you hadn't signaled first," Turlington explained. "We've been given orders from Port Royal to hail every vessel we encounter on the way back to rejoin our Commodore to warn them."

"Warn about what, sir?" Wormsloe asked, ever alert.

"There is a grave danger from piracy in the area," he spoke low. "If we may discuss the matter in your cabin, Captain Wormsloe? I've no wish to alarm your crew."

"Of course, sir. Follow me." He offered his arm to Carpathia then led the way to his cabin.

Once there, he offered Turlington a glass of port. The man accepted but wondered, "Should you not offer the lady something, Captain?"

"Captain Wormsloe is not being rude, Captain Turlington," she assured him. "I have traveled for several months aboard the *Lorelei*, and the captain knows that spirits do not agree with me. They give me indigestion."

"I did not know, ma'am."

"You said you had warnings of a pirate threat. What precisely is the threat? I thought the Royal Navy had all but eradicated piracy in the Caribbean," Wormsloe said.

"Would that it was so, sir, but alas, it seems the worst of the bastards have still to be caught or killed. Oh! My apologies for my language, ma'am. I fear I am more accustomed to speaking to seasoned sailors than I am someone of your station." He winced.

He found her laughter musical and entrancing. It distracted him almost enough to miss the brief glimpse of sharp, elongated canines. Even so, he wasn't sure of what he had seen.

"Do not worry about my delicate ears, sir. One does not spend months aboard a sailing vessel without hearing some very colorful turns of phrase."

He nodded and took a sip of his port then continued, "Anyway, as I was saying, the worst of them still manage to elude justice. It has recently come to light that one whom we thought dead months ago has resurfaced and has gotten his hands on a ship-o-the-line."

"Who is this pirate," Carpathia asked and leaned forward with interest.

"Bloody Vik Brandee, ma'am. I don't know if you have ever heard of him, but in these parts, he is the deadliest and hardest to catch pirate to sail since the days of Billy Black. The only other pirate to rival him is the Grimm Reaper. In fact, they used to sail together until about five or six years ago, when they had a falling out."

"You say this Brandee was presumed dead until recently? What happened?"

"Well, ma'am, I regret to say that one of our own did not do a very thorough job. Last year, the captain of the *HMS Bonnie Mae* chased Brandee's ship into a hurricane. The ship was destroyed in the storm, and no survivors were found, but he must've escaped in a small boat. If the Bonnie Mae had done a better search, he would have been caught and hanged. Now he has been reported active again. A Boston shipping house has lost two ships to him during the spice trade season. He took the second one within a day's sailing of Bermuda. He may have taken a third ship in that same area and time frame. A stripped vessel was found adrift with only three survivors, one of which died shortly after rescue. Their account seemed far-fetched, though. They did not claim to have been attacked by Brandee himself but by a female pirate or a male dressed as a woman. They said she was asking after Brandee and that she slaughtered the entire crew. Personally, I think they swallowed too much seawater, and it addled their brains."

Carpathia's eyes smoldering like coals, the only outward sign of her rage. She was old enough to prevent her body language from betraying her moods.

Wormsloe asked, "You said Brandee has a ship-o-the-line?"

Turlington slammed back the rest of his drink before he responded, "That is the worst news of all. We still don't know how he got his hands on it. But the report is that it's the prototype of its class, a dreadnaught designed for pirate hunting. The only ship in the fleet which is a true match for it is the *HMS Quicksilver*, built on the same lines. The *Quicksilver* almost didn't get built after the *War God* disappeared on its maiden voyage nearly four years ago."

"I've heard the stories about that," Wormsloe commented. "There was a lot of superstition around the disappearance. I always figured that her crew or captain was too green, and she proved too much ship for them to handle."

"That possibility had occurred to the Admiralty, as well, which is why the crew for the *Quicksilver* was carefully selected. We aim to completely eradicate the pirate and smuggling presence in the Caribbean," he confirmed.

Carpathia smiled at him. "You are very brave, Captain Turlington. I am sure you will be able to find this evil pirate and put a stop to his criminal ways."

"Yes, ma'am." His answering smile was of one besotted. Her eyes were like blackest night, but warm and inviting at the same time. He felt that in their depths he would be safe and loved.

Wormsloe frowned. "M'lady, please take your meal in your own cabin. I do not care to watch."

She laughed, openly revealing her fangs for the first time. Turlington remained oblivious, firmly under her spell. "All these years you have served our master, yet you have no stomach for how we feed. You are going to be a miserable creature, when he finally brings you over."

"He has not spoken of any such reward for my service, m'lady. I fully expect to serve until I am no longer of use and then to be discarded."

"Then why do you serve?"

"I have my reasons." He would say no more on the matter.

Not really caring, she stood and held out a hand to Turlington. He rose and came to her obediently. Once she reached her cabin and brought him inside, she shut the door.

He waited expectantly, while she stood and stared at him. Finally, she spoke. "Strip."

He did so without hesitation. Never in his wildest dreams could he have hoped to bed a noblewoman. He had always heard that the nobles were a decadent lot. It looked as if the stories were true. It mildly surprised him that she remained clothed.

She looked him up and down and decided she liked what she saw. "You will want to lie flat for this." She pointed at the bed. Once he positioned himself like she wanted, she knelt by the bed.

He jumped at her initial touch. Her skin felt like ice. "There is no need to be so nervous, my love," her voice soothed. "If you please me, I might grant you a boon. You do want to please me, don't you?"

"Oh yes." His voice was rough with lust. He still couldn't believe his luck.

"I need you to answer some questions for me. First, what is your Christian name? I like to know a man's name, if I am going to take him to my bed."

"Joseph."

"That is a good, strong name. I like it, Joseph," she sighed as she continued to caress and manipulate him. "I am glad we met. I have heard of this Vik Brandee. I was sent here to find him, as a matter of fact."

He propped up on his elbows to give her an alarmed look. "Oh, my dear Carpathia, you don't want to do that! He is very dangerous. I would hate to see you fall victim to him."

"It is he who would fall victim to me, my love." She pushed him back to the bed. "I have been sent to kill him. Will you help me?"

Tamara A. Lowery

Lost in her eyes and voice, he nodded. "Anything you ask of me, lover."

"Good."

He was ready for her when she put her mouth on him. The hard smoothness of her fangs sliding on either side was a new sensation. It didn't take her long to bring him. Just before he came, she slid him in deep and drove her fangs into his base.

He screamed.

She fed.

☠

Joseph slowly regained consciousness. At first, his surroundings disoriented him. He lay naked in a strange bed and cabin. How did he get there?

A beautiful woman came into view. She seemed vaguely familiar. He found that he feared her yet craved her touch. She was his goddess. He would do anything to gain her favor.

"I see you are awake, Joseph," she smiled.

"I know you. You're Carpathia?" He sounded uncertain.

She nodded and smiled. "That's right. I am glad you remember."

"Where am I, how did I get here?"

"You are aboard the *Lorelei*. We rescued you from pirates. They attacked at night, when most of your men were asleep." She placed a hand on his arm, sending an electric shock through him. "I am sorry, but you were the only survivor."

"I don't remember anything about that."

"You suffered a head wound. I have heard that can affect the memory," she told him. "You also suffered a leg wound and lost a great deal of blood. So, you may feel weak for a while."

He glanced down at his leg and saw a stitched wound that went from the top of his thigh into his pubic hair. He was both alarmed and grateful that he hadn't lost his manhood. Then he finally registered the fact he was naked in the presence of a lady.

It amused Carpathia seeing her new toy begin to blush. She thought it precious and found it mildly surprising he had enough blood to manage a blush at all. She handed him some trousers and smiled. "It is a bit late to be embarrassed, Joseph. I was the one who dressed your wounds."

He took the pants and quickly slipped them on, wincing as the fabric scraped across the stitches. Once he restored his modesty, he stood shakily and looked about for a shirt. She anticipated this and handed him his uniform shirt.

"I need to return to the *Quicksilver* and report to the Commodore."

"Of course. If you feel strong enough to walk, I will take you to Captain Wormsloe. You can give him the coordinates we'll need to return you to your ship."

"Thank you for everything, Carpathia. I am forever in your debt." He smiled down at her. She had to be the most beautiful creature he'd ever seen. What he wouldn't do for a taste of those lips.

The vampire smiled up at her toy. *"Yes, you are,"* she thought. Aloud, she said, "You are welcome, Joseph." Then she stretched up and gave him a light kiss. He had to fight to keep from falling over when she pulled away.

She led him out of the cabin.

☠

Later, in Wormsloe's cabin, she held a private conference with the captain. He quickly expressed his doubts.

"This is a dangerous game you're playing, lass. I hope you don't bring down the wrath of the entire British Navy on us."

"You are worried for nothing, Captain," she assured him. "Turlington is completely in my thrall. He will do what I tell him to and believe what I wish him to believe. I have already begun to implant false memories of a pirate attack into his dreams. He will never know they aren't his own. You scuttled his vessel?"

"Yes, although it was a shame to waste a craft that was in that good condition. But we can't leave any evidence of this encounter. There are still those who hunt your kind; why draw their attention to this part of the world?"

Her voice was dangerously low. "You do not need to lecture me on survival skills. I have been around for centuries. It was not by accident, nor luck."

"No need to be so touchy about it, lass."

She sighed. "I am still Hungry. His crew was so pitifully small, I was loath to share any with my slave. I only did so to prevent him from attacking any of your crew, since we need them to operate this vessel."

"Thank you for your consideration," he replied drily.

"Too bad I will not be able to hunt freely aboard this dreadnaught he claims to serve on," she continued, ignoring the sarcasm. "However, I want to continue to follow the trail of dead mers for now, Captain Wormsloe," she added. "If we can find Brandewyne that way, I will dispose of my new toy once I've tired of him."

Wormsloe nodded his agreement. "I hope we can. I would prefer not to involve the Royal Navy if it is at all avoidable. The only reason I'm not on the lists is because

I've kept a low profile and followed my employer's orders implicitly."

"Then be grateful that I have need of you and your ship, Captain. Otherwise, I would not think twice of sacrificing you or it to achieve my goal." Her tone was chilly.

His reply equaled it. "Duly noted."

Tamara A. Lowery

Chapter 13

They left Ferdinand with his grandfather, once they reached the little village. The boy wanted to continue with them, but Viktor would not break his agreement with Rosalia.

He eventually had to threaten to kill the boy if he tried to follow them. He made it clear to Ferdinand that he would not be able to sneak around to follow, either. He convinced the boy he could not only smell him but also hear his heartbeat from a distance.

As an added safety, Grimm quietly told the village elder he should tie the boy up for a couple of days. He knew his captain really would kill the lad if he had to. Viktor Brandewyne did not make idle threats. Fortunately, the old man believed him.

Viktor really didn't want to be so close to the port of Vera Cruz. It wasn't that he feared Alberto Villanova. He didn't. He just knew the man still held a grudge over the deflowering of his daughter and had enough power to make trouble for him. Viktor didn't have the time to deal with such a hassle.

Tamara A. Lowery

"I'd like to keep my presence here as quiet as possible," he told his men.

"Villanova still being pissy?" Grimm asked.

"Aye. The man will not let go of a grudge."

"That's true." Jon-Jon nodded. "That business with his daughter happened, what, six or seven years ago?"

"Eight, actually. I think the main reason he refuses to give up the grudge is the bastard I got on the wench. A pregnancy is not easy to hide, and talk got out," Vik surmised.

Grimm snorted his disgust. "Hmph, the man just doesn't know how to market. He could have still gotten a power match out of the girl, if he'd just explained that she was educated on how to please a man instead of needing training, and her fertility was already proven. Any randy old goat with money would be glad to have a wife that could give him an heir as well as good sport."

Viktor laughed, "Actually, he did try that approach. Theresa wouldn't agree to it. Why settle for an ugly old man, when she'd had the best?"

They all had a good chuckle at that.

The pirates made their way to the villages in the mountains west of Vera Cruz and started asking around for any local witches. More often than not, the villagers crossed themselves and ran away. Only a few had anything useful in the way of information.

Finally, Viktor located an old *brujo*. The old man lived, or hid, deep in the mountains in a shallow cave. The extremely rugged terrain made the cave nearly impossible to find.

The old warlock began to finger an old, beaded talisman he wore around his neck the moment he saw Viktor. "What do you want here? How is it you bear the sun's touch?" he demanded warily.

The warlock's fluent English briefly surprised the vampire, until Viktor noticed the man's mouth movements did not match the sounds. He had used some sort of spell to translate.

"I am not a dead man, *señor*. I am cursed," Viktor answered. He knew what the old man's question had hinted at. "I have come here for information, if you are able to give it."

"Ask your question, then."

Right to the point. Viktor appreciated that and found it refreshingly different from all the previous magic practitioners he had dealt with to this point. "I have heard there is a cave in these mountains where the devil is said to live."

"*Sí*, this is the cave. Why do you seek the devil, cursed one?"

"I was told to find and collect some devil's hoof."

The old man blinked at him for a few moments than began to cackle with laughter.

Grimm watched Viktor and the warlock closely. The captain had grown testy over the past week as his blood rations neared depletion. Laughing at Viktor Brandewyne all too often proved deadly for the one laughing.

Amazingly, the vampire held his patience. He looked more bored than irritated. Apparently, the directness previously displayed by the old man had been an aberration.

Though tedious, his current behavior was more in line with what Viktor expected of his sort.

Once he wound down, the warlock had mercy on the pirates and explained the cause of his mirth. "You are in the right cave, but there is no hoof to be found here. Some who don't know what they're talking about call me the devil. Others say I serve the devil. The Roman Church has cast a pall of evil on my religion, which is ancient. The priests have a tendency to call any of the old gods the devil, whether they are good or evil or neutral, or even regardless of whether they are male or female."

Viktor sighed. "It figures. We wasted a couple of weeks trying to find you. I should have known it was a false lead. Do you at least know what devil's hoof is, so I can ask the right questions to find it?"

"No, *señor*." He shook his head. "Although I have heard of it before, I do not know what it is or where to find it. I am curious why it took you so long to find me. Surely you could have gotten a straight answer by taking the mind of one of the villagers who still seek my services. Or do you not have that ability?"

"I did not think it prudent. I have already imperiled my quest by doing that once, when I was trying to find the one who set me to bring back some devil's hoof."

The old man gave a toothless grin. "Was Rosalia being bitchy with you?"

"How do you know the Sister?" Viktor turned suddenly more alert.

"Long ago, when I was a young man, she took me as a lover," he said with a wistful expression. "She didn't go by Rosalia then, however. She called herself Blancaflor and said she was the youngest of the devil's three daughters. I didn't give much credence to the claim at the time, but she does not age, or if she does, ages so slowly you do not notice it. And she is wickedly clever. She has a knack for getting men to do her bidding that surpasses that of any mortal woman."

"Did she discard you when she had no further use for you?" Grimm asked curiously.

The old warlock shook his head. "No, I escaped. She became over-confident of her hold on me and grew careless. Although I do not know what devil's hoof is, I know what she uses it for. She puts it in the food of someone she wishes to control. In small portions, over time, she has enslaved entire villages. The substance is very potent. A concentrated dose will cause visions, but it must be mixed very carefully. Too much will drive a man mad. I began to watch when she prepared my food. Any time she put some in it, I only pretended to eat. She never caught on until the night I fled and hid here in these mountains."

"I will take your warning into consideration. She has already tried that trick on me. I broke free, but I lost one of my men when I broke her spell on my crew."

The old man looked at the vampire with a new respect. "No man has ever broken her spell before, let alone freed others from it. She will be more determined than ever to ensnare you, *señor*. Be careful."

"I intend to be. Can you give me an idea of her influence on this coast?"

He grimaced and waggled his hand. "It is so-so. When I was young, it was stronger, but she has lost interest in this area, except for the trade routes overland and the few natives to have survived the Spanish."

"Thank you."

They took the leave of the old warlock. Viktor intended to do everything he could to avoid Rosalia's snares.

☠

"Lazarus, come forth."

Obediently, the cat materialized.

"Go find our ship. Let Mr. Brumble know it is time to come back. Have him meet us in Vera Cruz, not the original drop-off point," he instructed.

Rather than leave immediately to carry out the order, Lazarus turned his head sideways and looked at his master as if to say, "How am I supposed to tell him anything?"

Viktor frowned. "What is wrong? Why aren't you obeying?"

"Mrrurr?" the cat sounded confused.

Grimm offered a possibility. "You haven't fed in a few days, Captain. Maybe your concentration isn't strong enough for him to understand."

"No, that's not it." Vik shook his head. "He's always been able to understand me, regardless of my feeding habits."

"Y'know, I've never heard the critter speak, even when he's a bird," Jon-Jon said and scratched his neck. "How's he supposed to deliver your message, Cap'n?"

The captain and the first mate looked at their second mate. Jon-Jon looked back and started to worry about his life expectancy.

Finally, Viktor turned his attention to the rest of the crewmen. "Do any of you have a scrap of paper or parchment?"

Jon-Jon breathed a sigh of relief and began to dig through his bag. Warren found a scrap first and handed it to the captain. Jon-Jon found a charcoal stick that he kept for quick figuring navigational calculations.

Viktor took the implements with a nod of thanks and wrote a terse note then returned the charcoal to his second mate. He rolled the note into a tight roll and pulled a spare hair thong from one of his pockets.

Lazarus watched the proceedings intently, purring. He butted his head against Viktor's hand, as the vampire tied the note around his neck. When the cat morphed into his rave form, the thong dangled like a necklace. He launched and fluttered just long enough to let Vik see him grasp the note in his talons. He turned and soared in the direction of the sea.

As the group began to head east, Grimm waited until he and Viktor were out of earshot of the others to bring up the obvious.

"Thought you said you wanted to avoid Vera Cruz."

"That was while we were still trying to find this place. Now I am going to hunt. I don't want to go back on the ship Hungry."

"Soooo," Grimm drew the word out with one corner of his mouth lifted in a half-grin, "you are counting on Villanova to try to apprehend you."

"Precisely. Having my food come to me saves time."

"Welcome back aboard, Captain Brandewyne," Zach greeted them as they returned to the *Incubus*.

Vik nodded. "Good to be back, Mr. Brumble. I sense contentment from the cadre, and all hands appear to be accounted for, so I take it hunting was good."

"Aye, Captain, very good. I find that piracy agrees with me. Father will not be happy about the silver losses. The turquois was sparse but good quality stones," he reported. If watching his brother and the other vampires feed on the crew of the taken ships had bothered him, he didn't let it show.

Viktor found himself liking the man, which automatically made him suspicious of the younger man. He didn't take to new people that easily, and he had yet to secure a hold on Brumble's will beyond having the other Brumble boy as one of his vampires. Zach reminded him of himself, or at least how he might have turned out if he'd grown up a trader's son instead of an orphan in Savannah.

He'd have to see to it that Hezekiah slipped the young man some of the rum he used to keep the crew in line. Tainted with a few drops of the vampire's blood, it was almost as effective as biting without the risk of turning those it was used on. Of course, Brumble had a strong will and would require a larger dose.

Vik wondered if the young man's background as a trader could help unravel the mystery of what they were supposed to be looking for. Perhaps he could take care of two problems at the same time.

"Mr. Brumble, join Mr. Grimm and myself in my cabin. I want a full report and accounting, and there are a few other things I wish to discuss with you," he ordered.

"Aye, sir."

Grimm, ever observant, noticed Viktor surreptitiously jab his thumb and squeeze several drops into the half-full decanter of brandy. An almost imperceptible shake of the head warned him against accepting a drink. They'd used a similar ruse on the young trader when they took his cache of emeralds and his freedom. Viktor used a lot more blood this time. He wanted the spell to be long term.

"Have some brandy, Mr. Brumble," he said, more of an order than an offer of hospitality.

To his credit, Zach took the glass with a skeptical look. "No offense, captain, but accepting a drink from you is what landed me out of my father's favor and on this ship."

"Yes, it did. Drink."

Still, Zach didn't obey right away. "I have to know, sir, what is in this besides brandy?"

Vik raised an eyebrow. Yes, this one would bear watching, even under the blood spell. He was a clever one. "If you will do the honors, Mr. Grimm?"

Hezekiah was mildly surprised at his captain's reaction. In his experience, Viktor usually wasn't this patient. Single-handedly killing and gorging on the blood of the six goons Villanova had sent to apprehend them seemed to have put the vampire in a good mood.

He shrugged and went with the captain's whim. "He has put some of his blood into the brandy. It will make you subject to his will without risking turning you vampire. There is a good deal more in that drink than he usually uses, probably because of how strong your will is."

The look of horror on Zach's face was warning enough. Grimm caught his wrist before he could dump the glass out on the deck. He had his pistol out, cocked and the barrel pressed against the younger man's temple. The whole while, Viktor watched with a calm, almost peaceful expression.

"You can drink that and maybe accept a second, or I can paint the bulkhead with your brains," Grimm said pleasantly.

Zach gulped, angry and horrified at his predicament, but he saw no way out of it. Finally, and with resignation, he put the glass to his lips and quickly downed the contents.

"Would you like another drink, Mr. Brumble?" Vik asked.

He shook his head. "No, sir, thank you." He already felt himself being bound to the vampire's will, but he also sensed that he wasn't being forced to any decision at the moment. "I am not aware of having done anything to merit this enslavement, Captain. Why did you feel it necessary?"

"Hezekiah, you can put your weapon away." Viktor didn't answer the question immediately. His first mate didn't question him, although it was plain that he was worried that Brumble didn't seem to be fully under, since he was still able to question.

Viktor returned his attention to the young man. "You remind me too much of myself. I can't allow you to operate freely, or I'd have to watch my back constantly," he told him.

"Then why have you allowed me to live?" Zach was confused.

"You are useful. I wouldn't discard a sword or a gun just because they might injure me. I merely make sure I handle them safely."

"Oh." The argument made sense to him. It also told him that if he wanted to stay alive, he needed to remain useful. "Very well, how may I be of service?"

Viktor smiled. The young man got his point. "How widespread is your father's trading business?"

"Pretty much worldwide. If there's a profit to be made on it, the old man wants to deal in it."

"I see. How much do you know about the different commodities he trades?"

"I'm the eldest son. I was being groomed to take over the company. So, among other things he required of me, I had to memorize almost everything we trade in as well as the best ports to acquire them in."

Vik shared a look with Grimm. Could this be the break they needed? "Have you ever heard of something called devil's hoof?"

Zach blinked, surprised. "It's a cooking spice made from a hot pepper. The pepper used is grown to the east of India and is said to be the hottest pepper in the world. The spice is very potent, but there is only a very select market for it. We dealt in it for a while, but there isn't very much demand for it now."

"Mr. Grimm, take Mr. Brumble and go over our charts. I'm sure we have some of the Indian Ocean. I need a course set and a port to go to."

"Aye, Captain."

Tamara A. Lowery

Chapter 14

While Grimm and Zach worked on a course, Viktor summoned Jon-Jon to his cabin.

"You wanted to see me, Cap'n?"

"Have the lads make ready to sail, Mr. Jon. I want a full inventory of all supplies and provisions. We're going to head east and make the crossing. Then we have to round the Cape into the Indian Ocean. Mr. Grimm and Mr. Brumble are working up a course from there. I need to know how close we need to keep to the trade routes in order to pirate for fresh supplies along the way. I'd like to make the best possible time."

"Aye, Cap'n. I'm on it." The second mate turned and exited the cabin to round up men to aid in his task.

Viktor next turned his will to seeking out Belladonna. The siren's weather magic would be a great help in speeding him on his way as well as aide in hunting.

A mild wave of vertigo hit him, like he was falling into nothingness. At first, he thought she was blocking him again. He concentrated harder, trying to break through her shields like he had before. Again, he got the sense of falling. It was like pushing with all his might only to find there was nothing to push against.

"Belle?" he said aloud as well as projected. He got no response. He could not sense her at all. Surely nothing had happened to her. Since forming blood bonds with his crew, he'd felt the bonds break when any of them were killed. He'd had both a blood and flesh bond with the siren ever since she'd bitten a chunk out of his shoulder. He had not felt anything break the bond.

Maybe she had merely gotten too far away for him to sense her. He still wasn't sure of the range he was capable of.

Mildly irritated, but not too worried yet, he decided he would try her again later.

☠

Grimm knocked at the cabin door and waited for permission to enter. Once he got it, he found Viktor with his back to him looking out the windows and nursing a bottle of bloodied brandy. Obviously, something was bothering the captain. He considered asking about it, but he knew Vik well enough to know he'd tell him when he was ready.

"I've got Jon-Jon's report, and Mr. Brumble has mapped out some prospective courses."

The information got no response.

"Vik?"

"I can't find her, Hezekiah."

"What do you mean you can't find her? We already found her," Grimm replied, confused.

Viktor shook his head but did not turn around. "Not Rosalia. I can't find Belladonna. She isn't answering."

"She must just be mad at you again. Probably moping around somewhere nearby and shielding her presence. Just promise me you won't try luring her out by swimming again," he reasoned.

"I know better than that, Hezekiah. No, I can still sense her when she blocks me. I cannot sense her at all. It's as if she doesn't exist.

That bothered Grimm. Not only was the siren a useful member of the crew, but he also actually liked her, even if he didn't entirely trust her.

"I can't imagine anything being able to take her out."

"No, I never felt the bond break with her." Vik shook his head and went to his desk. "I think she has used the time we were seeking Rosalia to practice blocking me out. She probably is holed up on some island with some poor fool that's young, dumb and full of cum. If that's the case, I'd rather not know. We don't really need her help with the weather right away. That ability won't come into play until we make the crossing."

"Aye, the quicker we reach Africa the better. Catching any prizes, escorted or otherwise, on the open ocean is a chancy business at best," Grimm agreed. "Most traders like to stick to the coastal areas."

"Exactly. Now, what have you got to show me?" Vik was all business.

Grimm placed charts on the desk and pointed out the trade routes along both African coasts. "We agreed it would cut off at least two weeks of travel time to head northeast from Madagascar and make straight for the tip of India. Brumble assures me that, as far as he knows, the traders don't use that route solely because of all the business they do with ports around the Horn."

He looked at what his first mate pointed out and nodded. "What about the take from the prizes he claimed? I recall him mentioning turquoise and silver."

"I was wondering when you'd get around to that." Hezekiah grinned. "The turquoise is fairly good grade, and a couple of the pieces are as big as your fist. But there's not a lot of it. Brumble said that it may come in handy where we're going. The traders have found that the locals of that part of the world prize blue stones quite highly. Seems they think the things are holy. Makes sense to me to hang onto it for now. Just not that much demand for it in these waters."

"The silver is another matter," he continued. "The hold next to your cadre is over half full of ingots. The weight could slow us down. My agent in Havana can get a very good price on it."

"Havana." A wicked smiled tugged at the corners of Viktor's mouth. "Perhaps a visit to the Crescent is in order. Manuel will be glad to see you're back in business, and I've prepared for an extended session with Valerie."

Manuel looked up from his bar out of habit and curiosity. Habit because he had trained himself to notice any time someone crossed his threshold; curiosity because the Crescent Inn, which was usually a quite noisy place at this time of day, had grown deathly quiet. Now a hushed whispering electrified the air.

The barkeep broke into a broad grin as soon as he saw the men who caused the disturbance. He even came out from behind the bar, grabbing a bottle and a tray full of mugs on the way.

"*Capitans!*" he boomed happily. "Welcome back! It is good to see you again. Come, I'll give you the best table in the house." He bustled over to a table where a well-to-do family was eating and ordered them to find another table.

The husband protested the treatment and gave the pirates a condescending sneer. The pirates just stood there, looking intimidating and smug. Manuel decided to put the fear of the devil into the stubborn customer.

"This is Bloody Vik Brandee and the Grimm Reaper. You really need to leave their table and find another."

The man recognized the names and blanched. "I had no idea, *señor*. My apologies. We will leave right away." He rose and gathered up his family.

Jon-Jon put an arm around the waist of the man's wife as she tried to squeeze past. Grimm took an interest in the oldest daughter and snagged her to him.

"You ladies are welcome to keep us company," the first mate suggested.

"Javier!" the wife cried and reached for her husband as she struggled against the hulking pirate's grip. The daughter only struggled when she noticed her mother or father looking her way, a fact not lost on Grimm.

The moment Javier made a move to retrieve his wife he found Viktor's hand on his shoulder and the tip of a dagger just below his ear.

"Go on to your table, and you'll get them both back in a few hours unharmed and better educated in the womanly arts. Try to stop my men, and I will kill you, and you'll never know what their fates will be."

"Javier!" she nearly shrieked. Jon-Jon had started some exploratory groping with his free hand. She had never been handled like that in public.

"Lucita be quiet!" His voice sounded strained. "Are you so proud you would rather be a widow?"

"Smart man. Now take your other children and go away." Vik patted his shoulder in dismissal. Javier grasped the hands of the boy and little girl and quickly led them away from the pirates.

The men took their seats. Grimm and Jon-Jon pulled their captives into their laps. The daughter had given up any pretense of a struggle and relaxed into Hezekiah's arms. Lucita continued to squirm, but she had begun to resign herself to her fate.

"Oh ho! A wiggler! I like that," Jon-Jon grinned. His lap started to demonstrate to her just how happy he was. She blushed as she realized she was curious about the large hardness growing under her.

"I think she's starting to like you, Mr. Jon," Vik laughed. "Manuel, I've noticed you've never protested any time we've pulled this stunt here."

Manuel shrugged and set out the mugs then took his own seat with the pirates. "I used to be a pirate, too. Why spoil your fun? Besides, I never get tired of the show."

"Keep it up, and you'll lose all your respectable customers."

He shook his head. "Deep down, there are very few respectable people that come in here anyway. I've found that most of those who are truly decent people usually have no money to spend. So, I don't worry about offending them." He turned his attention to one of the barmaids. "Talia, go up and tell Valerie to kick out whoever she has up there and to freshen up. *Capitan* Brandee has paid for her services in advance."

"*Si*, Manuel."

"She will be glad to see you didn't bring that fiery red head with you this time. Where is she, by the way?" He looked around wistfully. "If you've grown tired of her, I wouldn't mind hiring her."

"She is on an errand elsewhere right now," Vik lied.

"You don't want her on staff, Manuel," Grimm warned. "She has a tendency to kill her playmates if they aren't wily enough to outwit her."

Manuel looked dubious, but he knew better than to question the Grimm Reaper. "I can see where that would be bad for business. Most of the *chicas'* customers are not much on the ability to think. That is why they are so easy to part from their gold."

"And you want them alive, so they'll go out and get more gold to be parted from."

"*Si.*"

"Speaking of…," Jon-Jon dropped a few coins down after downing his drink. "Where's the closest room not in use, Manuel?"

"Third door on the right just up the stairs," the barkeep replied and pocketed the coins.

Lucita picked that moment to grow vocal again. "Why do you need a room now? I thought you only wanted us to eat with you."

"No, you didn't, love. But if you don't want to use one of the rooms, I have no problem just doing you right here on the table."

"No!"

"Let's go then." He got up and grabbed her wrist. "Trust me, love. I think you'll enjoy this." When she tugged against his grasp, he just hefted her onto his shoulder and headed for the stairs.

Valerie arrived at the table a moment later. She had a wicked smirk on her face. "It's about time someone took the starch out of that cow's corset." She jerked her head at the pair disappearing up the stairs.

"Mama is always so prim," the daughter complained. "She hates that Papa brings us here to eat, but she cannot cook."

"Valerie, pet, it is good to see you again. I have come to collect on my investment," Vik leered at her.

She pouted back at him. "I ought to just keep your money as payment for having to endure that horrid woman you brought with you last time. You hurt my feelings."

He turned in his chair, grabbed her behind the knees and pulled her to him. Before she knew what was happening, he had her sitting astraddle of him and kissed her fiercely. She looked dazed when he pulled back.

"I imagine I'll get what I paid for, pet," he growled.

Her voice came out breathy when she answered. "Oh yes, and any way you want it. Mi Dio, you have grown fierce, Captain Brandee. I like it."

"Good, because I intend to wear you out."

Grimm saw that his girl paid close attention to their behavior. More importantly, he saw she was aroused by it. He slipped a few coins into Manuel's hand and headed for the rooms to take advantage of the girl's mood.

A few days later, they were back aboard the *Incubus* headed for the Florida Strait. Grimm knocked at the captain's cabin door.

"Enter."

"Danny said you wanted to see me, Captain?"

"Come in and close the door, Hezekiah." The greeting let Grimm know the conversation was private and there was no need to stand on formality.

Once the door was shut, Grimm asked, "What is troubling you, Vik?"

"Belladonna."

"You still can't reach her?"

Viktor shook his head. "I'm getting nothing. I even left our bond open while I was with Valerie in the hopes it would at least make her mad enough to yell at me."

"Speaking of Valerie, I thought you said you paid for her in advance. How come you gave Manuel more gold?"

"I want to keep our welcome open there, and she isn't going to be in any shape to make him any money for a few days. You heard me say I intended to wear her out. Of course, for that same reason I didn't feed on her."

"I see," he nodded, understanding the captain's reasons. A thought occurred to him. "Have you thought about seeing if Lazarus can find Belle?"

"I have, but I wanted to save that as a last resort." He sat down. "I am going to try to call her one last time. If I get no result, then I will send him."

To help concentrate, he closed his eyes. Then he focused all of his will on the siren, searching. As before, he could sense nothing, not even her will trying to block him. He just couldn't accept that she was powerful enough to shut him out like this. If she was, she would have done so months ago.

He drew all of his energy into himself, even what he used to maintain the links with his crew and his cadre of vampires. He focused all of it and sent it out as a mental shout. *"Belladonna!"*

For just the briefest of moments, he felt her. She was hundreds of leagues away, hunting. He almost got a lock on her, when the cabin was shaken by a loud boom.

"Vik!" Grimm ran over to his captain and friend where he had been blasted across the cabin. He had hit the bulkhead hard enough to knock things off a shelf as well as stun him.

Lazarus jumped up on the table and began to yowl loudly in distress.

Viktor picked himself up and shook his head to clear it. "Dammit, Jim, shut up!" The cat fell silent immediately.

"Are you alright? What happened?"

"I almost had her then something shut me out, Hezekiah," he answered. "Maybe that spell Rosalia cast wasn't completely dispelled. The power that is blocking me doesn't taste like Belle's magic."

Grimm thought about it for a while. "I guess that makes sense. She may want to make things more difficult and cutting you off from someone whose magic could aid you might slow you down."

"Yes. That fits with everything we know about the Sisters," Vik agreed. "Now that I know Belle isn't the one blocking me, I am left to wonder why she has not investigated why she hasn't heard from me."

"I can't answer that one. I know she often complained about wanting her freedom, but I always got the impression that she really didn't mind being bound to you as much as she claimed. She just as frequently reminded me that she was supposed to be helping you. It doesn't make sense that she would just make a run for it like that."

"Lazarus," Vik addressed the cat, "I want you to find Belladonna and let her know I have need of her. I know she can understand your thoughts to a point. Knowing that I sent you to her should get the message across."

"Mrrreh." The cat padded over to an open window. He changed into his raven form, launched into the open sky and spiraled outward from the ship as he began his search.

Tamara A. Lowery

Chapter 15

Lazarus searched a wider and wider area. He'd flown for weeks and seen many things, but he had found no trace of the siren.

She hadn't been on any of the islands he'd encountered. He'd not searched the larger islands thoroughly, granted. But he'd reasoned that she wouldn't venture very far inland. Belladonna was a saltwater creature and would want to keep close to her element.

He couldn't help but wonder if he had passed her location, but she had been too deep underwater for him to see her.

Without warning, a fog bank sprang up around him. It was impossible to see, so he was forced to land. Once on the ground, he shifted back into his feline form.

The fog hovered about a foot above the ground, which allowed him to see for a short distance. The ground was rocky and barren. It also seemed to be bowl-shaped, because every direction he looked the ground sloped upward. He found it very disorienting.

When he realized his eyes wouldn't be much help, he began to sniff the air to see if that would give him any more information. He smelled wood smoke coming from one direction. Mixed with it was the aroma of roasting fish.

A pitiful, mournful sound escaped him as he suddenly realized how very hungry he was. He hadn't stopped to hunt the entire time he'd been looking for the siren.

He followed his nose to the source of the mouth-watering aroma.

He soon realized he'd landed on Hell's Breath, and Uncle Zeke had a couple of nice-sized sea bass propped over his fire on spits. Since it was the old wizard, he restrained his initial urge to just steal one of the fish. Instead, he sat and stared patiently but pointedly at the old man.

"Hello, Jim Rigger." Zeke smiled at him then reached for one of the spitted fish and offered it to the cat. "Thought you might be hungry. It's not good to go so long between meals."

"Mrrrow." Lazarus nodded his head to thank him for the meal. He snatched the fish and began to devour it. As he ate, he felt his energy replenish. Even the bones got chewed to bits and eaten, although the skull gave him a bit of a challenge.

Zeke nibbled his own fish and watched the cat with a cryptic smile as he ate. Finally, he broke the silence. "Y'know, they say you are what you eat."

As the cat swallowed the last bit of fish, his body convulsed then went amorphous, changing involuntarily. When Lazarus reformed, it was as a fish. He lay there thrashing on the ground and gasping for water that wasn't there.

Zeke took mercy on the creature and waved his hand over him. Where there had been a fish, there once again sat the huge black cat.

He quickly grasped the implication of the old wizard's words and the change he had undergone. He eyeballed the other fish and made a try for it. He reasoned that turning into a fish would allow him to search the seas for the siren.

Zeke anticipated this and held the fish out of reach. "Sorry, boy-cat, you ain't getting' my dinner."

Lazarus gave a growl, switched his tail and laid his ears back.

"Don't you sass me. I know why you're out and about. Your captain has you out looking for that wild girl. She's on an errand for me. I don't want him distracting her, so I'm shielding them from each other. She'll come back once she's finished the task I've set her."

"Mrrreh murr?"

"No. You can stop looking for her. Go back to your captain and give him my message. Oh," he added, "tell him if he tries to break through the shields again, I'll put him through the bulkhead instead of just against it. What Belladonna is doing has to be done, and done as quickly as possible."

Without warning, the fog rolled in thick. Lazarus sensed he needed to fly, so he launched and changed in mid-leap. As quickly as it had appeared, the fog vanished and left him hovering just above the waves.

Tamara A. Lowery

Chapter 16

Lazarus opened his senses, mentally following the thread of energy that tied him to Viktor. He knew the Captain would not be happy to learn about Zeke's interference with Belladonna, but he would be interested in the new ability the old wizard had introduced. Finally, Jim would be able to relay news to his master directly.

He found his bearings and headed in the direction he knew the *Incubus* to be. It would take him a few weeks to reach the ship. Vik had caught the trades and was already nearly to Africa. He was making good time even without the siren's weather magic.

Lazarus would make a point to hunt along the way. If he followed the trade routes, he should have no trouble finding a ship or two he could steal food from.

Three days after encountering Zeke, Lazarus saw a ship below him. It was soon enough after his last meal that he considered passing it by to wait for the next one he spotted, but something looked familiar about the vessel's lines. He went lower to investigate.

He recognized the *Shining Star*; the ship Zach Brumble had been captain of when they'd taken him. He decided to land and snoop around. Scuttlebutt would let him know where the ship might be found when Vik was back in these waters and if they would be carrying anything worth taking.

Confusion and speculation ran rampant among the crew of the *Shining Star*. They'd left behind the Navy ship they'd rendezvoused with well over a month ago, yet they hadn't returned to Boston or done more than stop to resupply. They hadn't done any trading.

Some had been very apprehensive about the dreadnaught. Its lines were almost identical to the pirate ship that had taken their former captain. The pirate had masqueraded as a Navy ship, as well. However, this one had all its attending flotilla of support ships, and all had been in uniform. The sailors seriously doubted the pirate could pull of that elaborate of a ruse.

The speculation had been about why they had met with the small armada. Most suspected it was to make report of the two attacks on their shipping line, presumably by the same pirate. There was talk that it had been Bloody Vik Brandee, who was supposed to be dead.

There was also talk about the captain's new cabin boy. He was still too young to sprout a beard, but tall for his age. His voice hadn't even started to change. He also strongly favored their former captain, Brumble, so much so that some thought he might be the man's son or maybe a bastard brother.

Something was odd about him, though. Captain Bainbridge had given him his own quarters instead of giving him a hammock in the officers' quarters or putting him in with the crew.

And, the boy seemed very interested in their business. Some even wondered if, going on the idea that he was some kin to the Brumble family, he had somehow convinced the captain to seek to avenge Captain Brumble. Of course, others argued that Captain Bainbridge would not be so foolish as to go after a pirate like Brandee. That would be suicide.

The talk among the crew peaked Lazarus' curiosity. Quietly and unnoticed, he made his way to the captain's cabin. Before he even got in, he caught a scent that wasn't common on a merchant ship. It was stronger from just behind the door.

He managed to hook the edge of the door and pulled. It wasn't locked and swung wide enough for him to squeeze inside. Once in, he kept to the shadows to avoid notice. All ships kept cats to control the rats, but this captain might not like them in his cabin. He didn't want to be thrown out.

The captain was arguing with his cabin "boy." Lazarus recognized the man as having been Zach's first mate. He had never seen the person dressed as a boy before. The crew had been right about the strong resemblance to Zach, but this was neither a son nor a bastard brother. The cat knew female when he smelled one.

"Sam, I really would feel better if you went home. The Navy is searching, and I promise to keep an eye out for the ship as well."

She shook her head emphatically. "We've been over this, Captain Bainbridge. I want to try to ransom my brothers, if they're still alive. I do not trust Commodore

Critchfield, and I will not return to my father's house without my brothers."

"Dammit, Samantha! You realize that your disappearance may kill the man? He was always a total bastard to Zach and Thomas, but you know he dotes on you. I've never even heard him utter a harsh word to you."

She gave him a stony gaze. "I will grant you he never struck me, but in private he never restrained his verbal rage. He might not have directed it at me, but that didn't make it any less frightening. If I were to go back now, he would be quick to marry me off, whether I said yea or nay to the groom. The last thing I want is to be tied to some abusive brute or any man not of my choosing. I will not go home. I have no home."

"You are a stubborn woman."

"I am a determined woman."

Lazarus found this young woman very interesting. He thought he remembered Zach and Thomas mentioning a sister, but he had never imagined she would be anything like this woman, or that he would ever encounter her.

Yet here was this young woman bravely, if foolishly, gone to sea in search of her brothers and the pirates who took them. He was sure Viktor would want to learn that someone was looking to ransom the Brumbles, but the part of Lazarus that was still Jim Rigger wanted her more than the money.

He'd never encountered a woman like her. In his experience, women just didn't do what she was doing.

Samantha found the large black tomcat that started haunting her perplexing. It seemed like every time she turned around, there was the cat. She assumed it was one of the ship cats, but she didn't understand why it had attached itself to her.

After a couple of weeks of this, she resigned herself to the cat's presence. In fact, she started to find it comforting. Although he seemed vicious to anyone else, he was quite gentle with her. He'd even taken to curling up on the pillow next to her.

A brief commotion on the deck of the *Shining Star* occurred that day. A line had gotten out of control, and the man working it lost a finger.

Lazarus hadn't eaten anything since boarding the ship, and the smell of fresh blood drew him like a magnet.

The sailor bled quite a bit before his shipmates could get him calmed down enough to wrap the wound. As the ship's smith seared the stub with a hot iron to seal it, Lazarus lapped up the blood puddle as quickly as he could, before it could soak into the planks or get washed away by sea spray. He sniffed around until he found the severed digit, but he didn't eat it right away.

Tamara A. Lowery

Chapter 17

That night in Samantha's cabin, he waited for her to start to doze off before he ate the stolen finger. As soon as he finished with it, he leapt up on the bed to snuggle up with her, as he'd been doing since he discovered her identity.

"There you are, kitty," she mumbled sleepily. She stroked his fur and adjusted to accommodate him. He began to lick her hand then her chin, his sandpaper tongue making her giggle a little.

Then he morphed, and instead of Lazarus the cat, Jim Rigger lay naked next to Samantha Brumble. She was just sleepy enough that it didn't register immediately. Before she could wake up enough to scream, he began to kiss her.

As an added precaution, earlier in the day he had bitten his paw and put the blood in the captain's stew when the man wasn't looking. He hoped the magic would work for him the same way it did for Viktor. He didn't want to be interrupted this night. He didn't think another opportunity would present itself anytime soon. He knew he had to leave and find his master before long.

Sam began to wake up during the kiss. At first, she thought she was still dreaming. She'd been having a recurring dream about a roguishly handsome man visiting her in the night for several nights. The dreams had grown increasingly erotic.

Something felt different this time. She'd only had her imagination to go on before. This felt real. He was warm, and his weight had her pinned. The kiss felt much more sensual than she'd ever dreamed and fired reactions in her body which made her skin hyper-sensitive to every touch.

Her mind fought against it, screaming warnings at her. Something must have gotten through to her. She came fully awake just as he pulled back from the kiss. It wasn't a dream; there really was a man in bed with her, and he was completely naked.

She drew in breath to scream, but he clasped a hand over her mouth to stifle the sound.

"If you cry out, Sam, the others will hear. Then your secret will be out." He smiled as he warned her. "Bainbridge might not be willing to send you home, but can you take the gamble that his mates will go along with him? I know the crew won't. I've been listening, and they are teetering between loyalty and mutiny."

Sam glared at him, furious that he was right. She struggled and tried to throw him off. He had far more experience with wrestling however, and he had the advantage of leverage and more weight. He managed to pin her wrists and get full length on her in the process.

"Now, now, Miss Brumble, that's no way to be," he chided. His eyes shone with both mischief and lust.

She stilled as fear began to override her anger. She was acutely aware of his erection pressed against her hip. "How did you learn who I am?"

Jim smiled at her. "You don't smell like a man, and anyone who knows your brothers could see you are related with one look at you, love. At least half the crew thinks you are Zach's bastard or a bastard brother."

Just like that, her anger returned. "Who are you? How dare you speak so familiarly of your betters?"

"I am someone who knows where they are and how they are faring. As for them being my betters — that is open for debate." He lifted up enough to look her over and admire the way the thin night shirt outlined her form. And now we have a dilemma, Sam, or should I say you have a dilemma. Do you reject me and suffer exposure as a female on a ship full of men, or do you accept my advances and keep your secret?"

"Bastard," she hissed at him.

He nodded but took no insult. "Yes, I am. Of course, if you grant me what I want, I can promise that you will be reunited with your brothers in time." He did not add that the reunion would be dangerous and bittersweet at best.

Sam bit her lip. *"Damn, he would dangle that in front of me,"* she thought. Aloud, she said, "What do you want?"

"For now, you." Jim made sure his expression conveyed exactly how he meant that. He was rewarded with a blush from her but could tell she was still undecided. He thought he knew what was holding her back.

"I know you are still a virgin, Samantha. It will hurt just a little at first, but the pain is short and fades quickly. There are things I can do that will make the pain barely noticeable."

She looked at him nervously. Her upbringing made her frightened of doing this, but her body had started to relax and respond to the weight of his on top of her. He was an attractive man and remarkably clean, for a sailor. His eyes were a mesmerizing hazel, not quite green and not quite brown, but a multi-rayed mixture. "I guess it wouldn't be so bad," she replied, her voice a husky whisper.

"Oh no, love." He leaned down to kiss her again. "I can guarantee that it will not be bad; it will be marvelous."

Jim was grateful that his captain's little trick had worked on Sam's captain. The man never heard a thing.

Samantha lay sleeping next to him, exhausted. She had proven very responsive to him. He wished he could afford to spend more time with her, but he already felt the drain of remaining in human form. At least he'd gotten to enjoy himself this time.

He sensed he would have a long flight ahead of him and decided to feed. He crouched between Samantha's knees and pushed her thighs apart to gain access to the large artery there.

The pure human blood intoxicated and invigorated him. He made himself stop, although he didn't want to. But he didn't want to kill her, either. As it was, she might sleep for a day or so before she built back up enough to function normally.

For a moment, he thought he wasn't going to be able to return to being Lazarus. His human body didn't want to morph. That would be bad for him for several reasons. He was a pirate away from his crew on a ship full of people that had been hunting him. He also doubted he would be able to function in daylight in this form. Not to mention the only way to get back to his captain would be to lead these people to him. Without a way to communicate what had happened, Vik might take it as a betrayal rather than a gift.

Then the change took him, and he was once again the large black cat. He breathed a sigh of relief and changed over to his raven form.

He had a ship to find.

Sam woke to someone shaking her and calling her name repeatedly. It seemed to take forever to struggle free of the soothing darkness that enveloped her mind.

"Huh? Wha...?" She couldn't seem to make her mouth work right. The confusion and disorientation vaguely reminded her of how she'd felt after drinking half a decanter of her father's brandy on a dare from Thomas.

"Sam! Wake up!" Bainbridge's voice was laced with worry and urgency. She'd always risen before dawn. It was three hours past now, and he'd been trying to wake her for nearly half an hour. He also didn't like how clammy cold her skin felt. He was already sweating from the oppressive tropical heat.

"Captain? What's wrong?" She finally got control of her ability to speak.

He sighed in relief. "I was going to ask you the same thing. Sam, its three bells past dawn and you're still abed." Her eyes widened in surprise. He held her down when she tried to get up. "No, stay there. Your skin is like ice."

"I feel dizzy, like I've had too much liquor but without the euph... eupho...," she frowned, frustrated.

"Euphoria?" he supplied.

She nodded then whimpered and held her head. "Ow! I know I didn't have anything to drink last night. What's wrong with me?"

"Offhand, I'd say you might have contracted one of the many diseases that thrive in these climes. Perhaps we should have the ship's surgeon examine you."

"No! He can't! I can't hide who I am from a doctor." She clutched his arm, desperate to stop him.

Bainbridge gave her sad eyes. "Sam, these things have to be taken seriously. I've seen strong men brought low and waste away to nearly nothing in a matter of days. You can't help your brothers if you're dead. Rest today, but if you're not better by tomorrow morning, I'm going to have Dr. Grogan check you out. Don't worry; I promise he'll keep your secret."

Sam saw she wasn't going to win this argument. "Alright, but I don't like it."

"It's for the best, Sam. Now rest."

He was almost out the door, when she was struck by a vivid memory of the night before, one that filled her with dread and despair at the same time it secretly thrilled her.

"Captain, wait!"

Chapter 18

He turned back at the note of desperate fear in her voice. If anything, she looked paler than when he'd come in to check on her. "What's wrong?"

She bit her lip and looked off to the side. "I think someone else on board knows my secret already."

That got his full attention. She acted as if she were guilty of some transgression. "Who? How?"

"There was a man in here last night. I don't know who he was. I had just dozed off when he woke me. He called me by name and knew I was Zachary's sister," she told him.

Bainbridge frowned. "Did he make you eat or drink anything? Poisoning could explain your pallor and clammy skin."

She shook her head. "No, he did not poison me. I just hope he didn't get me with child. I kept hoping you would hear and come remove him."

"He raped you? Could you recognize him among the crew? I could hold an inspection as a pretext for looking for him." The captain was outraged.

"If you single him out to be flogged, the crew will want to know why, Captain. You can't tell them the truth, but he might. He said there've been rumors among the crew already about my possible parentage," she protested.

"I'll have the blackguard's tongue cut out to silence him!"

Sam reached out to touch his arm. She smiled sadly at him. "I appreciate your outrage, Captain Bainbridge. However, I would ask for leniency."

He looked at her incredulously. She laughed, but it was shaky. As the facts sank in, her emotions were in turmoil, and she wasn't entirely sure how she felt about it all.

She was sure about one thing, though. "I never held with my father's brutal ways. This isn't worth such a severe punishment."

"Samantha! He has impugned your honor! You are a young lady from a family in good social standing."

"And I jeopardized that honor the moment I decided to pursue my current course. Face it, Captain, once it becomes known who I am, my social status in Boston will no longer exist. Even if I'd been kidnapped and carried off, I would forever be tainted in the eyes of polite society." She half-sighed, half-laughed. "Just the fact that I grew up without a mother put me at a disadvantage with that snobbish lot of old harpies. Honestly, I don't care."

Bainbridge refused to give it up, although he softened somewhat. "Still, he brutalized and raped you, Sam. That crime cannot go unpunished."

She looked away, a guilty, confused look on her face. It wasn't lost on him.

"What is it you aren't telling me?"

"He wasn't brutal. He was very gentle. It may have started out as rape, but in the end, I was seduced." Almost inaudibly, she added, "Just like in the dreams."

Bainbridge's hearing was sharper than she thought. "What dreams?" he asked sharply.

"For several nights, I have had a recurring dream in which a man comes to me and seduces me. The man in the dream looks a lot like the man last night."

He was silent for a while as he absorbed this information. Finally, he spoke gently, "Are you sure you didn't just dream this?"

"I'm not sure, but I don't think it was a dream this time." She shook her head. "It felt real, and it hurt a little at first. Also, he was always clothed in the dreams. He was completely naked when he woke me."

"What do you want done with him when we find him?"

Sam thought about it for a while before she answered. "I want to talk to him. Something he said made me think he might be an agent for the pirates that took Zachary."

He raised an eyebrow in silent question. She explained, "He claimed to have information about my brothers' whereabouts. He might be able to help us find Brandee."

Bainbridge hadn't expected that, but it explained a lot to him, he thought. "I'll make plans to locate the man, but right now, you need rest. If you think you can eat something, I'll bring you some food."

She nodded and lay back. "Thank you." She was asleep before he was out the door.

He closed it quietly and went in search of his first mate. He personally doubted that this raping bastard on his ship was really connected with the pirate they hunted. That just didn't jibe with all he'd ever heard of Vik Brandee. Granted, the man was unpredictable and rarely used the same method back-to-back to take a prize. He definitely liked to mix it up, but Bainbridge had never heard of him planting a spy on a ship, ever.

Probably, the man had merely figured out who Sam was and deduced why she was here. From there, it was a quick jump to using the information to blackmail her into bed. It wouldn't surprise him if the man was hoping to force a marriage to gain a stake in the company, now that the owner's sons were out of the way. Blackguard.

Still, he wouldn't know for sure until the villain was found and questioned. The trick was to do so without betraying Sam's secret.

He had to admit, considering what had been done to her, she bore up well. She was stronger and more practical than he would have ever thought a woman could be. But then, being a bachelor sea captain, he wasn't around women that often. The few times he had been, it had either been the whores who haunted the dock districts or the socialites who attended functions hosted by his employer. Most of the latter he found to be silly creatures. The former, he had merely used to satisfy base needs in his youth, but he'd never given them much thought.

"Mr. Warding, a word with you, sir," he called when he spotted his mate.

Obediently, Warding followed him to his cabin.

"Captain?"

"I need you to do a boat count, Henry. Young Sam informed me he overheard someone claim to know where Captain Brumble and his brother are being held. I want to make sure this person hasn't left the ship. We're still a couple of days out from land."

"Aye, sir. Can the lad point the sailor out?"

"He thinks so, but I want this done without alarming the rest of the crew. There's been murmuring lately, especially about Sam. I don't want to fuel the rumors. They're wild enough as it is."

"Understood."

The next morning, Samantha felt more like herself. She greeted the captain with his breakfast and had set aside a hearty portion for herself, as well.

"Good morning, Sam." He was pleasantly surprised. "I see you're feeling better today. You still look a little pale, but you've got more color than yesterday."

"Yes, Captain, thank you. Have you learned anything of my — visitor?" She hesitated, unsure of how to refer to the man who had taken her virginity.

"Unless he can turn into a fish, he is still aboard. All the boats are accounted for. I've told the mates to organize a rat hunt. It will make a good pretext for us looking the crew over," he told her. "I told Mr. Warding about your theory that the man may be a spy for the pirates. I said you overheard someone talking about knowing where your brothers are, but I did not reveal your true identity."

Several rats died aboard the *Shining Star* that day, but they did not find the man that had seduced Sam.

It shook her confidence somewhat and killed a small bit of hope she'd had for finding her brothers. She was forced to admit to herself that it must have been a dream after all.

In an effort to comfort her, Bainbridge suggested that maybe her mind was trying to put a more pleasant light on what the Commodore had almost done to her. He also pointed out that she was actually a few years past the age most young women were married off. He supposed it was only natural for her mind to turn to such thoughts.

The day after the rat hunt, he approached Sam about something he'd been putting off but could no longer be ignored. He found her rummaging around her small cabin and muttering under her breath.

"Blast it! Where is it at?"

"What are you looking for, Sam?" he asked.

"Oh! Hello, Captain. You startled me." She jumped at the sound of his voice. "My locket is missing. I've been keeping it in a small box under my pillow. Now I can't find it anywhere. There's just the open box with some claw marks on it."

Bainbridge took the box from her and examined it. "These marks are from cat claws," he said, surprised. "I expected rat. Hmm. Now that I think of it, I haven't seen that monster of a black cat in days. You know the one. It adopted you for a while."

Sam blinked. "You're right. The last time I remember seeing it was the night I got sick and had that bizarre dream. Maybe he took the locket. He was batting at it, when I was cleaning it."

"That is probably what happened. It's not the first time I've seen a ship cat steal some odd trinket or object for a toy. I'm sure it'll show up when the cat does."

"I hope so. It had miniature portraits of my brothers in it," she sighed.

To break the awkward silence, Bainbridge broached the subject of why he was there. "Sam, eventually your secret will come out. There is no avoiding the fact."

"I know. I supposed you are going to try to convince me to go home yet again."

He shook his head. "No, I've given up on ever being able to do that. However, you need to be prepared for when that time comes. Sailors, as a whole, are a rather uncivilized lot and unfit for polite society. Often, the only real difference between the crew of a merchant vessel and a pirate is their employer. There is a very real threat that you will have attempts against your virtue."

"So, what do you suggest I do to be prepared for that?"

"You already know the rudiments of fighting from growing up with your brothers, but you are outweighed by and lack the sheer physical strength of most men. I would like to train you in weaponry. I believe you'll need to learn to fight dirty, as well, to offset the inequity of any would-be attackers," he told her.

Sam grinned in relief. "Thank you, Captain. I've wanted to ask you to train me with sword and gun for some time now. But I was afraid you would use it as an argument for sending me home. As for fighting dirty, I already know how to do that."

He blinked, remembering their encounter with Commodore Critchfield. "True that; very well. Be prepared to choose a weapon to train with this afternoon. For now, go find the chief rigger and let him know I want him to inspect and repair the lines. I noticed the rats had chewed the spare ones badly."

Tamara A. Lowery
“Aye, Captain.”

Chapter 19

Thankfully, the pirating proved good during their voyage. They experienced a dry spell about mid-Atlantic, but Viktor expected that. Any of the few times he'd made the crossing in the past, it had been touch-and-go to spot prey, unless of course, he'd stalked a convoy. It was a big ocean and easy to miss an entire fleet simply because of a few degrees difference in courses.

The winds turned out favorable, so the crossing took just over a month. In the roughly three and a half months since they left Mexico the *Incubus* had already rounded the Cape of Good Hope and sailed northeast along the eastern coast of Africa. Provided the charts he had were accurate, he expected to reach the southern tip of Madagascar within the week.

He had Grimm, Zach and Jon-Jon in his cabin pouring over the charts he possessed. Some did not agree with the others, depending on the cartographers that drew them.

"My God! I've never seen such detailed charts of the Indian Ocean before," Zach referred to ones taken from a recent prize.

Grimm had to agree. "Aye. I think these are the ones we should rely on in these waters. The men from that prize said most of their trade was done solely in this region."

Viktor stood and stroked his beard as he listened to his men. "I didn't know you'd spoken with any of them, Hezekiah."

"Aye, Captain. I knew they were destined for the larder, but I've always made a habit to gather information whenever I'm in unfamiliar waters. Never know when it might be useful."

"Admittedly, a good habit to have. Perhaps I should have kept one alive, but it is too late now. My plan is to follow the west coast of Madagascar around and cross to India from its northern tip." He pointed to the charts.

Jon-Jon said, "Doesn't look like any of the trade routes go that way. Why is that?"

"As far as I know," Zach answered, "there are too many rich ports to make along the coast and taking the long way around. Traders are a greedy lot by nature, and there is more profit to be had in the long route than the short route."

"The prizes have been rich and well-stocked lately. If we take one more before the course change, there should be plenty of provisions to see us across," Vik declared. "I'm more interested in reaching our destination and finding what I need than sticking close to our prey right now."

"That makes sense. Lord knows old Zeke harps enough about time limits," Grimm muttered.

"Indeed," Vik concurred. "Mr. Jon, have the lads keep their eyes open for a fat prize. Mr. Brumble, I want you to relieve Mr. Bland at the helm."

"Aye, Cap'n."

"Aye, Captain."

Silent Fathoms

The two men left to fulfill their orders. Grimm remained. He'd received no orders and sensed Viktor had something on his mind.

The vampire noticed his first mate still there and asked, "Was there something you wanted, Hezekiah?"

Grimm leaned his butt against the table and crossed his arms. "Something's bothering you, Vik. I can tell."

"I don't know what you're talking about."

"Bilge. You miss her."

Viktor frowned. "I have gone longer than this without a woman."

"Belle is not a woman. It's been too quiet around here since she left."

Grimm momentarily wondered if he had pushed the matter too far with his captain. The vampire just stood there and stared at him with an unreadable expression. Then he turned silently and retrieved a bottle of his blood-brandy mix. He uncorked it and took a long pull then replaced the cork.

Without turning, he admitted, "I am worried. The few images I get from Lazarus are of open sea or passing ships, although it seems he rested a few days on one of them. There has been no sign of Belladonna. You are right; it has been too quiet. Not being able to sense her at all after her being an almost constant irritation for months is like losing an eye. It throws all my perceptions off."

Grimm nodded. "That's what I suspected. The past few prizes we've taken, it has seemed like you were only going through the motions."

Tamara A. Lowery

"Aye. That's how it has felt. I don't like it, but I am starting to adjust to the possibility that we won't have Belle's aid anymore in this venture."

It was Grimm's turn to frown. "That's going to make finding the rest of these bitches a royal pain."

"Aye. I hope that Zeke will offer an alternative solution the next time we encounter him, but I won't count on it." He grinned to break the dolorous tension. "Hell, man. It's been a hell of a run, and I don't intend to go down without a fight. I'll figure out a way to finish this business with the Sisters. I'm looking forward to going back to living each day for itself instead of having to constantly worry about the future."

"Damn right. We are the best at what we do. Here's to the next prize."

Two days later, Madagascar was a blur on the horizon. Showing bold and bright were the sails of a medium-sized merchantman in between the *Incubus* and land.

"A double portion to Collins for spotting her," Vik declared. It was a reminder that, in the years before he was cursed to vampirism, he held his crew's loyalty through a balanced combination of terror and generosity. Keep him happy and serve well, and he would give bountiful rewards. Cross him or shirk your duties, and death was swift to follow.

"What plan of attack do you want to go with, Captain?" Grimm asked.

"I'm feeling bloody today, Mr. Grimm. Chase them down. Subtlety is not necessary," he decided.

"Aye, Captain. Riggers aloft! Full sail! Mr. Farmer, set a pursuit course; we're going to run her down!" Grimm barked orders to the crew.

Within seconds, the rigging and decks were swarming with activity. The *Incubus'* copper clad hull let her slice through the water far more swiftly than one would expect of a ship her size. The copper didn't keep the barnacles off completely, but it was harder for them to get a purchase on. It also protected the timbers from shipworms, which cut down on repairs.

Vik and Grimm both felt the old hunting blood come up as their prey realized what was about to happen. The much smaller crew of the merchant ship had to scramble to get all her sails set. Viktor grinned at the scent of panic the pirates had incited.

"They're running scared, Mr. Grimm. Let's put the fear of Hell in them," he announced and flew to the bowsprit and whooped.

Taking the cue from their captain, all the pirates in the rigging and on deck let out a roar in unison, just as they were catching the other ship up.

Still, the prey tried to run. Vik pointed at the masts and made a cut-throat gesture. Grimm nodded that he got the signal and ordered the forward gunners to take out the merchant's masts. The prey was soon too crippled to run anymore.

The riggers on the pirate quickly furled sails or turned them to create drag and slow the ship. As the *Incubus* neared her target, enormous corkwood buffers were suspended over the side nearest the other ship. Swivel guns on the railing fired harpoons and lines into the side of the victim. Bells sounded to signal the crew on the gun decks below to push the counterweights out the gun ports. The harpoon lines ran through a pulley system and quickly pulled the other ship to the side. The buffers absorbed the shock of the two ships as they collided.

"Stand down and prepare to be boarded!"

A volley of musket fire answered the pirates. Most missed since the merchants were not experienced in combat. One mini ball, however, struck very close to Mr. Grimm, and another pirate took a shot in the leg.

Two merchants fell to the deck with stilettos quivering in their chests. Viktor had thrown them with deadly accuracy and superhuman strength.

"Take them, lads!" he ordered and flew into the fray, a sword in either hand.

The battle was short. Viktor's ferocity took a lot of the fight out of the merchant crew. The pirates hardly had a chance to get their blades bloody by the time the merchant captain ordered his men to surrender. Only three sailors were dead, but his crew had been small to begin with.

Viktor made a terrifying sight. The blow he had dealt one man had resulted in an arterial spray. The vampire was soaked from head to toe in blood spatter. The blood with his usual black clothes and his glowing eyes was enough to chill any man to the bone.

He stalked over to the erstwhile captain of the merchant ship like the predator that he was. The man stood tall and refused to show weakness in front of his crew. Viktor could smell his fear but admired his bravado.

"You were wise to order your men to stand down but foolish to resist in the first place," he told the merchant captain. "It cost you three men."

"Our cargo is yours for the taking, sir. I only ask that you let these men go home to their families."

Viktor grinned and bared his fangs. The man only flinched a little. "The cargo was always mine for the taking, sir. As for you and your men, I'm afraid you'll never see your families or homes again. Your blood is even more precious to me than your cargo."

"Our blood?" The man didn't seem to understand.

To get his point across, Viktor slowly and deliberately licked the blood off the back of his hand and made a show of savoring it. When he looked back at his victim, his pupils had dilated, making his eyes nearly pure black with a thin ring of green fire to separate the pupils from the whites.

"Oh yes. It is like the finest ambrosia," he laughed. "But, for your bravery I will grant you a swift death."

At a silent signal from his captain, Jon-Jon brought an empty keg and a length of rope over to them. Before the man could say anything, the burly pirate knocked him unconscious. He tied a slipknot around the victim's ankles and tossed the other end over a spar with a practiced flick. He hoisted the man up then lowered him headfirst in the keg up to his shoulders. With the loose end of the rope, Jon-Jon tied the man's arms up to his waist. This kept blood from gathering in the hands as well as freed him from holding the rope.

While Jon-Jon tended to that, Viktor retrieved his dagger from the first man he had killed. Once the victim was trussed and in position, he reached into the barrel and slit the man's throat. To keep his word of granting a swift death, he plunged the dagger into the base of the man's skull. Death came instantly. Gravity ensured the corpse bled out.

Lazarus finally reached the *Incubus*. He felt like he'd been flying forever since leaving the *Shining Star*. As he circled before landing, he saw that the pirates had just taken a prize.

He landed close to his captain and returned to feline form. He leapt to Viktor's shoulder.

"Hello old friend." Vik reached up to scratch the cat's head. "I take it you had no luck finding her."

"Meh," the cat replied and started to lick blood off Vik's face. The vampire laughed and put the cat down on the deck.

"Meeyaaaah!" he protested.

Jon-Jon had just lowered the drained body of the merchant captain, and other pirates herded the prisoners to the larder hold or worked to transfer cargo and provisions over to their ship. Lazarus bounded over to the body and started to tear into the throat ravenously.

"Oh, so you're hungry. Eat your fill then."

The sun had dipped while all this activity went on. They'd captured the ship late in the afternoon. Viktor sensed his cadre as they began to stir and sent them a mental message to go to the larder hold to choose their meals. He didn't see a need for their services during the crossing to India and planned to will them dormant for that portion of the voyage. The direct feeding would ensure they weathered the prolonged "sleep" well.

Unexpected movement near the corpse caught his attention. The second the sun fully set, Lazarus dissipated into a dark smoke as if to transform from cat to raven.

"You are going to hunt some more?"

Something wasn't right. The transition stage lasted longer than usual. It seemed like the smoke cloud was much larger than usual, also. As it finally coalesced into a solid form, a familiar voice he hadn't heard in months emanated from it.

"No point in hunting for her anymore, Captain. Zeke has her off on some errand and is blocking the two of you from each other until she's done." Jim Rigger stood over the now mangled corpse.

"How?" Viktor was visibly surprised. Several others were startled, as well.

"New trick the old man taught me when he intercepted me. He said, 'You are what you eat.'"

"Interesting." Vik recovered quickly. He filed the information away for future experimentation. "Why is the old man interfering?"

Jim shrugged. "He doesn't want her distracted while she's off doing whatever it is he's got her doing. He's a strange bird. I swear he can hear my thoughts."

"I wouldn't be surprised, Jim. Damn, but it's good to see you again. Will you be able to keep this form?"

"For a while. The first time I tried it, I was able to hold it for a few hours. I made the mistake of feeding and nearly wasn't able to change back right away. Almost thought I was going to get caught."

"I suspect you have an interesting tale for me. Let's go back to my cabin, and you can put something on. Jon-Jon's looking a bit excited by the sight of you," Vik laughed.

Jon-Jon made a vulgar gesture at them for the comment.

"I see what you mean," Jim grinned. "You might want to include Mr. Grimm on this conversation. I've learned some valuable information."

To say Grimm was surprised to see the man who'd been his predecessor as Brandee's first mate would have been an understatement. "Jim? What? How?"

"Relax, Mr. Grimm. This is only temporary. It's just a new trick that weird old wizard taught me. You're still first mate."

He turned his attention back to the captain. "You're back on the lists, Vik." He was blunt.

The vampire nodded. "I expected that would happen eventually. Brumble report me?"

"Aye. I'd still like to gut that bastard," Jim confirmed then grinned, "and I may have found the instrument to do it with."

Vik's curiosity peaked. "What would that be? We have his sons, and by their account, he'll not really suffer from their loss."

"He also has a daughter, Samantha or 'Sam' as she calls herself. She's taken it upon herself to run away from home to try to find us and ransom her brothers. She is masquerading as a cabin boy aboard the *Shining Star*."

"I know that look, Jim. You seem entirely too pleased with yourself."

"For a virgin, she was very lively in bed." He grinned.

Grimm laughed. "You always have been a bit of a tomcat."

"I enjoy wenching, and it'd been months since I'd had any. She also has the sweetest blood. I had to make myself stop before I took too much."

"Ah, now I understand why you said you were afraid you'd get caught. If she was so lively, how did you keep her captain from bursting in to protect her honor?"

"Used one of your tricks, Vik. I put a couple of drops of my blood into his stew that day. He never heard a thing. Oh, I almost forgot about my trophy."

He held out a small locket. Viktor took it and examined it. When he popped it open it revealed finely painted miniatures of Zachary and Thomas Brumble.

"She'll be missing this. I thought I spied something shiny around your neck when you showed up, but it was hard to tell with that thick fur of yours."

Grimm brought up a problem that might arise from Jim's exploit with Samantha Brumble. "I don't think any of this news will sit too well with Zach. I vote that we don't let him, or Thomas hear any of this."

Vik handed the locket back to Jim. "Zach is working out well as a navigator, but he does still have a strong sense of honor. He definitely wouldn't respond well to the news that you deflowered his sister. We should let them know she's looking for us, though. I refuse to run from a headstrong female. It will be better if it's not a surprise should we encounter her."

Jim looked thoughtful for a while. He handed the locket to Grimm. "Give this to Zach when you tell him about Sam. It will let him know you're telling the truth. Just say that Lazarus brought Vik the news. I don't bear them any ill will, just their father."

Vik raised an eyebrow and teased his friend. "Why Mr. Rigger, if I didn't know better, I'd say you love the wench."

"I love every woman, when I'm with them." He laughed but did not meet the Captain's gaze.

"Did you learn anything else aboard the *Shining Star*?" Grimm brought the conversation back to business. Jim shot him a grateful look.

"Aye. The crew had been spooked when they found a Navy ship to report us to. Their captain had sought out one Commodore Critchfield."

"I've heard of him. He built up a reputation fighting and hunting pirates around the Barbary Coast. He's known as a vicious bastard."

"Oh, it gets better." Jim smiled without humor. "He sails the sister to this ship."

Neither liked that news. "That definitely removes a huge edge in battle," Grimm stated.

"Aye, it puts us on an even footing as far as vessels go," Vik agreed. "What I'd like to know is how the man thinks in battle. If we know what attacks he's most likely to use, we can prepare a better counterattack."

"There's also the cadre," Jim reminded. "If we can destroy his crew's Navy discipline with sheer terror, it would give us back much of the edge taken away by sailing sister ships."

"True," Grimm agreed. "I'd wager that he's never encountered a pirate crew capable of the discipline and teamwork our lads have under your control, Vik."

"Don't think I haven't enjoyed that control, either. I no longer have to constantly watch my back against potential mutiny or the occasional malcontent. That has always been a chief weakness among the Brethren: everyone wants to be captain, present company excluded."

Silently, Grimm was grateful Vik hadn't reminded him of the events that had led them to part company all those years ago. It was part of the reason that, although they were on friendly terms, there was a lingering tension between him and Rigger. When he'd walked in to find the former first mate instead of the demon cat, he'd been sure Vik was going to reinstate his old friend as first mate.

"Mr. Grimm." Vik's voice brought him back to the present. "See to it that Zach Brumble is given at least a double, if not triple, dose of the special rum. We've trusted him so far, and he has proven valuable and loyal, but this business with his sister could change all that. He's too strong-willed and charismatic to allow him to become a free agent again."

"Aye, Captain." He left to do so.

Once the door closed, Jim spoke. "Thank you for making that call on Zach. It's harder to sense when I'm Lazarus, but he still entertains a faint hope of escape. If he were to turn on you, I might not be in a form where I could stop him."

"In all truth, that hadn't occurred to me. You know, I thought Hezekiah was going to piss himself when he saw you."

"I know. I could smell his fear. I always thought he was a bit jealous of our friendship. It's the only reason that makes sense to me for him to leave the crew in the first place. You never did talk about that."

"No, I did not."

"Mm-hm. You still aren't going to tell me what took place during that month you two went off to scout out that suspected treasure shipment, are you."

Viktor just looked at him.

Jim raised his hands and shook his head as he laughed. "I thought as much. Well, since there are no wenches on board…," he trailed off as he returned to his feline form.

Tamara A. Lowery

Chapter 20

About a week after they left Madagascar behind, they no lo longer made good headway. The winds began to die down. They'd hit the doldrums.

At first, Viktor and Grimm weren't too worried. They'd encountered the phenomenon before, and in their experience, it usually hadn't lasted very long. As if to justify this belief, the winds picked back up after a couple of days.

It died again after barely one day had passed. This time, they were left at the mercy of the currents for over a week.

This cycle continued sporadically for what seemed like forever. The wind would pick up just long enough to tease them, then, it would die again. It was maddening.

Viktor stood staring out over the glassy water. The sky above was cloudless. The sun was blistering hot. Some of the men milled about doing busy work to fight the boredom. Others sat around and gambled or found some place to doze. Very few went below deck during the day. It was just too hot and stifling without a breeze or draft.

Grimm joined the captain. "We're still not too bad off, for now. I had Stubby and Mr. Bland cut all rations to three quarters. What we've got should last another month and a half at that rate."

"Good. Has Mr. Brumble been able to determine how far off course the currents have pushed us?"

Grimm scratched his head, clearly not happy about the information he had to share. "Yes," he dragged the word out. "The good news is that we aren't that far off, actually."

"You imply there is bad news, Mr. Grimm."

"Aye. We've apparently hit a stretch that isn't in any of the currents. Until the wind picks up, we are stuck exactly where we are."

Viktor continued to stare out to sea and digested what his first mate had told him. The situation did not look good. Belladonna would have been very useful about then. She could have given them the wind they needed.

But she wasn't there, and he had no idea when she might return. No, he would have to figure out some other way to get them out of this fix before supplies ran out.

"Well, now we know another reason all the trades stick to the coastal waters," he sighed. "Too bad this isn't a galley…," he trailed off as an idea struck him. "Mr. Jon!"

"Ho!" the second mate called back.

"Lower the boats and attach tow lines!"

"Aye, Cap'n."

Grimm blinked at him. "Now why didn't I think of that? Not only will it get us to a sea current, but it'll give the lads something to do besides busy work."

Viktor's laugh betrayed the stress he'd felt up to that point. "I know. Would you believe I entertained the thought, for a split second, of trying to convert the *Incubus* to a galley?"

"That would've been tricky. We've got enough timber and sailcloth to fashion makeshift oars, but we'd either have to use the lower gun ports or try to cut oar ports."

"Aye. And the copper hull would be ruined, if we did that."

The two friends lapsed into a comfortable silence and watched Jon-Jon organize the boat crews. They knew that towing a ship as large as the *Incubus* would make for slow going. But it was better than the motionless drifting they'd endured so far.

Viktor found his mind wandering. The forced inactivity had been frustrating and infuriating. He had half hoped, half expected Hell's Breath Island to manifest and transport them out of their predicament. After all, he was supposed to be operating under a time limit, although he'd never been told exactly what time frame he had to work with.

He had even, for a while, entertained the paranoid fantasy that Zeke had something to do with the doldrums lasting so long. He just couldn't figure out why the old wizard would try to sabotage his quest. It really didn't make sense, so he quickly discarded the idea.

He grew bored with watching the activity and returned to his cabin. He poured himself a glass of brandy. He didn't feel the need for blood at the moment.

It dawned on him, as he sat down, that his Hunger had almost grown dormant. He had been taking blood regularly, but more out of habit than a desire for it. It seemed odd, now that he thought about it. He tried to think back to the last time he'd really felt the Hunger. It hadn't risen since shortly after the last ship they'd taken.

He wondered why. The one being he knew might have an answer was not there to ask, however.

Knowing that no one was near enough to hear, not even Lazarus, he wondered aloud, "Belle? Where are you? When are you coming back?"

"Are you coming back?"

Chapter 21

The *Lorelei* tracked mermaid kills for months. Captain Wormsloe and his passenger were of the opinion they would lead them to Brandee.

It soon became clear that more than one pod had fallen prey to the vampire. Some kills were days or weeks apart, and the course steered to reach them grew increasingly erratic. Wormsloe wondered if that was a sign of the mental state of their prey or if word had gotten out amongst the merfolk of the monster preying on them.

"We are getting close to our quarry, Captain," the woman told him. "You should reach a fresh kill by noon."

"How fresh?"

She turned glowing eyes to him, her fangs showing just the tips. He carefully avoided direct eye contact. He recognized the signs of her Hunger stirring.

"I felt them die not a full hour ago," she told him. "Judging by the power they released, I'd say he has grown addicted to them."

Tamara A. Lowery

"Why the erratic course?"

"I have been thinking about that. Many of the merfolk are much more clever than humans, if naïve about their culture. The kills have been smaller and farther apart lately. I would say they've been dividing their groups in an attempt to evade their predator. He can't chase all of them at the same time, so it raises the odds of survival."

"Hmm, that makes sense. It will be dawn soon, milady. You should go below."

The vampires nodded acknowledgement. "Yes, I can already feel the day approaching. Make sure the bodies are properly destroyed, Captain."

"I will."

As predicted, the *Lorelei* came upon the remains of a mermaid pod about midday. Wormsloe noticed something different about this one, though.

They retrieved five dead mermaids, but the fifth had not been fully drained. Her throat had been torn, as if the vampire had pulled away quickly before he had finished feeding. The captain reasoned that they had probably been close enough for Brandee to sense the female on board, causing him to cut things short.

Wormsloe made a note to warn her to shield her presence. Brandee was a wily bastard, and they would need every advantage they could get. He definitely did not want to give the pirate any advance warning of an attack.

Once the dead mers were beheaded and their hearts removed, the crew threw the remains back into the ocean for the sharks and other scavengers.

Satisfied that no other bodies were to be found nearby, Captain Wormsloe retired to his cabin to get some rest before nightfall.

Finally, Belladonna sensed she was getting close to her prey. She had scented mermaid blood a day ago and headed in that direction. A few times, she had come across the remains of Alyssa's kills. Once, someone else had already mutilated the bodies.

The siren would not touch the kills. She wasn't squeamish about it, but it was clear that Alyssa was turning while still alive. Belle didn't want to risk creating a link with the creature, or worse, strengthening her bondage to Viktor.

It surprised her to find she really missed the connection to him. She knew Zeke was shielding her from her master to the point that the bond was virtually broken for all intents and purposes. She enjoyed her freedom, but there was a small blind spot in her senses where the vampire should be.

Maybe Grimm had been right when he'd guessed that she loved Viktor.

Belle shook her head to clear it of thoughts of the vampire. She needed to focus on catching Alyssa.

"Damn," she thought, "how fast can a pregnant mer swim?"

Maybe an hour before sunset, she finally caught sight of her prey. She arrowed toward the mermaid.

A slight change in pressure warned Alyssa of the approaching siren. A wave of terror chilled her. She had caught scent of her natural predator during her last kill. Instinct caused her to abandon the meal unfinished. Even though she had become a predator herself, feeding on her own kind, she hadn't considered that she was now capable of holding her own with a siren in a fight. All she knew was she had to live long enough to calve.

She fled.

Her speed was now greater than that of other mers, but the siren gradually gained on her. Ahead, she saw the bottom of a ship's hull. That meant humans. She could get them to shelter her from the siren.

A labor pain struck and caused her to double. Belladonna used the distraction to her advantage and closed a good deal of the distance between them.

The mermaid turned glowing, fear filled eyes to the siren. "He promised me he would not allow you to harm me or my child," she accused.

Belle stopped short. Alyssa's eyes had turned emerald green. There was a powerful magic in her voice. "Viktor?"

The magic felt so similar, she actually felt a tremor of fear and longing. Then she remembered why she was hunting the mermaid. "He is not holding my leash at the moment. I have been sent to destroy you. You have become something you were never meant to be."

"No! My daughter will need me! My pod is dead."

"Yes, by your hand and Hunger." Belle grew irritated. "Do you have any idea how much prey you have ruined for me? I can't eat your leavings. Hell, I won't even be able to eat you!"

"Then let me go!"

Belle shook her head. "I can't. I have been charged to put you down before you create more of your kind. You are no longer a mermaid. You are a predator."

Another labor pain hit the pregnant mer. She cried out involuntarily.

Silent Fathoms

The siren eyed the nearby ship. Without a pod for protection, the birthing would draw other predators to them. Zeke had forbidden her to kill Viktor's offspring. She had to get them out of the water.

"Go to the humans and calve your son, Alyssa. Just as I must eventually kill you, I am forbidden to harm him."

"Son?"

She nodded. "You carry a merman; one who will be unlike any other. The Elder wants me to bring him to Hell's Breath."

"You will never have him!" Alyssa snarled and darted toward the ship.

"I don't really want him," Belle muttered, letting her go for the moment.

"Captain Wormsloe! We've got a live one!" the call came, as Alyssa was spotted by the crew of the *Lorelei*.

"Help me! Don't let it kill me!" the distressed mermaid called out.

"Our quarry must be very close," Wormsloe reasoned. "Lower a line and bring her aboard. I want every other hand to prepare the ship for battle! Chances are Brandee is not far off."

The ship became a hive of activity. One of the men helping Alyssa aboard called the captain over.

"Sir, she is pregnant!"

"Not just pregnant, man. She's in labor," he corrected as he observed the convulsions in her extended belly. "Damn, she's not going to be any use for questioning until she's whelped. Mr. Borescue, fetch the ship's surgeon."

"Aye, Captain."

Alyssa's screams unnerved the crew. There was great relief when the child was finally born. The tiny boy had a shock of coal black hair and appeared to be fully human. The doctor cut and bound the cord. He examined the child before he handed it to its mother.

As Alyssa suckled her son, Wormsloe decided it was a good time to question her about Brandee.

"How far behind you is Vik Brandee?"

"Too far. He was not here to protect me or his son from her."

It clearly wasn't the answer he had expected. "Who are you fleeing? We've been following a trail of murdered mermaids. We are hunting the vampire that killed them. We thought it was Brandee. And what do you mean 'his son'?" He had no idea he was giving her too much information.

Alyssa had been quick to learn the weaknesses of human males, as were all her kind once exposed to humans. The mers had used human men for mating for centuries, due to a rarity of mermen. If these humans learned she was the source of the corpses they had found, they might destroy her. Her son was too precious to risk leaving him unprotected. She knew she would have to choose her answer carefully.

She stroked the hair of the child at her breast and spoke softly. "My son was sired by the one you call Vik Brandee. You are right that he is a vampire, but he is not the creature I was fleeing. I am being hunted by a siren. She is the natural predator of my kind, but this one is different. She wants him for herself. I do not know why she did not eat the bodies of my pod mates."

Chapter 22

Belladonna clung to the side of the ship; her talons buried deep in the wood. She'd made sure she picked a spot out of sight of the men on deck. She growled irritably to herself. She should have killed the rogue mer when she'd had the chance and just cut the brat from the body. Now the clever bitch had implicated her as the one these humans should be hunting. That was going to make retrieving the whelp much harder.

She toyed with the idea of screaming and destroying the minds of all the humans on board, but she didn't want to risk permanently damaging the infant mer. Zeke had specifically forbidden her to kill the whelp and had ordered her to bring it to him once the dam was dispatched. The old fart was always making things complicated for her.

She would just have to bide her time. She was wondering how best to get at Alyssa to kill her, when the sun disappeared below the waves. Belle was shocked to sense at least three vampires aboard the vessel. Alyssa bore Viktor's unmistakable power signature, but the others were very different. One was very old and frighteningly powerful. That was not good.

Tamara A. Lowery

Alyssa gave Wormsloe permission to take the child and show it to his female passenger. She reasoned a human female would protect it. She knew the siren still remained close, waiting for a good time to try to kill her. She had to prepare for the coming battle and wanted her son safely out of the way.

Using her mer wiles and raw sexuality, she lured a sailor close to her. The vampirism she had gained magnified her seductive abilities. All of the men near her fell mesmerized by her glamour, even when she embraced the hapless sailor and bit deep into his throat, feeding greedily. Birthing had taken more out of her than she'd realized.

She was so concentrated on feeding that she never sensed the vampires come on deck. In a split second, Alyssa found herself dislodged from her prey and fighting for her life.

Belle could smell the blood. It drew her to climb up and peer over the rail. She had not fed on human flesh in weeks. Every eye was focused on the battle between the vampire and the mermaid.

The vampire pummeled Alyssa and stunned her long enough to grab a sword from one of the sailors. With one powerful stroke, she beheaded the mermaid.

Belle blinked and breathed a sigh of relief. She had not dealt the death blow; therefore, she would be able to avoid Viktor's wrath. She ducked back down out of sight and listened to learn what had become of the infant.

"It appears we were on the wrong track, milady. I think this was the source of the kills we've been cleaning up." Wormsloe indicated the dead mer.

The female knelt and examined the body. "We are only slightly off course, Captain. She was the rogue, but she has been fed on. There are bite scars on her breasts." She stood and looked at him. "I may be wrong, but I would almost swear she was still alive when I took her head. There have been legends of vampires that were turned without dying, but I have never seen a verifiable case in all my centuries and travels."

"What about the baby? Does it need to be destroyed?"

"I will have to observe it longer to know. I find it odd that the creature appears to be human rather than mer. He also reeks of magic, much stronger magic than I would expect of a newborn. As tempting as it is to drink it, I know the reasons behind our laws against feeding on the sea folk."

Wormsloe considered the situation for a while. "He'll need milk. I think one of the goats is a nanny, if the cook hasn't killed and cooked it yet. She said Brandee got the whelp on her. Perhaps there's a way to use him to track the bastard."

"Perhaps. You know more of this pirate we're hunting than I do, Captain Wormsloe. Would it be a viable plan to use the child as bait?"

"It might, but I doubt it, milady. Given his reputation when he was human, I imagine he's got little bastards floating around all over the Caribbean. I never heard of him being particularly attached to any of them."

"Very well, I will think on what we've learned here tonight. For the present, I will keep the child in my cabin."

She turned to leave the deck, but he stopped her. "Now that we have the whelp, we shouldn't need Turlington anymore." He sincerely hoped she would let him dispose of the Navy man. He viewed the prisoner as a liability.

"You have already pointed out that the child might not be bait enough for our fish, Captain. Therefore, I will keep the option to use my toy's Naval connections." Her answer came as more of a command than anything else. "Now that you mention him, though, I've noticed that his health has been deteriorating. I've probably been feeding on him too much. We need to get fresh provisions; otherwise, I'll have to turn him to keep him."

The last thing Wormsloe wanted was another vampire on board. She'd brought one with her and already made one more since the voyage started. It had cost him one of his best bosons. He would not betray his chosen master's wishes where this female was concerned, but he'd be damned if he was going to lose any more of his crew to her or any of her "offspring." At least he'd been able to convince to finally dispose of one of them. Unfortunately, she executed the newer vampire. He consoled himself that she bore ill will toward the one she'd brought aboard and kept him starved most of the time.

"We will take the next vessel we encounter or put in to a port, should it come to that. I will send the doctor around to Turlington to see if he can give the man anything to bolster his strength."

"Good, as long as it is not laudanum. In his current state, that would only speed his death and rebirth. I shall await the sustenance for the child in my cabin." She turned and quickly vanished back below deck.

He resisted the urge to shake himself. He'd been working for her kind for nearly two decades, but there were still some things they did that just made his skin crawl.

Back in her cabin, she gazed at the infant. It had slept since shortly after its birth and initial feeding. She was still puzzled by its human form. Everything she'd read about the merfolk indicated that it should have had a tail rather than legs. The only sea folk she'd read of that could pass as human were sirens.

The wild magic in the child's aura did not taste the same as the mother's, although she'd had a slight hint of it, like an echo of a whisper. The father must be the source.

She was beginning to understand why her master had dispatched her to hunt the pirate down. Already, his magic was causing unchecked changes in the order that had stood for millennia.

If such wild magic could not be controlled, it must be destroyed before it could become a serious threat.

The baby woke with a small hiccup and blinked around at his surroundings. She was struck by the fact his eyes were a bright emerald green. Infants she had seen in the past had always had blue eyes. They also seemed to be focused, unlike the bleary gaze of a human infant.

She found herself smiling when he burbled and gave a toothless grin. She had to admit he was a beautiful child. The power he emanated was more potent now that he was awake.

Perhaps she would keep him as a pet. Being part mer would guarantee he would last longer than a human pet. It would also be interesting to see how his magic developed and how she could put it to use.

Reaching down to feel the texture of his hair, she let him catch her fingers. His tiny hands were so very warm. He popped one of her fingers into his mouth and started sucking on it. An alien emotion shot through her at the sensation. She found herself feeling protective towards him. There was a stirring in her long-dead womb. She had never borne children when she had been alive. She had never regretted that until now.

A wild notion planted itself in her mind. If Brandee could sire children, even though he was vampire, perhaps his magic was powerful enough to revive her womb. Even more than the mer baby, a child from such a union would give her the leverage to overthrow her master and rule in his stead.

She had to be careful to never reveal that secret to anyone. If her master even suspected the slightest hint of rebellion, he would destroy her.

There was some relief that the nanny goat had not been slaughtered yet. There was even more that the baby accepted the goat milk.

Wormsloe and his passenger had both worried the child would reject the milk. Despite his appearance, he was not human. Nothing in all the lore the vampiress had read gave any indication of what mers ate.

The baby went back to sleep after his feeding. Wormsloe ordered a small hammock rigged up in the passenger's cabin. Once the vampiress was sure the child was secured, she turned in for the day.

Chapter 23

Belladonna moved to the keel of the ship after she was satisfied the vampire wasn't going to drain the baby. She had been mildly surprised to learn there was a vampire law against feeding on sea folk. Apparently, more was known about her kind than she realized.

It worried her to hear that this vampire was hunting Viktor. She wondered if it had anything to do with his involvement with the New Orleans kiss, or if it was something more sinister.

She could curse Zeke for requiring her to retrieve the brat and bring it to him. She knew it was eventually going to breed out her favorite food. Viktor's bloodline would create a hybrid mermaid population that would quickly supplant the pure blood mers. To eat one of the hybrids would bind her that much closer to the pirate's will.

If not for the brat, she would be making spells and plans to dispatch the entire crew of this ship. It was bad enough the humans were hunting Viktor without drawing a vampire of this one's age and power after him, too.

Tamara A. Lowery

She would destroy the vampire, if she could get to her without endangering her chances of getting away with the child. Apparently, she was going to keep him in her cabin.

It was just a matter of waiting until daylight.

Shortly after dawn, a dense fog enveloped the *Lorelei*. A haunting female voice could be heard from everywhere at once, as if the voice was the fog.

Wormsloe had his hands full keeping his crew from panicking. The fog grew so thick anything moving two feet in front of one was seen only as a shadow.

Belladonna climbed aboard the ship once she was satisfied the fog was thick enough. If no one could see her, she wouldn't have to waste time killing them and risk raising the alarm. Her senses allowed her to move easily and silently about without even brushing against any of the sailors.

She had to be more careful once she got below decks. The fog didn't reach within the ship. The quicker she found the cabin the child was in, the better.

It helped that the child's aura tasted strongly of Viktor. She knew the flavor well.

She entered the cabin cautiously. The vampire's power indicated she might be able to stay awake past dawn, and Belle's fog had darkened the sky enough that it would allow the vampire to move about without fear. The siren had seen enough of the fight with Alyssa to know the vampire would be a deadly opponent.

She found no sign of the vampire in the cabin. Her scent was strong, indicating she wasn't far away, but Belle did not see her. She must've had a hidden and secure daytime resting place. It would make sense, especially if there was worry one of the crew might try to destroy her while she was dead to the world.

Belladonna found the baby in a small hammock hanging in the corner. Nearby was a water bladder full of goat milk.

He was awake, when she started to pick him up. She was struck by his green eyes, so like Viktor's. He even had his father's black hair. He burbled at her.

"Sh, little one, we don't want to wake anyone." She lifted him and snagged the milk.

The baby's eyes latched onto the leather bottle, and he made a small whine. His chubby arms waved towards it. Belle took the hint and gave him the neck end of it. Someone had tied a kerchief over the mouth in a way to mimic a teat. The infant popped it into his mouth and began to feed greedily.

The blissful look in his eyes caused her to fight not to chuckle. He was definitely Viktor's son.

She sensed her fog start to thin. She wasn't sure how long she had been standing there holding the baby while he fed. There was no time to hunt out the vampire to kill it. She had to get off the boat.

She put the milk down and cradled the infant to her shoulder. Quietly, she exited the cabin. She didn't encounter anyone in the corridors, but she almost ran into Wormsloe when she came on deck.

Hastily, she shoved him back, before he could react. She darted for the rail.

"Stop her! She has the baby!"

A couple of sailors made a grab for her. They only received gashes and blistering welts, as she one-handed the infant and extended her poisoned talons from her other hand.

Before anyone else could get close enough to try to subdue her, she dove over the side.

In the water, Belle retracted her talons to avoid harming the baby. Just as the siren took her true form, now that she was back in her natural element, so the child revealed his mer nature. The black and silvery green scales on his tail were almost a match for Belladonna's black and silver shark tail.

His instincts kicked in, as well. He seemed to recognize her as a predator and started wriggling, trying to get free.

Oddly, the siren realized she had no urge to eat the young mer. She wondered if that had anything to do with how similar his aura was to that of his sire.

She made her features as human as possible in an effort to soothe him, although there was nothing she could do about her tail. She had never been able to maintain legs in sea water. She was able to return her eyes and teeth to their human façade, however.

The ruse seemed to work. The baby calmed considerably. He even burbled at her and caught some of her hair as it drifted around him. He promptly pulled it then popped his fist into his mouth and began to gum it.

Belle was still smiling, bemused at the child's antics, when the open sea around her closed into a lagoon. The lagoon gradually drained until it was only a foot deep.

For the siren, the transition back to full human form was smooth and nearly thoughtlessly automatic. For the young mer, it was frightening and traumatic. He screamed and clung to her as his tail split to form legs and feet, and his scales and fins were absorbed back into his skin. She thought it odd that he hadn't reacted to his legs transforming into a tail.

"Sh, sh, little one. You are safe," she cooed. "No one is going to hurt you."

"Heh. Never thought I'd see you go all maternal, girl."

She shot Zeke a glare as she walked out of the lagoon and onto the shore of Hell's Breath Island.

"All right, I'll leave off teasing." The old man smiled. He reached out. "Let me see the boy."

Belle was reluctant to hand him over. "What do you want with him?"

Zeke shot her a look then smiled wryly. "You're already under his spell. His magic must be powerful indeed to ensnare a siren so easily. He wants a mama since you killed his real one, and any female that gets near him is going to fall in love with him until he finds the one he wants."

"I didn't kill the mermaid." She figured she might as well get this over with.

"You have to finish the job, girl. Her taint cannot be allowed to spread." His tone was stern.

"I didn't say she wasn't dead, old man." She finally handed the baby to him. "The same one that killed her has been cleaning up the kills she left behind before I could get to them. They followed the dead mers to track her. They thought they were tracking Viktor."

"Who?" Zeke's eyes glowed like coals with ultra-hard diamonds in them.

"At least two of them are vampires. One is very old and powerful, much more so than any I have encountered on this side of the world. She is the one that dispatched Alyssa.

I didn't get a good look at her, but I think I will be able to remember her voice and scent. She sails on the *Lorelei*, captained by a human named Wormsloe."

"What was the vampire called?"

"I do not know. It seemed almost as if everyone on board was careful to avoid saying her name."

"Hmmm. It seems odd that I have not seen this creature. If she is hunting the One and someone or something powerful is protecting her from my 'sight,' it does not bode well."

"If I'd had the time, I would have ferreted out her hiding place and destroyed her while the sun rode high."

"Let's hope that not doing so does not prove fatal."

Wormsloe was glad of the guarantee of protection by the vampire's master. Otherwise, he feared she might kill him for the loss of the baby mer.

Although she was not pleased, she was calm about the matter. "You say a fog of unusual density sprang up, and shortly after a strange female took the child and went over the side with him?"

"Yes, milady. I am ashamed to admit she caught me off guard. She was unnaturally fast and strong. It was hard to tell in the fog, but I think she was naked. The two sailors who managed to reach her tried to stop her escape. I don't know what kind of weapon she used, but the cuts have festered and won't stop oozing. They also have noxious welts close to the wounds."

"Was there singing heard at any time?" she asked sharply.

He blinked. "Why yes there was, now that you mention it. It started shortly before the fog arose."

She nodded. "There was a siren on board. The two men shall have to be killed, unless you want them to have a slow and excruciating death. The venom in a siren's talons causes a gangrenous rot in human flesh."

"Damn! I should have taken better heed of what the mermaid said. I thought her account of fleeing from a siren was just a lie to cover the fact that she was the predator killing other mers. She said a siren is a mermaid's natural predator. It must have stolen the child to eat it."

"I don't think she intends to eat the child. I don't know her reasons for kidnapping him, but if she had been after a quick meal, why did she feed him?" She held up the almost empty milk bladder.

She wasn't really that upset about the theft of the child. Now that he was gone, she could see that he had cast some sort of spell on her that compelled her to be protective of him. She was a very old and powerful vampire. As far as she knew, only a handful of vampires were more powerful than her. If this creature had enough power as an infant to affect her so much, she could not afford to let it survive to adulthood and full strength.

She hoped the siren's instincts proved more powerful than the child's magic. If so, she was sure the sea monster would make quick work of such a tender morsel. Otherwise, she would have to hunt it down and destroy it, just like its sire.

She found Wormsloe on the bridge the next night. "Did you ever get coordinates from Turlington for that dreadnaught he sailed on?"

"I did."

"I think it's time we paid his Commodore a visit."

He resigned himself to involving the Navy. In all fairness, she had followed every other option that had been made available to them. "Very well. We need to get a good look at the ship. If it truly is the sister of Brandee's ship, I would like to know its capabilities and lines. I don't want the bastard to take us by surprise. Are you still planning on enthralling the Commodore?"

"Yes. He is already hunting the same prey. He can be my hound and drive Brandewyne to me."

Chapter 24

The towing was making progress, but it was very slow. Supplies dwindled dangerously low, even with strict rationing. After over a month of cut rations, the men had grown weak and thin.

Worse, Viktor could feel his grip on them begin to fray. The rum he'd tainted with his blood and used to keep them in his sway had been exhausted. He would have to do something about that soon. He knew there were some among the crew that might incite a mutiny, even though they had no better ideas on how to get out of the fix they were in.

Even Lazarus was having a hard time of it. Viktor had sent him out daily to search for land or at least spot signs of an ocean current. With no air currents to ride, it was hard work.

Almost at the end of their supplies, some good news finally arrived. Lazarus found an island. Better yet, there was fresh water and abundant fruit. The visuals he sent

Viktor told him that it was just beyond the horizon on their present course.

"Mr. Grimm!"

"Aye, Captain."

"I need eight men in good condition and two long boats. There's an island that should come into sight within the hour at our current speed. I want to lead out a foraging party."

"Aye. Do you want me to come with you?"

Viktor shook his head. "No, I need you here to keep the rest of the crew in order. Once the island comes into sight, call in the tow crews and give them a ration of water and a rest period. I'll take Brumble with me in the other boat. I want to keep an eye on him personally."

Grimm nodded his understanding. Neither of them really trusted Zachary. The man was clever and resourceful. He had pledged his loyalty to the Captain, but he thought too much like both Viktor and Grimm for either of them to risk turning their backs on him without the bloodied rum to ensure it.

A current ran not far from the island, which was an atoll of four narrow islands and three islets surrounding a deep-water lagoon. It was a relief to Viktor. He knew they could use it to give the tow crews some time to recover their strength. But it proved a bit of a trial for the foraging party. They had to fight the current to get to the atoll.

Lazarus had shown him that the island was occupied. There seemed to be a plantation system set up at different points about the islands. Viktor would rather the place be deserted, but at least he'd had forewarning enough to prepare to bargain with the locals.

They had to make for the entrance to the lagoon at the north end of the atoll. The current was proving too difficult to navigate to make landfall on the outer shore.

As expected, they were spotted not long after entering the lagoon. By the time they reached the dock, there was a throng of curious islanders waiting on them. Most of them appeared to be either Africans or some unknown olive-skinned race Viktor had never seen before. A couple of white men on horses rode up at the back of the group, dismounted and headed out the dock to greet them.

"*Bon jour*, what fate brings you here?"

"*Bon jour*," Viktor returned the greeting. "Our ship was becalmed almost two months ago. We hope to be able to resupply."

"Come ashore, *mes amis*. We will have our people prepare a meal for you," the shorter of the two men said. "I am Emile, and this is my business partner, Julian."

"Thank you. I am Viktor, this is my navigator Zachary, and these are some of my crewmen." He accepted the invitation, grateful that full names had not come into it. He wasn't sure how far his reputation had spread or if anyone would know him in these waters. There was also the question of Brumble's reputation. He would be more well-known, but Viktor wasn't sure what kind of standing Brumble & Sons had among the locals.

On the whole, their hosts were very hospitable. It was one of the best feeds any of them had enjoyed in months. Everything was fresh, even though some was a bit exotic to them.

"Excuse me, but what kind of meat is this?" Zach asked. "It tastes vaguely familiar, but I can't quite place it."

Tamara A. Lowery

"It is the flesh of the coconut crab," Julian answered. "They are a gigantic native species. Tomorrow, we will hunt and trap them so you can take them back to your ship. If you keep them in seawater, they will remain alive for several days, until you boil them."

"I look forward to it."

They discovered their hosts had not exaggerated about the size of the coconut crabs. The creatures were large enough to take off a hand with their claws if a hunter wasn't careful. The guides Julian and Emile sent with them bore the evidence. A few were missing some fingers and toes.

The pirates caught on quickly, however. Before the tide changed, they had enough crabs to fill one of the boats. They filled the other boat with coconuts, small kegs of liquor made from fermented coconut milk, casks of water and some vegetables that were grown to feed the slaves and the Indian laborers.

Emile asked Viktor to talk with him in private. He left Brumble to oversee loading the boats and went to see what the older man wanted to talk about.

At the main house, Emile handed Viktor a glass of port and smiled a knowing smile.

"It took me a while to put it together, but I figured something out last night."

"And what is that?" The pirate was careful not to let his wariness show. To all but those who knew him well, he appeared perfectly calm and at ease.

"Who you are, Captain Brandee. Old Billy Black described you quite well." He watched for a reaction.

Viktor regarded his host for a while before he spoke. "*Le Comte du Mer*. I remember Captain Black mentioned your exploits on occasion. I was not aware you were still around."

"*Oui*. Much like Billy, I was wise enough to get out, once I'd made my fortune and set myself up in business. Our little home here in the Chagos is ideal for my temperament. It is far enough from the shipping lanes to keep it private but sustains quite a profitable crop of coconuts. Coconut oil is a much more easily obtainable resource than whale oil."

"And much safer to harvest, I'd wager." Vik laughed.

"That it is, *mon ami*. How is old Billy these days?"

"Dead from pneumonia about five years ago." He sobered somewhat as he remembered his old mentor. "Not how I would choose to go. I prefer a swift death in battle to a drawn out and painfully unmanning death like that."

Emile smiled sadly. "You almost make me wish for the old days. But I have grown too old and soft now."

They drank in silence for a while. Finally, the old French pirate spoke again. "Your navigator is a Brumble, isn't he? I'd say keep a close eye on him, especially if he's anything like his *pere*. I made the mistake of doing business with the man about a decade ago. He managed to cheat me out of a great deal of the profit from that venture. If I had him here today, I'd slit his throat."

Viktor nodded. "Aye, Tobias Brumble has done much to earn the vengeance of several men. So far, young Zachary has proven to be a better man, but I know better than to trust him. He has the kind of charisma and leadership skills that could easily win over a weak-minded or ill-treated crew from their captain. That is why I brought him with me rather than leave him with my ship. I would like to have a ship to return to."

Emile chuckled. "I was warned you were a shrewd and clever man."

"Oh, I doubt the Captain used language that polite."

"*Non*. He was quite colorful whenever you came up in conversation." His host laughed. "Well, *mon ami*, I thank you for the company and the news."

"And I thank you for the supplies, *Comte du Mer*."

Both boats were loaded by the time they returned to the dock. Looking out across the lagoon, they could see the *Incubus* approach the natural harbor.

"*Mon Dieu*! Is that your ship?" Emile asked.

"It is." Vik smirked.

"How did you manage to get your hands on a ship-of-the-line?" Julian asked.

"It was a gift."

"A gift." The young planter was incredulous.

"Let it go, *mon frère*. If he says it was a gift, it was a gift."

To Viktor's surprise, Julian heeded his partner's advice. Smart man. The pirate did not have much patience for being questioned.

He was further surprised by the next thing Emile said. "Are you sure these two boats will be enough?"

"Are you offering more?"

"I like to help the Brethren out whenever I can. One never knows when they will need a favor returned." He shrugged.

"I can see why you have been successful in business. You hedge your bets."

"*Oui.*"

"Thank you for the offer, sir. I'll send the boats back for a second load."

"It will be waiting on the dock. *Bon voyage*. I would wish you *bon chance*, but you strike me as a man who makes his own luck."

"I know that look. What has you so amused?" Grimm asked upon Viktor's return.

"Our benefactor on the island is *le Comte du Mer*." He hooked a thumb behind him. "We're going back for a second load."

"Emile de Champ? He dropped out of sight years ago. I figured he was dead by now."

"No, he said he went into business after he made his fortune. He and his partner are running a coconut plantation."

"Partner, is that what he's calling him?" Grimm snorted.

Viktor raised an eyebrow. "You know something I do not?"

"Aye. I doubt Billy Black ever warned you the Comte prefers men. He probably figured the two of you would never meet."

"But he warned you?"

"No." He smiled wryly. "I found out the hard way. I met him once, when I was between ships, a few years before I met you. He propositioned me."

Viktor had to tease. "That was only because you are such a pretty thing, Hezekiah. What man could resist you?"

"One that wishes to continue breathing."

"Hmm, and yet he is still around. Are you sure I'm getting the whole story. Mr. Grimm?"

"Captain Black stepped in and properly introduced us before I could draw my blade, or I'd have slit the man's throat. My sense of humor was not so strong in my youth." He smiled. He recognized the teasing for what it was. "It's best he did, too. Given the Comte's reputation with a blade, I'd have at least a scar or two to show for the encounter. I'd probably have had half the man's crew after my hide, as well."

"Aye, old Billy did tell me about how loyal his crew was. I used his fairness and generosity to his men and his ruthlessness with those who'd crossed him as some of the models to develop my own leadership style."

"You've always had a habit of adopting the best from those who've gone before you, and it has served you well, Captain."

Chapter 25

Brumble was put in charge of the second supply run. Everything went smoothly until they passed the mouth of the lagoon on the way back to the ship.

A breeze had kicked up and made the sea choppy. Because of this, the crew of the trailing boat didn't realize right away that they'd been bumped from below. The second collision was more noticeable.

They looked around but couldn't see what had hit them. They doubled their rowing speed, wanting to reach the ship as quickly as they could before whatever it was came back. Then, a sudden and rapid succession of thumps threatened to capsize them.

Without warning, something grabbed two of their oars from below. Luckily, one man managed to let go of his oar just in time. The other man didn't fare as well. He was pulled into the water along with his oar.

Before the man could even scream, he was ripped to pieces. Sharks swarmed and roiled around the boat. They churned the water to blood-tinged foam. The remaining pirates quickly hoisted their oars out of the water. They didn't want to join in their shipmate's fate.

Zachary heard the cries of horror and looked back to see what the commotion was. He immediately ordered the lead boat turned about.

The crew chief on the besieged boat waved them off and shouted to warn them away. "Go on to the ship! The buggers will go for your oars! That's how they got Jackson!"

Zach saw that the aggressiveness of the swarm prevented the other boat from rowing to safety. He took the heaving line and tried to toss it to them. The idea was to tow them out of the sharks.

The line fell short by only a couple of feet. Zach began to pull it back in to make another attempt. A shark grabbed the line and tugged, almost jerking him off his feet. He released the rope and let the creature have it, but he suffered severe rope burns.

He would have to go back to the ship for help.

The sharks continued to pummel the stranded boat, trying to capsize it. Viktor watched the drama unfold, desperate to find a way to salvage the situation. He didn't want to lose the men, and they really needed those supplies.

A strange sensation washed over him. It felt familiar, but it made him doubt his senses. Could it be, after all those months?

The crew that was stranded huddled and murmured nervously. The sharks had gone. They peered cautiously over the side and looked into the water. The breeze laid, and the water calmed. They could see about a fathom down before it grew too dark for details.

Not a single shark was visible. Just moments ago, the sea had worked alive with the predators.

"That's mighty unnatural," Grimm commented. "Wonder why they left so quickly."

Viktor reached out with his senses for a connection he had given up trying to find. It was weak and stretched thin, but it was back.

"Belle?"

Grimm looked at him, surprised. Before he could comment, the siren appeared and climbed up the mooring line. By the time she reached the railing and swung herself over, legs had replaced her tail.

Belladonna stood by the railing. She looked both feral and vulnerable. Viktor stood still and stared at her. She looked as if she wanted to bolt back into the sea. Grimm stayed back and looked back and forth between the siren and the vampire.

"Belladonna." Viktor wanted to call her to him, but he knew the link they shared was too weak, and she might flee at the attempt. He didn't want to scare her away. It was time to rely on the seductive skills he used on human females.

He approached her slowly. His expression was carefully guarded. He did not want to spook her. Only Grimm watched on.

Viktor retained enough of a hold on his crew to ensure they paid him and the siren no mind. They were busy helping their mates aboard and hoisting the boat and supplies up, before the sharks decided to return.

Belle watched Viktor's approach. It wasn't a predatory stalk. Rather, it was a very cautious approach. She didn't sense any fear from him, but he did harbor some apprehension. She blinked and realized he was worried she would flee from him. It was a valid concern. Just seeing him wakened emotions she had tucked away in a dark corner. Part of her did want to run away. Another part wanted to run to him. He was the only man who had ever made her feel that way.

She was so intent on her inner conflict that he reached her before she realized it. Gently, he reached up to touch her face with just his fingertips.

"You came back," he whispered. There was a look of wonder in his eyes and a tone of hope in his voice.

Her mind screamed at her that this was a trap. But she couldn't quite manage to make her body react to the instinct. She had never seen him appear this vulnerable, and it confused and worried her. Was he truly so attached to her that her absence could weaken him so?

If that was the case, his mission could easily be doomed to failure without her help. She could not allow that to happen. Other than Zeke, Celie, and perhaps Gloribeau, she was the only one who knew the full scope and reason for what he had to do. Viktor might think he knew the why of it, but he really only knew enough to motivate his cooperation. If he ever suspected he was being manipulated, it would not go well for those trying to pull his strings. Dorada had already learned that lesson. Belle held no doubt Rosalia would learn it, as well.

With a sigh, she realized she would not abandon the pirate. What disturbed her was that she really didn't want to abandon him.

"Yes," she said softly. "I came back."

Viktor turned to his first mate. "Mr. Grimm, see to it that the men get that cargo stowed securely. Have the riggers unfurl the sails. We're about to get a good wind and current. I need to talk to Belle in private and am not to be disturbed."

"Understood, Captain. Welcome back, lass."

Belladonna stood in Viktor's cabin suddenly feeling very awkward. She hadn't been there in months. Her one comfort at the moment was that the vampire seemed to be equally ill at ease.

"I would have stopped by my cabin and grabbed some clothes," she muttered.

The comment both surprised and hurt him a little. He didn't want her to be that uncomfortable around him. It just seemed so uncharacteristic of the normally uninhibited siren.

"Would it make you feel better to be clothed?"

She nodded but would not meet his gaze. He retrieved a shirt and pair of loose breeches from his trunk and handed them to her. He then turned away to give her a little privacy.

Belle held the clothes and looked at his back for a few moments. He was being very careful with her, as well as patient and considerate. She wasn't sure what to make of his mood. She put the clothes on quickly. She was amazed at the security the thin layer of cloth gave her. Perhaps it came from the fact she was now enveloped in his scent.

Vik watched her surreptitiously in the reflection on the large cabin windows. Once she was clothed, he turned back around. He caught her sniffing the fabric and noted the calming effect it seemed to have on her.

She noticed his scrutiny and the small smile that tugged at the corner of his mouth. "What?"

His smile widened as his amusement grew. "You look adorable. I keep forgetting how tiny you are. Your personality is so formidable."

She narrowed her eyes at him. "I'm trying to figure out if that was an insult or a compliment."

"Now you sound more like yourself. I've missed you, Belladonna."

"Then your aim has gotten really bad."

Before she could react, he clasped her to him and kissed her fiercely. She felt amazing in his arms. It took him a few moments to realize something wasn't right.

Belle wanted to relax into the kiss, but she just couldn't bring herself to. The panic of feeling trapped tried to creep in. She knew if she allowed that to happen, she would struggle, which would fire his Hunger. So, she allowed him to kiss her, but she had to stiffen up to fight the panic.

He pulled back from the kiss but didn't release her completely. "What is wrong? You reek of fear."

She had to fight the panic even harder. She'd momentarily forgotten about his heightened sense of smell. She forced her voice to remain even and said, "It's been a long time, Viktor. I need to ease back into this, and you are making me feel a bit trapped."

She saw him close down as he stepped away from her. The emotional walls were coming back up. He did it so smoothly that she wasn't sure if it had been hurt in his eyes she had a glimpse of or not. If she'd been human, she might have apologized and tried to draw him back out. But she was a siren, and remorse was alien to her.

She breathed a sigh of relief that he had gone back to hiding his vulnerability, which translated to weakness to her predatory nature.

What she didn't count on was his aggression manifesting to mask the hurt. "So, where have you been for the past several months, and why were you blocked from me?"

She had expected the question, but the rage behind it caught her a little off guard. "I didn't block you. Zeke did that."

"Why?"

He loomed over her, but she didn't feel trapped this time. Violence she understood far better than the softer emotions.

"Because he didn't want you to know what I was doing." She stepped right into him and got in his face. "Until Zeke decides to inform you of his business, I will not tell you where I was or what I was doing. Just be satisfied that it was something that needed to be done."

"I could force you to tell me, pet." His voice was a deadly purr.

"I wouldn't suggest trying it, Captain. It wasn't as strong on my end, but I sensed the blast he sent at you when you tried to force our link back open."

He had to admit she had a point.

Tamara A. Lowery

Chapter 26

To make up for lost time and to mollify the vampire, Belle sang up a wind to speed them on their way. They reached the Bay of Bengal in a few days, rather than a couple of weeks.

They followed Zach's trading information and sailed to the northern end of the bay and the saltwater swamps of the Sundarbans. Lazarus was dispatched to locate a port or village and save them time on sailing the coast to find one.

Within a day, they moored offshore from a good-sized village. Several small boats came out to meet them. The villagers brought their wares to the ship rather than wait for the crew to come ashore. Luckily, only the men of the village came out. If Viktor hadn't administered a fresh dose of liquor tainted with his blood, the crew might have given him trouble. Except for the ones that had gone for supplies at Emile's, they'd all been on the ship a very long time.

Viktor learned that none of the merchants, who could speak in broken Portuguese, dealt in the pepper he sought.

The best he could discern, he needed to speak with their elder.

Although the villagers offered to ferry him over, he preferred to use one of the *Incubus'* boats. He'd been a pirate too long to depend on a local for a quick getaway, if one became necessary. He had Grimm, Belle and Brumble come with him. Jon-Jon was left in charge of the ship and crew.

He brought Zach because the man had the best grasp of Portuguese. It was the primary language in that part of the world for trading with Europeans. Zach picked it up during trade runs to Brazil for his father's company.

Children swarmed them as they were led through the village. The men ignored them. Belle watched them curiously. She'd never been around that many juvenile humans at one time. She didn't really count the ones the pirates had captured during their quest for the Mermaid's Tear. There hadn't been this many, and they hadn't been milling about like this, either.

"What are they saying?" she asked.

"I think they are begging," Zach answered. "Their Portuguese is very broken, and I do not understand Bengali."

Grimm decided he'd rather be able to walk freely. He'd never like to be crowded. He pulled out a handful of silver coins and tossed them so they would scatter away from the pirates. The children dashed after them like chickens after corn.

"That should keep them busy long enough for us to pass," he muttered.

His prediction proved correct. They were able to move much quicker and soon reached the dwelling of the village elder.

A series of catwalks surrounded and connected the buildings on this edge of the village. Mudflats stretched out beneath the stilts, and a narrow creek separated the village from the jungle.

Zach took the initiative and asked one of the locals why the houses were on stilts. He was told it was to stay dry during the monsoon season. When he translated that for the others, Vik gave him a sideways glance.

"I'm surprised you hadn't already figured that out, Mr. Brumble. You say you've traded in Brazil. They have similar weather, and the Amazon drops considerably during the dry season."

Silently, he reached out to the siren. She jumped at the mental contact but did not try to shut him out. *"Keep a close eye on him. He may just be trying too hard to be useful, but he should have had no need to ask that question. I have recently been counseled not to trust him."*

"You don't trust anyone anyway, but I will be your eyes in this instance."

The toothless old man greeted them at the door. He peered closely at Viktor and Belladonna before he stepped aside and motioned them in. A young boy stayed close to his side and acted as translator.

Viktor sighed. Two translators would make this a long and tedious conversation, and it increased the potential for miscommunication.

He was surprised when the old man bypassed the translation and spoke directly to him in English. "What have you come seeking, Lord of the Sea?"

Tamara A. Lowery

"I was told a pepper grew here that some call the Devil's Hoof."

The old man nodded. "The naga pepper grows deep in the forest. It is protected by the Tiger God and the Forest Goddess. It can burn a man's hand with its flesh and seeds, but there is a rich honey which can be found in the forest, as well. That will coat the naga and make it safe to carry. Why do you seek it?"

Viktor sensed there was more than mere curiosity behind the question and answered cautiously. "Why is it important?"

"Because of *Daskin* Rey and Bonobibi."

He knew this game. Mother Celie had used it as a teaching tool when he'd been a child. As the old man expected him to, he asked, "Are they the Tiger God and Forest Goddess you spoke of?"

"They are. You and she will have to be especially careful if you enter the forest."

Belle asked, "Why did you single us out to warn us about this 'Dawkin Roy' and Bonobibi?"

The old man gave them a benign smile. He reminded them a bit of Uncle Zeke, but he did not emit the sheer power of the old wizard.

"They, like you, are very powerful and very jealous of their territory. I will tell you the story then you will understand the warning."

"*Daskin* Rey means Lord of the South in my native Bengali. Long ago, he came to rule over the forest of Sundarbans. He was a great ruler and was brave, handsome and very powerful. He could even turn himself into a tiger, his magic was so great. He owned all the riches of the forest: the trees, the fish, and even the wild honey. He was also kind, just and generous, sharing his riches with the people of the villages. However, he punished the ungrateful ones who used his gifts unwisely or were greedy and took more than they needed, failing to pay tribute."

"How did he punish them?" Grimm asked.

"He would send his army of tigers, crocodiles and sharks," he answered then continued the story, "*Daskin* Rey ruled alone for many years. Then, one day a woman was lost in the forest on the very day she had to give birth. She bore twins, a boy and a girl, but she could only carry one child back to her village. Although it broke her heart, she chose to take the boy and left the girl behind."

"The girl was found by some chital deer that took pity and raised her, teaching her the ways of the forest. Young Bonobibi grew to know the forest's magic and became a powerful goddess. She could command sharks and crocodiles and protected both people and animals. All of the creatures of the forest are her children, and she, their mother."

Viktor perked his ears at that. He wondered if she was one of the Sisters of Power he still had to deal with. If she was, it could be good or very, very time consuming. Who knew what quest she would have for him to complete.

"Of course, *Daskin* Rey was jealous of the power of Bonobibi. He transformed into a tiger and went to war against her. He slipped into the river and ordered his army of sharks and crocodiles to attack her."

"But, her power had grown so great, they could not harm her. They fought for a long time, but neither could overpower the other."

"Realizing this, *Daskin* Rey, the Tiger God, and Bonobibi, the Forest Goddess made peace with each other and formed a pact of friendship. And, to this day, they rule the forest together," the old man finished.

Tamara A. Lowery

Viktor thought he understood the point of the story. "So, if I understand this correctly, we should only take what we need from the forest and give thanks for it."

The village elder nodded, his wispy white hair dancing around his face as he did so. "It is also important to be out of the forest by nightfall. The tigers will come like ghosts and take men right off the boats without making a sound."

The siren spoke up. "Surely the creatures do not live so close to the shore. The water here is more salt than fresh. I can smell it and feel its power."

"The tigers of the Sundarbans drink the salt water and hunt the rivers and mangroves at night. Only Bonobibi's magic prevents them from entering the village." His answer seemed to satisfy her.

Grimm had a question that had been bothering him since they'd met he old man. "Tell me, elder, how is it that you speak our tongue so fluently?"

The old man laughed. "Many years ago, when I was young, men speaking this tongue came to our village. They called themselves missionaries. They taught those willing to learn their words." His face grew stoic. "They also tried to tell us our gods were not real but were demons trying to keep us from their god, whom they called the Lord. Not only would they not listen to our stories and warnings; they punished those who told them. Finally, they went into the forest. They planned to spend the night and return to prove our beliefs false."

"What happened to them?"

"They never returned to the village." He shook his head sadly. "Their boat floated out of the forest still laden with their things. Some tiger claw marks in the wood were the only sign of what happened to them."

Viktor decided it would best serve him to tell the old man why he needed the pepper and honey. If he didn't, it would make getting a jungle guide difficult if not impossible. Plus, if this Bonobibi was one of the Sisters of Power, he couldn't afford to anger her.

"There is a sorceress in a far land whose help I need. She needs the naga pepper, which she calls devil's hoof, to work her magic to help me."

The old man gazed at him for an uncomfortably long time before he responded. "There is a great aura of destiny about you, Lord of the Sea. Your future is hidden from me, but you have spoken the truth."

He turned to the boy and spoke quickly in Bengali. The youngster nodded and ran out of the house. "I have sent for guides to help you find the naga pepper and harvest the honey you will need to safely carry it. Remember the warning I have given you."

Viktor bowed. Grimm and Zach followed his lead. Belladonna inclined her head.

"Thank you for your aid, elder. We will heed your warning and abide by the rules of *Daskin* Rey and Bonobibi. Is there any specific tribute that they require?"

"Only that you obey their laws while you are in the forest."

Tamara A. Lowery

Chapter 27

They embarked into the forest at midday or just after. Viktor and Grimm both watched Belle. They stayed alert for any signs she might be weakening as they went further from the sea. Zach just watched her like a wistful puppy, hoping for a smile or even a glance from her.

Belladonna was very aware of the scrutiny but chose to ignore it. Even deep in the mangroves, the water remained very brackish. With her magic tied to salt water, she was in her element. She was also aware of other eyes on them that were more of a threat.

"We are being shadowed. I have not been able to catch a glimpse of them, but I can smell at least three large cats following us in the mangroves. There are also a number of crocodiles in the river. The water is too shallow right now for sharks, but they have been here in the past, probably during the rainy season, when the rivers are up."

The announcement had two effects on Viktor. First, he relaxed, grateful that this swamp did not drain the siren like the Louisiana bayous had. Second, he focused his senses on the surrounding forest. He was surprised he hadn't scented the tigers, as well. He realized he had been too focused on the siren.

Now that he was aware of their presence, he could smell them also. He listened carefully and could make out four heartbeats coming from the forest, two on each side of the river.

"There are four of them."

One of the tigers broke cover and padded out onto the mudflat. It stood and watched them pass.

"*Bagh*," one of their guides whispered as he looked back at the cat.

"What does that mean?" Zach asked.

"Tiger."

☠

Amazingly, they hadn't gone very far into the jungle when they came across several pepper plants growing in a cluster. They decided to cut the stems to harvest them after a minor disaster.

Zach made the mistake of grabbing one bare-handed to pluck it. At first, he was fine, but he inadvertently squeezed the pepper. Some of the juice was forced out near the cap and touched his skin. Within seconds, the skin blistered, and he was in tears. Belladonna's speed was the only thing that saved his eyes.

He'd moved to wipe the tears away, but she grasped his wrist and stopped him. He protested, when she didn't release him right away. "Please, Miss Belladonna, let me regain some dignity. I am ashamed to be so unmanned in front of you."

"Be quiet. If you had rubbed your eyes with this on your hand, you would have blinded yourself." She examined the hand then took her flask and poured some of the contents over the blisters.

At first it stung then grew numb. Belle grasped his hand tightly for a few moments. When she finally released him, the blisters were gone.

"What have you got in that flask, lass?" Grimm asked. "I've never known you to drink before."

"Sea water. It seems that these inland excursions are going to be a regular part of the quests each Sister sends us on. I feel better if I have some of my native element with me. I don't want to repeat what happened in the bayous."

"Good thinking, pet. We can't really afford another episode like that."

"I know, and I'm not your pet, Viktor."

"Think what you like." He turned his attention to their guides. "We were told we need honey to transport the peppers in."

After Zach translated to Portuguese, the guides nodded eagerly. They hadn't understood why these strangers were after the peppers. The things were really too hot to use on a regular basis.

Dhirindro had no qualms about hunting for honey, however. With some extra, he could make a profit large enough to allow him to not work through the rainy season.

Once they had a small barrel half-filled with naga peppers, they boarded the boat and poled further up the river. As before, the tigers shadowed them.

It took a couple of hours to find a honey tree. They located it by the bees swarming around it. Now they had the dilemma of how to harvest the honey without getting stung.

"Too bad we don't have smudge pots," Grimm commented.

Gautam, the other guide, had done this before with his brothers. He took a small torch made of palm fronds that were tied tightly at one end and loose at the other. Stuffed into the loose end were matted plant fibers. He used flint and steel to strike a spark to it. It blazed to life, but he blew on it until the flames died down to a dull red glow and smoke billowed out.

He carried the smoking torch slowly to the honey tree. As the bees calmed or flew away, he reached carefully into the tree and broke loose a large section of honeycomb.

Zach brought the half keg of peppers over so Gautam could place the honeycomb in it. Some of the thick liquid, a rich golden brown, dripped onto Zach's hand. He licked it off, and his eyes grew wide.

"My God! I've never tasted honey like this! It's incredible!"

"It's honey," Grimm muttered. "How incredible can it be?"

Belle was curious. "What is honey? I have heard sailors speak of it, but I've never seen it."

The first mate answered, "It's a sweet sticky kind of syrup made by bees. I'm not sure how they do it, but they collect nectar from flowers and somehow change it into honey."

That peaked Viktor's curiosity. "For an old pirate, you seem to know a lot about the stuff, Hezekiah."

He made a face. "My family's business was bee keeping. I grew sick of honey and anything to do with it. It's the main reason I went to sea."

"Pity you don't like honey. One of my fondest childhood memories is of Mother Celie's corn pone with honey and butter." Vik smiled. "But I guess you would get tired of something most consider a treat, if you were around it in abundance all the time."

"Exactly."

Zach had been talking with Dhirindro while they had their honey discussion. He came to the captain with a report.

"Dhirindro says that there wasn't enough honey in this tree. There's still some left in it, but he said to leave some for the bees so they don't starve before they can rebuild. He also wants to harvest a little extra, so he can sell it in the village."

Viktor looked up to check the sky, but they were far enough into the forest to make it difficult to judge the time of day. He really needed to pick up a small chronometer to carry with him. The one on the ship was too bulky to lug around.

"Very well, but I don't want to be in this forest too long. The old man said to not be here past dusk."

"Aye, Captain. I'll tell him."

It took longer than expected to find another bee tree. They were so far into the forest that the water had started to become fresh. The gloom was such that it was hard to tell if it was nearly dark or just the thickness of the canopy. Everything seemed to be in shadow. Gautam grew nervous.

"I don't like this, Captain," Belle complained. "We are in an area we are not welcome in."

"You sense them as well."

Tamara A. Lowery

"The tigers and the water creatures are just a warning. They were sent to watch, but they are growing restless."

"Mr. Brumble, tell Dhirindro he needs to move as quickly as possible. We are close to wearing out our welcome. Mr. Grimm, make sure the boat is ready to launch, but be wary. The tigers are closer, and several crocodiles have started to show themselves. They're just as fast and, going by reputation, much more vicious than gators."

"Noted, Captain. I'll keep an eye out."

Before long, they were distracted by the sound of arguing. Walking further from the boat, Viktor and Belle found Gautam and Dhirindro yelling and gesticulating at each other. Zach stood to the side just trying to keep up with the conversation.

The vampire quickly grew irritated. They didn't have time for this. "What is going on?" he barked in his most commanding tone. It had the desired effect of stopping the argument.

To his credit, Zach did not flinch when Viktor turned a baleful eye on him. Both the vampire and the siren could scent the man's fear, but he seemed determined not to show it.

"They disagree about how much longer to harvest the honey, Captain. Gautam is very afraid and wants to leave now. He says *Daskin* Rey and Bonobibi are angered by our prolonged presence. Dhirindro believes that Gautam and the village elder are just superstitious old fools. He says he has seen how white men now rule in the ports west of here and believes the old ways are dying. He wants more honey to sell, so he will not have to work through the monsoons."

Viktor stared at the younger guide. His eyes started to glow emerald with ire. "We have enough honey for my needs. You know where this hive is. If you want more honey, come back on your own time to get it. I have a long voyage ahead and do not have time to satisfy your greed."

Zach started to translate but saw he didn't need to. Dhirindro understood the threat, even though he didn't understand the words. He closed up both casks and picked one up to carry back to the boat. Gautam took the other one.

Grimm was glad to see the return. "The crocs are getting closer, and if I've any sense of smell at all, one of the tigers has sprayed."

Belle scrunched her nose even as the first mate made that announcement. "Gah! I can't stand the smell of cat piss, and this makes Lazarus smell like a flower!"

"It is rather strong, but we're leaving now," Viktor agreed.

It grew dark while they still worked their way toward the village. They'd brought no lanterns, since they'd planned on being out of the forest before sundown. What little bit of moonlight could filter through the canopy and an abundance of fireflies provided the only light.

That allowed just enough for the vampire's hypersensitive sight to guide them through the maze of tidal rivers and mangroves. He took point and directed them with the aid of Zach's translation.

Gautam gave more feedback than Dhirindro. He knew these waters better, and Dhirindro was still sulky over being forced to leave earlier than he'd wished.

Just as they got to sparser tree cover, the siren caught scent of tiger. She turned just in time to see a silent blur of orange and black pull Dhirindro into the water. There was no splash, and he didn't even have time to scream. The boat barely bobbed; the kill was made so smoothly.

"Impressive." She admired the cat's predatory efficiency. "Captain, we've lost one of our guides. A tiger took Dhirindro."

"Everyone face outward. Don't let them sneak up on you. Watch for the crocs, as well."

Gautam reeked of fear. Even Zach was nervous. Only Viktor, Grimm and Belladonna remained calm.

Two things happened at once. Viktor spotted a tiger swimming toward him, and Belle dove off the opposite side.

"Miss Belladonna!" Zach cried out. He was on the same side and saw her go in. He also saw at least three crocodiles and one shark fin converge on her.

Grimm had to grab him and knock him unconscious to keep him from going in after her.

Viktor couldn't spare any attention for the siren. He had to trust that she knew what she was doing. She was in her own element and was a formidable predator and sorceress. He had to concentrate on the big cat in front of him.

A second tiger had entered the water, when Lazarus manifested, unbidden. The demon cat crouched low on the side of the boat and growled menacingly at the tigers. Viktor had been about to shoot the lead one before it could get on the boat.

Both tigers paddled in place, ears forward, looking curiously at the large black cat. The lead tiger made a chuffing noise. Lazarus replied with a complex vocalization.

"What's going on?"

Vik shrugged. "I'm not sure what he told them, but it seems to have worked."

The tigers swam back to shore and melted back into the forest. One roared briefly before disappearing from sight. A second later, both pirates would have sworn they glimpsed a man loping off through the trees.

"*Daskin* Rey," Gautam whispered in awe. He was still so frightened the whites showed around his eyes. He nearly fainted as a female form emerged from the forest. "Bonobibi!"

The forest goddess stood on the muddy shore. Although barefoot, she was richly dressed in gold and scarlet. The silks and jewelry set off her black hair and blue skin. Power seemed to roil around her.

Viktor performed a half bow, his eyes never leaving her. "Milady."

Bonobibi spoke, but they could not understand what she said. Even Gautam was unsure. Her language was similar to Bengali, but of a higher form.

The siren reappeared halfway between the boat and the goddess. She spoke to Bonobibi, opening her link with the vampire to allow him to follow the conversation.

"*Greeting Bonobibi. Our apologies for not leaving sooner. Your lord has already punished the one who delayed us.*"

"*He is not my lord, merely my co-ruler.*"

The siren smiled wryly as she recognized her own irritation with Viktor in the goddess' tone regarding *Daskin* Rey. "*My apologies. I know that sometimes we must allow them to believe they are in control.*"

Bonobibi laughed, a clear, bell-like sound. "*Yes, it does make them easier to influence.*"

Tamara A. Lowery

Viktor held his tongue. He did not want to reveal how close the bond was between the siren and him. He did make his mental presence "warm" in the back of her mind as a warning, however.

Belle ignored him for the moment. *"We did not mean to offend. We have what we need and wish to leave in peace."*

"Not so, sea siren. You have more than you need. Dhirindro took honey that he did not require. His wish was to be lazy during the monsoons by profiting from something he would not ordinarily acquire."

Belle turned to speak to the men on the boat. "We need to get rid of the extra honey."

Grimm had just picked up the cask and was preparing to toss it over the side, when the forest goddess held up her hand to stop him. To say that he was startled by her sudden presence on the boat would have been an understatement.

Gautam groveled on the deck, terrified. Zach was still unconscious. Viktor was startled but hid it well. Belladonna tried to hide her irritation at having to swim back to the boat to translate.

"Do not waste it. That would be worse than stealing it," Bonobibi said. She stooped and touched Gautam on the shoulder. *"Take this honey to Dhirindro's family. His wife and sons are not to blame for his greed. After the monsoons, his oldest son will be old enough to hunt and work to provide for them. Be sure he knows why his father died, so he does not repeat his mistakes."*

Gautam nodded a little too rapidly, assuring the forest goddess her wishes would be carried out. Only later would he come to know and appreciate the honor of having been blessed by Bonobibi and the prestige it would bring him among his people.

Viktor took a step toward her, which was enough to bring Belladonna out of the water. She recognized the look in his eyes. It was lust mingled with curiosity. She had to fight the growl of jealousy that wanted to rise in her throat.

"Bonobibi, I seek the Sisters of Power. Are you one of them?"

After the siren translated, the goddess smiled and shook her head. *"No, I am not one of those you seek, Daskin Sagor. But I must admit you are the most beautiful white man I have ever seen. You are not like the others who came before, either. You show respect for our ways, even though they are not your own. If not for the jealousy it would engender in Daskin Rey, I would invite you to stay and become my lover."*

"I am honored, but I must complete my quest, Bonobibi." He bowed and smiled wistfully, deciding it wasn't important to point out he was only half white. "I would not be able to stay. My very life depends on finding the Sisters before it is too late."

She nodded her understanding. *"Go in peace, Daskin Sagor. May you find what you need."*

Tamara A. Lowery

Chapter 28

The village elder had called Dhirindro's eldest son to his house and was awaiting their return. They didn't question how the old man had known ahead of time of the tiger attack. He sent Gautam in to break the news to the boy while he stayed outside to speak with the pirates.

Zach had wakened and now nursed a sore spot on the back of his head where Grimm had struck him. The first mate had threatened to cudgel him again if he didn't calm down. It had taken a few minutes to convince him that Belladonna was unharmed and had returned to the ship.

He had a disbelieving look in his eyes as Viktor and Grimm related the encounter with Bonobibi to the elder. He still had a hard time accepting that Belle wasn't human, and his upbringing didn't allow for the actual existence of pagan deities. He'd always been taught that they were merely man-made idols based on imagination, not real beings.

The old man smiled at him as he would at an inexperienced child. "You were not touched by the goddess, were you, my friend?"

Zach shook his head. "I saw no goddess. The only woman I saw in the forest was Belladonna."

"How is this possible? Your aura does not show that Bonobibi is displeased with you. Why would she deny your eyes the honor of seeing her?"

Grimm answered, "She had nothing to do with that. Belle went into the water to protect us from the crocs and sharks. I had to knock the lad senseless to keep him from going in after her."

"I didn't want them to attack her!"

Vik chuckled. "They should be more worried about her attacking them, Mr. Brumble. She considers shark an appetizer."

"I don't think he really believes us, Captain. Perhaps we could convince her to give him a demonstration of her feeding habits the next time we take a prize."

"You are a cold-hearted bastard, Mr. Grimm."

"Well, I do have my reputation to uphold."

The old man cleared his throat to get their attention. "I am starting to see why you won the favor of Bonobibi, as well as why it would not be good for you to stay. *Daskin Rey* is much like the tiger he represents. Tigers are solitary hunters and very territorial. In your own ways you, *Daskin Sagor*, and your co-leader are as dangerous and accomplished predators as the tiger. If you remained, there would be war."

Vik nodded. "Very probably. But, for us the sea is home. Land is mostly a place to rest and resupply. I will not be tied to one port for long, nor will I be ruled by any female, be she goddess, siren, witch, or human."

"Yes, it is good that you only took what you need and are leaving. The Tiger God and Forest Goddess rule together in peace, but it is a delicate balance, and someone of your nature would destroy that balance completely. I wish you good fortune on your journey, and I pray it does not bring you back. This is not meant as an insult but as a wish for peace."

The vampire bowed. "No insult taken, elder. Thank you for your guidance. We will take our leave now."

The old man held up his hand to stall them a moment and locked eyes with Zach. "Young friend, you must learn to open your eyes and your mind. Before the end, you will see many things more wondrous or monstrous than you've ever imagined. If you keep both closed, it will drive you mad."

Unsure how to respond to the advice, the trader's son merely bowed and said, "Thank you."

Viktor called his mates to meet in his cabin a few hours after they had set sail. For the time being, they had headed south to exit the Bay of Bengal, but a course needed to be decided upon.

"We have a choice of returning the way we came or continuing east and cross the Pacific," he announced.

Grimm and Zach looked over the charts spread out on the table. Jon-Jon towered over their shoulders. Belle perched on the sill by the large windows of the captain's cabin, seemingly uninterested.

"Going back the way we came is a known course now," Zach said. "It will take about the same amount of time to hug the coast as what we lost to the doldrums. However, once we round the Cape of Good Hope, we'll have to fight the wind to go northwest."

Grimm grunted his agreement. "Aye, then there's the over land trek to get back to the Pacific coast."

Even Jon-Jon could tell where this conversation was headed. He felt it necessary to point out a major drawback. "We don't have any charts of the waters east of China. We have no idea of how many leagues it is from there to Mexico or where any islands are in between."

"A good point, Mr. Jon, but remember that we didn't have any reliable charts of these waters until we neared Madagascar," Viktor replied. "I've come across too many cargos from the east of East to think that the charts we need do not exist. As we head that way, we should encounter a prize or two that has some."

He noticed the siren had seemed a bit detached ever since the encounter with Bonobibi. He hadn't forgotten the banter she had shared with the goddess, but he would wait to discuss that with her in private. Had they spoken in a language any of his men could've understood, he would've had to call her out on it in front of them. He would not tolerate any hint of disrespect or challenge from any of his crew. If one was allowed to get away with it, others would start to think they could, as well.

He did want her input on this course decision, however. "What say you, Belladonna? Have you ever been in the waters to the east of us?"

She jumped at the question. She hadn't really been following the conversation. She blinked and replied, "Yes, I've swum all the oceans. It's really only one ocean, if you think about it. It just has these humongous land masses placed around in it at inconvenient locations."

The vampire looked at her blankly for a moment, as he failed to make sense of her response. He rephrased his question. "What do you have to say of the idea of continuing east across the Pacific?"

"Hmm. At this time of year, it would be quicker. The winds will be favorable, and I can bend them to double your speed, if you think the ship will hold up to that kind of beating. It is a wider and wilder sea than the Atlantic. There are island groups, but they are easily missed in such vast waters. I can guide you to them and help you avoid the reefs and shoals that have not grown into islands yet. I would suggest pirating as much as possible in the islands you will be sailing through soon on that course. They are plentiful, close together, and have a lot of sea traffic."

Viktor smiled. The prospect of good hunting appealed to him. His cadre had been kept dormant for close to two months now. They needed a good feed, and so did he.

Grimm and Jon-Jon shared his enthusiasm for getting back to doing what they did best. Even Zach seemed to show some eagerness.

On the Atlantic crossing, he'd discovered he truly had a taste for piracy. He doubted his sister would even recognize him, now. It bothered him that Sam was looking for him and their brother. He wished there was some way he could get word to her that she shouldn't. It would break her heart to learn of Thomas' fate. And Zach held no illusions about how her safety and virtue would be forfeit if she ever did succeed in locating them.

Viktor's voice brought his mind back to the present. "It's decided, then. We'll sail east through the Straits of Malacca, taking what prizes come our way, then cross the Pacific, island hopping with Belle's help."

"Mr. Grimm, inform the helmsman. Mr. Jon, have Mr. Bland take inventory of our provisions and supplies. Tell

Mr. Murph to inspect the spare timbers and spars. Then, take a group of riggers and inspect all the lines and lanyards. Mr. Brumble, assemble some gangs to clean and inspect the guns."

The men all acknowledged their orders and filed out of the cabin. When Belle started to follow them, Viktor stopped her. "Stay a moment, Belle. I'd like to have a word with you in private." His tone was gentle, which took her off guard.

"Very well," she replied with caution.

Once the others were gone, she looked at the vampire uncertainly. His silent regard would have been unnerving, had she been human. But she knew better than to respond like prey. Rather than make her nervous, his stare irritated her.

"What?"

"There is no need to be so testy, pet."

"Then stop staring at me and speak your mind, Viktor. You said you wanted to talk to me, but you've been sitting there like a lump. I know you're not happy about what I said to Bonobibi."

Vik felt a half-smile tug at one corner of his mouth. This was the Belladonna that he'd come to know and, if he'd admit it to himself, love. Of course, the smile irritated her further.

"What. Do. You. Want?"

In a split second he stood next to her, his lips only a breath away from her ear. "Oh, I think you already know the answer to that, pet."

Belle closed her eyes as a wave of desire so strong it felt like a lightning strike crashed through her. She both loved and hated that he could do that to her so easily. He never failed to confuse and frustrate her.

It was his turn to be confused and frustrated when she gently, but insistently, pushed him away. He'd caught the scent and heat of her body's reaction to him.

"Viktor, please, just tell me what you wanted to talk to me about." She sounded tired.

He half-sighed, half-grunted and crossed his arms. "Very well, yes, I was not pleased with your banter with the forest goddess. But the lads couldn't understand you. If they had been able to, there would have been repercussions for you. I cannot afford to let any of my crew show me disrespect in front of the others."

"Believe it or not, I do understand that reasoning. If I had been using a human language, I would have merely apologized for calling the tiger god her lord. I will admit I got a little too comfortable in my speech to her. It is rare for me to encounter a female with that magnitude of power that I don't see as a rival."

He raised an eyebrow. "I'd been wondering about that. I was surprised you didn't go into a display of jealousy when she transported herself to the boat."

"I wanted to, but we needed to get out of there alive. I doubt asserting territorial rights over you would have been a good move." She shrugged and looked at him with an uncertainty he wasn't used to. "You surprised me, as well, Viktor. I did not expect you to reject her, and in such a way as to not insult her."

"It was a gamble. She was testing the waters." His smile was smug. "She may not be human, but I've met her type before: women who think they can use their favors to control a man's will. My rejection of her was a case of both speaking the truth and letting her know I am not one who can be controlled."

"Hmph." She didn't know why she'd been foolish enough to hope that she was the reason he'd spurned a goddess' favors.

"Think what you like, pet. She lost interest in me fairly quickly after that. If she had truly wanted me just for a lover, do you think she would have let us go our way?"

"No."

Finally, it dawned on him what was bothering her. Careful not to spook her, he walked over to her, gently brushed her hair back with his fingertips, and tucked it behind her ears.

Belladonna looked at him warily, unsure of this change in mood. His smile was not cruel or malicious. It wasn't even teasing. It took her a moment to register that he still stroked her cheek with his thumb. Her wariness turned to confusion then desire.

Once he saw her relax and her eyes dilate, he leaned down and kissed her. He was gentle at first, but then, they both put everything into it.

He tasted blood and broke off from the kiss, but he didn't release her from the embrace. "Damn!"

"What is it?"

"I taste blood. It must be mine, not yours, since I'm still breathing. But I don't want you to think I'm trying to trap you, Belle." He held her tight enough that she couldn't angle her head up to see his face.

"I don't mind," she whispered into his shoulder.

He wasn't sure if he was more surprised by her admission or that he could sense she really meant it. It was frustrating that he couldn't take advantage of her mood.

"It's not just that, pet. My Hunger is up."

She growled her frustration. "It's always something. I swear, it seems like someone, or something doesn't want us to be together." Resigned to being denied again, she asked, "How long has it been since you fed?"

"Close to three months now. We have to take a prize soon. I've kept the cadre in a dormant state all that time, and I can sense them — withering, for want of a better word."

She mulled the problem over for a few minutes. "I'll scout out a prize for you and lure them this way. I would suggest waking your vampires the evening I return. You can take the ship at night."

"That is generous of you, pet."

She shrugged. "I need to hunt, as well."

A week later, they had taken not one but two prizes. Belladonna had scouted their course for about four days sailing ahead of them and had reported that the Malacca Straits were heavily travelled.

Viktor and Grimm were both pleased that the hunting would be so good. They knew they needed to be discreet about it, though. It was decided that they would only take ships at night and keep most of the gun ports hidden during the day. They reasoned it would make them harder to pinpoint as the pirates who would soon be terrorizing that stretch of water.

Of course, Viktor didn't plan on lingering long enough to arouse suspicion either.

Thomas visited his brother's cabin on a night between prizes. It was the first time they'd really had a chance to talk in months, since the young vampire had been kept dormant along with the rest of the cadre.

Zach decided to confide in his brother. There'd been many worries that he just wasn't comfortable sharing with the rest of the crew. Even having been on board for the better part of a year, he felt like an outsider. He had more education than most of the crew, and he was well aware that the captain and his mates still did not trust him.

"I understand the reasons behind taking this course, but I feel useless, Thom. I don't know these waters. Even if we had charts, I wouldn't be much use, because I don't know the currents."

"The Captain doesn't expect you to know all the seas, Zach."

He gave him a look. "If he decides he has no further need of me, he won't hesitate to dispose of me. I have no delusions about that. To be honest, I'm surprised he's let me live after that debacle with the doldrums."

Thomas shook his head. "He knows you didn't plan that. He'd only kill a man over something like that if it had been a deliberate act of misinformation."

"I guess. I did my best to prove my loyalty. I know Mr. Grimm has been watching me very closely, since we got the news about Sam." He stopped and blanched as he realized he hadn't said anything to Thomas about their sister. "Damn! I'm sorry, Thom. I forgot you hadn't been told."

"I've known since your master returned to the ship."

"My master?" He didn't know what his brother was talking about.

Thomas smiled at Zach's confusion. "Lazarus."

"The cat?" he half-laughed.

"Yes, and he is also the Captain's former first mate, Jim Rigger. I don't know how it is so, but it is."

"Jim Rigger. I remember the Captain telling me that. That's the name Captain Brandee mentioned he was avenging on Father by taking us."

Thomas nodded. "The same. He's the one who spotted her aboard the *Shining Star*. At least she's got George Bainbridge to keep her safe."

"He should have made her go home."

"Since when could anyone make Samantha do anything once she set her mind?" He laughed.

"There is that. Well, I hope she never finds us."

"So do I."

Tamara A. Lowery

Chapter 29

Sam and Captain Bainbridge finally got a lead on Brandee and the *Incubus* during a stop in Port au Prince.

They stopped there to change out the better part of the crew. The crew they'd been sailing with had grown dissatisfied with the lack of active trading. All of the officers worried about mutiny.

While Bainbridge recruited new crewmen among the docks and port-side taverns, he kept his ears open for rumors of the pirate. He asked some discrete questions in a few establishments, as well.

Samantha insisted on tagging along. He tried to talk her out of it, but she remained adamant. He was slowly becoming resigned to the fact that once she set her mind to something it was an exercise in futility to try to dissuade her.

Tamara A. Lowery

She separated from him to procure them some food while he interviewed some prospective riggers, when a boy approached her.

"You there, do you serve the master of the *Shining Star*?"

"Aye, I do."

He handed her a scrap of parchment. "Tell him Remiere wants to meet him tonight. These are the directions. He said to bring gold."

She took the scrap and nodded that she understood. Then, she took the food and went to find her captain.

Bainbridge had to threaten to lock her in her cabin to keep her from going with him to meet his informant.

"Trust me, Sam. You do not want to meet Remiere. I don't like dealing with the slaving bastard, but he is a reliable source of information, especially when gold is involved."

"He's a slaver?" She curled her lip in disgust. "I saw a slave shipment unloading once, when I'd followed my brothers to Father's warehouses. The stench was unbelievable, and the poor creatures looked so frightened and emaciated."

"It is an ugly business, but a profitable one," he sympathized. "I'm just grateful your father doesn't engage in it."

Samantha's face went stony. "Actually, he does; just not openly. I've seen his books, and I know the encryptions he uses. The Commodore only partially funded the emerald venture. The rest of the funding came from the proceeds of slaving done through a third-party shipper."

"I had no idea. But Remiere is not a dealer in just African slaves. He also deals in white slavery."

"White slavery?"

"Aye, he's a procurer for several brothels here in Port au Prince. He's very skilled at what he does, and he'd recognize you as female in a heartbeat. So, I will not risk you around him. Stay here," he ordered.

"Why should I care if he knows? He's not on the crew!"

Bainbridge gripped her forearms and fought the temptation to shake her. "Stay here, Samantha. That is an order. You don't understand this man. He is completely unscrupulous about how he acquires some of his — merchandise. He has been known to arrange kidnappings before. I would just as soon he not even know of your existence."

She glared defiantly but nodded her submission. "Very well. I will stay on the ship."

"Thank you."

Sam was surprised when she answered the knock at her cabin door. She'd expected Captain Bainbridge's return. Instead, she found herself face to face with the boy who had brought her the message arranging the meeting with Remiere.

"What are you doing here? Where is Captain Bainbridge?"

He made a grab for her wrist, but she moved back out of his reach. "He's been hurt. He needs you to come help him back to the ship."

She narrowed her eyes. That didn't sound right. "The Captain gave explicit orders that I was to remain on this ship. Besides, why would he send you to me instead of to his first mate?"

"How should I know? I'm just the messenger. All I was told was to fetch his cabin boy." He made another grab for her wrist and caught it this time. He gave a tug and tried to lead her out.

She kicked him in the knee hard enough to make him let go.

"Bitch!" He hissed as he struggled to catch himself. That one word was all the warning she needed.

The boy had lied and had been trying to lead her into a trap. Somehow, the slaver must have gotten wind of her and sent the boy to make the grab.

He'd fallen in the corridor when she'd kicked him. She tried to shut the door before he could get back up, and she almost made it. He moved faster than she expected. Before she could stop him, he'd forced the door back open and shoved her back.

Gratitude flooded her for the combat training the captain and his mates had given her. She put it to good use.

She dodged a fist that would have knocked her unconscious and ducked inside the boy's reach. He thought she'd made it easier for him to grab her, but she caught him off guard with a jab to his gut. He doubled over with a startled "oof!"

Quickly, Sam brought her knee up and elbow down at the same time to catch his head in between them. He dropped to his knees. He spat blood and shook his head to clear it.

She didn't expect him to recover as quickly as he did. While he was still down, he snaked out his arm and hooked her ankle. The move caught her off balance. She fell back and banged her head on the deck in the process.

She was momentarily stunned, but not as badly as he expected. He was used to fighting on land. Sam had spent the first two weeks of her time on the *Shining Star* learning the hard way how to control a fall. The weather had been rough at the time, and even seasoned sailors had difficulty staying upright while the ship pitched and rolled in the heavy seas.

The boy spit the tip of his tongue into his palm and glared at her. "I don't care if Remi said not to mark you," he slurred. "You're going to pay for that, bitch. He can still get a good price for you without your tongue."

He drew a blade and started to lean over her. Adrenaline jolted through her, and she reacted without thinking. Still on her back, she brought her foot up sharply and kicked him in the side of the head.

He crumpled to the deck.

Mr. Warding rushed into the cabin just as she got to her feet. He quickly took in the scene.

"Sam, what happened? Who is this?"

She kicked the knife away from the boy's hand and knelt to check his pulse before she answered. "I don't know his name, but he was a messenger for Remiere. The bastard sent him to kidnap me."

"Was? He's dead then?"

"Aye, I had to kick him in the head. He threatened to cut my tongue out." She hugged herself as the adrenaline wore off and shock threatened to take over. "I've never killed a man before. I didn't mean to kill him. I was just so scared."

"You don't look so well, lad." He caught her as she swayed. "Sit down, and I'll get you a glass of rum to steady you."

"Thank you, Mr. Warding. I hit my head pretty hard when he tripped me up." She accepted the glass and had half of it drunk before it left her gasping and coughing. She felt like throwing it back up but fought the sensation. Damned if she would show that much weakness in front of the first mate.

"Easy lad, it's not a good idea to drink it that fast if you aren't used to it."

She finally caught her breath. "Mr. Warding, you need to send some men to check on the Captain. I don't trust this slaver, especially after this. The meeting place is a tavern called the Crouching Dragon Inn."

"I know where the place is. I'll have Mr. Charring take some lads to check on him. I'm surprised he didn't take you with him, Sam. I've seen you practice your combat lessons, and this incident proves you can handle yourself in a real fight."

"He gave me explicit orders to remain on the ship." She shook her head and instantly regretted it. She must've hit her head harder than she'd thought. Blinding pain lanced through her skull, and her stomach rebelled against it and the rum. She barely reached the chamber pot in time to avoid making a mess on the deck.

Warding handed her a damp rag to wipe her face with. She thanked him shakily. Then, she stood up too fast and passed out.

He stuck his head out the door and snagged the first sailor to pass by. They lifted her onto her bunk then carried the body of her assailant to the officer's mess and laid it out on the table.

He dispatched the sailor to find Mr. Charring and go fetch the Captain. He then returned to Sam's cabin. He noticed she was drenched in sweat, so he opened the porthole and started to remove her shirt to cool her down.

The revelation of her true gender shocked him, at first. Then, some things that had always puzzled him about her finally made sense. It didn't take him long to realize who she really was and what she was doing or trying to do aboard the *Shining Star* for all these months.

Sam feigned sleep while awaiting Bainbridge's return. Warding stood guard by her bunk. She'd started to come to when he'd tried to cool her down. He knew her secret, but she wasn't sure what he planned to do about it. Until she knew that, she didn't want him to know that she knew he knew.

An involuntary groan escaped her. Just the effort of thinking about the whole mess made her head hurt worse.

Warding looked over at the sound. The girl appeared to still be unconscious, but he started to have his doubts about that. He wanted to fetch Dr. Grogan to check her head wound, but he wanted the Captain's approval first. He was pretty sure the man had known for some time about the cabin "boy's" true identity.

George Bainbridge soon entered the cabin. "Henry, I was on my way back when Darius met me with news of a ruckus aboard. What happened? Is Sam alright?"

"She needs to be seen by Roger. She took a pretty hard knock on the back of her head, it looks like."

Bainbridge looked sharply at his first mate. "She. So, you've discovered our little secret. I apologize for keeping you in the dark all these months, but we both felt that the fewer who knew, the safer she'd be. I'm honestly amazed that no one has discovered her before now."

Henry saw the relief in his captain's eyes. Now he wasn't the only one who knew the secret. "Some things make more sense now, but I have to admit that she is an excellent actress. And, she's handled herself as well as, if not better than, many men her age."

"What exactly happened, Henry?"

Before he could answer, Sam groaned and sat up slowly, holding her head. "The messenger that Remiere used tried to kidnap me. We fought, and I killed him. I didn't mean to, but he had a knife. Ow!"

She had another pain. When she pulled her hand away, there was blood on it. She looked at her pillow and saw more blood there.

"Are you alright?"

She started to shake her head but thought better of it. "No. the bastard tripped me up. I controlled the fall, but I must've caught the edge of something on the way down. Mr. Warding is right. I need Dr. Grogan to look at this and stitch it up. We might as well stop hiding my identity now."

Warding left to fetch the doctor. The captain sized up his charge. "The doctor already knows, Sam. Don't you remember?"

"Oh, that's right. I'd forgotten."

"Do you think it's wise to let the crew know? You've seen how the lads are around women."

"I'm sure, Captain. Most of the crew is new to this ship now. The old ones left are loyal to either my family or to you, so they can help keep the new ones in line. And I think I've proven myself with this incident."

"Hmph. I guess you have at that."

☠

After the ship's doctor examined and stitched the small gash on the back of her head, he scolded her for what she was trying to do. Bainbridge reminded him again that she had not only passed herself off as a male successfully but had proven herself a capable sailor, as well.

Dr. Grogan harrumphed and packed up his surgical kit as he grumbled about uppity females that had no place on a ship. Sam laughed and told him not to be such a sour old fart. He just grumped his way back to his cabin.

Bainbridge told Sam what'd he'd learned from the slaver about Brandee's activities. She accepted that it was old news by several months, but it was a start.

Remiere had purchased some brothel workers from another slaver who had trained them. He said that Delacroix had driven a hard bargain for them, claiming that he'd gotten them from Brandee and the Grimm Reaper, who'd forced him to overpay.

The news that the Reaper and Brandee were partnered again sent a chill through Bainbridge and his mates. Separately, they were bad enough. Together, they could wreak pure havoc on the shipping trade.

Tamara A. Lowery

Chapter 30

How to learn the location of Delacroix's island caused some consternation. Remiere had not provided that information, and Bainbridge was loath to have any further dealings with the man. Luckily, a few men among the new crew members had traded with him directly.

They were reluctant to give up the location at first. They feared retribution from the slaver's network of agents. The sight of the body of Remiere's lackey strapped to the mizzen changed their minds. It also gained Sam a measure of respect among the old hands and awe, if not downright fear, among the new hands. The lack of any mark on the body had some convinced she'd used witchcraft to make the kill.

The reaction to and acceptance of the revelation of Sam's true identity surprised Bainbridge, but he felt gratitude for it at the same time. It was evident none on board would dare touch her without her leave.

☠

It took them a couple of weeks to reach the slaver's island. Sam no longer had to argue for a place among the landing party. What they found on the island soon turned her stomach, though.

Theoretically, she expected to see women being trained in the sex trade. But nothing she ever imagined could have prepared her for the degradation and depravity she witnessed.

It became immediately obvious that most of the women were not willing wantons. Several were chained. Some bore bruises from frequent beatings. At least one that they passed was tied down while Delacroix's men took turns with her.

Sam saw her eyes. She could see that the poor creature's spirit was broken and dead.

As they neared the slaver's house, a new horror presented itself. Several children wandered around naked and hobbled. Through a window, a man could be seen forcing a child's head to his groin. Sam almost vomited.

She whispered to Bainbridge, "We have to get them out of here, Captain. All of them."

"It sickens me, as well," he whispered back. "But that won't stop this from continuing."

"Be that as it may, I could not sleep at night knowing I had willingly left anyone to suffer like this, especially the children. Once we get the information we need, we have to free them."

He could tell from her expression that her mind was set. She would act, whether he backed her or not.

Delacroix took his time covering himself when they entered. He was none too happy about the interruption and planned to beat whoever had allowed them in before he was ready.

Still, business was business, so he did not let his displeasure show. The blonde young woman dressed as a lad piqued his interest. He eyed her with a leer and asked, "*Bon jour, mes amis*. Are you buying or selling?"

Something hardened in Sam. Her revulsion quickly became a steel hard hatred, as cold as ice. She wanted nothing more than to slit the man's throat. A half-smile crept onto her face when she realized that a scant few months ago such violence would never have entered her mind.

Bainbridge noticed the expression and recognized it immediately. Even though he'd never seen it on her face, he'd seen it several times on her brothers' and father's faces. It always presaged a usually violent outburst. He took charge of the situation before it could get out of hand.

"We are buying information."

"Pity, that one would fetch a grand price. What information do you wish to purchase?"

"A customer of yours said you'd recently had dealings with Vik Brandee. We are trying to find him." Bainbridge settled for a direct approach.

The slaver's face darkened for a moment then he laughed. "You might as well leave her here with me now, *mon ami*. She'll just end up back here anyway if you find Bloody Vik."

"Do you have any information on his whereabouts or not, Delacroix?"

"I do, but it will cost you. Fifty gold and an hour with your wench."

"She's not a trade commodity. I'll pay the fifty gold, if I think the information is good."

Tamara A. Lowery

"Seventy-five gold or no deal."

Bainbridge jingled a pouch of coins then opened the top to reveal the color of the metal. "What have you got?"

Del sighed. "I did buy a group of women and children from Brandee and the Reaper a few months ago."

"How many months ago?"

"Close to a year now. It takes a long time to train a prime whore. I had to make sure I sold the best to make up the loss I took on buying them. The pirate you seek will take nothing less than full market value on the goods he sells."

Sam had to ask, "What would have happened if you hadn't met his price?"

"He would have slaughtered them all and probably me as well."

"Did he mention where he was headed afterward?" Bainbridge steered the conversation back on course.

"He did not, but there was scuttlebutt among the few men he allowed ashore about the Islas del Roques."

"Pay him," Sam said. "I want to be away from him and this place as soon as possible."

Bainbridge counted out the coins and handed them to the slaver. Delacroix couldn't resist a parting shot. "I will give you the gold back if you leave the wench with me. I can promise I would be a kinder master than Brandee or the Reaper."

They glared at him and walked out. They didn't stop until they were back to the pier.

Once aboard their skiff and rowing back to the ship, Bainbridge commented, "I know that look, Sam. I've seen it too often on your brothers and father."

"And how often did they act on it?" She still wore the half-smile, but her eyes were hard and cold.

"Often enough that I know it bodes ill for someone. I'm surprised that you didn't do something rash back there."

"I'm not so foolish as to try to free them without a plan or preparation, Captain. I do have an idea that I believe will work, though. If you agree, we can implement it tonight."

"Very well, but if I think it too risky, we will hail the first Navy ship we meet and ask them to shut this place down. I will not risk your life or freedom. You cannot do anything for your brothers if you are dead or enslaved."

She frowned but nodded. "Agreed."

The plan she'd come up with impressed him. They moved the ship out of the lagoon and made a show of sailing off. It had been late in the day when they left, so they didn't have to go far to manage the ruse. Once full darkness descended, they turned about and anchored just outside the lagoon with all the lanterns doused or shuttered. Overcast skies rendered them practically invisible to anyone on the island.

They darkened their skin with pitch and put on their darkest clothes then rowed all the small boats into the lagoon with muffled oars. A couple of the better swimmers among them went over the side and made their way silently to the pier. Very soon, the lone sentry was disposed of. Bainbridge and Sam had been very clear that any kills needed to be swift and silent to avoid raising the alarm.

They planned to take out or at least incapacitate all of Delacroix's men before they tried to free the women and children. Warding pointed out that the prisoners probably wouldn't be quiet or calm.

Tamara A. Lowery

While the crew carried out the liberation, Sam slipped away from the others and made her way to the slaver's house. She slipped inside to find him asleep. A youngster lay quietly sobbing next to him, pinned by the weight of his arm.

Gently, she lifted Del's arm, doing her best not to wake him. She motioned for the child to remain quiet and helped him slip out of the bed.

She stooped to remove his hobbles and whispered, "Don't worry. We're going to get you out of here."

The look of sad horror in the boy's eyes was the only warning that she may have made a fatal mistake in turning her back on the slave trader. She soon found an arm around her neck.

"Where do you think you're going with my toy?" Del growled in her ear. He began to squeeze and cut off her air.

She dug into the soft underside of his forearm with the nails of one hand in an effort to get enough air to not pass out. With her other hand, she managed to slip her marlin spike from its sheath. With all her strength, she stabbed straight backwards and caught him in the groin.

She gasped as his arm dropped from her throat. "I am taking them someplace they'll be safe from you," she snarled as she recovered her spike.

Blood gushed from the wound. She saw she'd impaled his testicles and nearly severed his penis. Going by the amount of blood, there was a chance she'd killed him. She felt absolutely no guilt about it.

Delacroix couldn't even scream. The pain and shock were so great he lay paralyzed. His eyes bugged and began to grow glassy. Sam couldn't be sure, but it didn't look like he was breathing. She wasn't inclined to get close enough to him to find out.

"Come one." She held her hand out to the little boy. He looked at her then at his tormentor. He squatted down and picked up the wooden hobbles that had worn his ankles raw and threw them at the slaver's head. He then scurried over to her and took her hand.

She smiled as she led him from the room, but he tugged against her hand when they neared the exit.

"What's wrong? You don't have to be afraid anymore."

"There are more of us here."

"Take me to them.

Before it was over with, the crew of the *Shining Star* rescued about fifteen children and twelve women. Sam was glad to be able to reunite some of the children with their mothers, but a few had already been sold off. Five children were now orphans.

Gregory, the boy she'd fought Delacroix over, was one of the orphans. He'd shown her where the other children had been, and he'd also shown her where the slaver kept his money. She made a point to clean it out. Her reasoning was that those rescued would need cash to make their way back to their families from Santo Domingo, the nearest safe port.

Bainbridge suggested that port. He knew of a mission there which would be able to shelter the refugees until they could contact their families. He reasoned with Sam that the lead on Brandee was so old an extra week or two wouldn't make much of a difference.

Once they off-loaded their unexpected passengers and re-provisioned, they set a course for the Isla del Roques. Hopefully, someone there could give them a clue where to look next.

☠

Fortunately for Delacroix, the crew of the *Shining Star* hadn't killed all of his men. Some had merely been knocked unconscious and tied up. Eventually they managed to work themselves free.

They found their employer badly mangled in a pool of blood but still breathing. The slaver managed to heat his knife over the lamp flame and sear the wound Sam had dealt him. It stopped the bleeding immediately, but the previous blood loss and the burning pain left him unconscious.

The slave camp physician was among the survivors of the raid. He washed the groin wound with rum and stitched Del up. He knew he'd have to watch the wound to see if it would heal well. A strong chance existed the organ would rot off and leave the slave trader a eunuch.

The prospect did not make Delacroix happy. "I want that crusading bitch dragged back here. Then, I will make her pay for this insult. Tell every pirate, smuggler or slaver that puts in here to keep an eye out for the *Shining Star*. Tell them I want the mad woman aboard, who seeks Bloody Vik Brandee, brought here alive and intact. Tell them I'm offering five hundred gold."

Chapter 31

"Does this ocean never end? Viktor growled and paced the deck near the helm. As the islands thinned out, so did the trade ships. He, Grimm and Zach kept track of the distances they'd covered, and he'd grown irritated that they hadn't finished the crossing yet.

"All oceans are one," Belladonna replied. "The land just gets in the way of travelling a straight course. I told you it was a longer crossing than the Atlantic."

He glared at her. "I'd like to make it to an inhabited island or at least a well provisioned prize soon. I need fresh blood, and I'd rather not feed on my crew."

As if in answer to his wish, the winds died suddenly. As the sails drooped and the ship slowed, a dense fog rose from the waters around them.

Grimm, grateful for the distraction from the irritating siren and the irritable vampire, reacted quickly and shouted the order, "Drop sea anchors fore and aft!"

"Reef the sails!" Jon-Jon added in a shout to the riggers. In seconds, the orders were relayed throughout the rigging and across the deck.

The fog moved to envelope the ship then cleared to the port side. As suspected, there lay Hell's Breath. A rock jetty rose from the sea and stretched from the ship to the shore.

"Looks like he wants to see both of us," Vik muttered. He'd almost reached the cargo net ladder before he noticed the siren hadn't moved from the spot he'd left her in. "Belle! Get a move on!"

She jumped at his bark but still didn't move forward.

"If the old man wants you there, he won't say his peace until you are." He frowned at her.

She followed him to the side, but her body language made it clear she didn't want to. He didn't understand her reluctance. He only knew that she was slowing things up, and he wanted this over with. The crossing was taking too long as it was.

They were surprised to see a small thatch hut on the far side of the clearing where Zeke made his fire. Viktor thought he caught a faint but familiar scent. Then the fire flared as the old wizard threw some strange herb in, and he lost the scent.

"Sit." Zeke pointed to a couple of rocks. They formed a triangle around the fire with Zeke's rock on the same side as the hut.

Viktor raised an eyebrow at the seating arrangement. Belladonna was grateful for the spacing but apprehensive. She knew what was coming, and she didn't look forward to it.

Zeke let them stew on their own thoughts in silence. He took it as a good sign the vampire didn't immediately demand an explanation of what the old man wanted with them. He knew Viktor was an impatient man.

When he judged enough time had passed, he broke the silence. "There are some things you need to know, boy. Some I will tell you and some you will hear from Belladonna. Then, there is someone I want to introduce you to."

Viktor had to admit his curiosity was peaked. "Very well."

"First, you need to hear what this girl has to say about the errand I sent her on."

Belle gaped at him, dumbfounded by how he'd just saddled her with the whole thing. "I thought you were going to tell him that."

Zeke shook his head. "I wasn't there, and I couldn't watch while I was shielding you from each other. He needs to hear it from you."

She had been unaware of the old man's blind spot. Both she and Viktor were amazed that he would admit to one. It brought home how seriously Zeke took this.

She took a deep breath and met Viktor's expectant gaze. "He sent me to clean up your mess. That mermaid you caught had turned vampire. She had to be put down before the natural order was completely disrupted."

The vampire had the siren pinned to the ground with one hand around her throat faster than Zeke could anticipate. His eyes blazed green fire. "I gave Alyssa my word that you would not harm her. She was bearing my child." His voice was low and dangerous.

Tamara A. Lowery

She had to use all her strength just to pry enough leeway to breathe. She had poor leverage, and he seemed much stronger than she remembered.

"Your son is safe, and I'm not the one who killed the mermaid," she managed to croak out. She lay there and gasped when he released her.

"You were sent to kill her, but you didn't, and my son is safe? Where is he if he's safe?"

"We'll get to that later," Zeke dismissed the question. "Right now, she needs your help."

Belladonna still lay on the ground, writhing and fighting to breathe. Without access to seawater, it took longer for her body to heal, and he had badly damaged her throat. If she'd been human, she would have already been dead.

Viktor scooped her up and started toward the rise that led out of the hollow and back to shore. The fog rolled in around the depression and formed a ceiling over them. He found it to be an almost solid barrier beyond which he could not pass.

"Let me out, old man. I need to get her into the water so she can recover."

"I can't. One of the aspects of Hell's Breath is that it won't release anyone until what they started has been finished. It was a fact I discovered the hard way shortly after I first arrived here. She has to finish her report."

"How can she if she can't even breathe, let alone talk?"

"Help her, boy. You know what will speed the healing."

The look the siren gave the old man would have curdled milk. She wondered why he had even offered her freedom from the vampire. What he now suggested would seal her bondage.

Viktor quickly grasped what the old wizard had hinted at. He bit into his wrist and deliberately made the wound wide to prevent it from closing too quickly. He held the bleeding wound to Belle's lips.

She tried to turn her head away, even though the predator in her wanted nothing more than to latch on and feed.

"Take it, Belle. You know it's the only way open to us now."

She knew she was trapped. Her gaze tormented and with no other choice except death, she took the offered wrist. She kept her mental shields up, but immediately realized that he had not. In a flash, she saw everything he'd experienced since they'd parted company, when he'd gone in search of Rosalia. It overwhelmed her. How much he'd missed and needed her tinted it all.

She cut her eyes up to his face while she drank. She didn't think he'd intentionally shown her all that. In fact, she was almost positive he wasn't even aware she had seen so much.

"Do you feel better now?" He kept his voice and expression carefully neutral. He was well aware of how much she hadn't wanted to do that; just as he had not wanted to force it on her.

"Yes." Her reply was just as neutral.

He crossed his arms and sat back on his rock, but she wasn't fooled. She knew how fast he could move. "Tell me about what happened to Alyssa."

"Zeke sent me to hunt her down, since I'm the one who told you it was safe to feed on her. He said to save the child and bring it to him, but the mother had to be destroyed to prevent the rise of a new form of predator. I came across a couple of her kills and properly disposed of them, so they wouldn't rise. She had already begun to turn and was feeding on her pod-mates. I found her shortly before she gave birth. There was a ship nearby. I allowed her to escape to it so she could calve."

"And…?"

"The ship had been tracking her, as well. There was a very old, very powerful vampire on board. They had been following the trail of Alyssa's kills and cleaning them up. I heard the vampire tell the captain that it was against their laws to feed on any of the sea folk. She killed the mermaid not long after the baby was born. She said she would have to study the child before deciding whether or not to let it live."

"Why would an old vampire be tracking Alyssa in the first place? How could one even learn about her? I never mentioned her in New Orleans."

She gave him a serious stare. "They didn't know they were tracking her. They must have come across the kills by chance, but they were definitely hunting someone."

"Who?"

"You."

"Hmmm. I wonder if Jeorge had anything to do with that?"

She shrugged. "I don't know, but I doubt it. This vampire was wondering if the child could be used as bait for you. Once it was daylight, I sang up a fog and retrieved the baby."

"Why didn't you dispatch this vampire while you were at it?"

"Two reasons: she was not readily in evidence when I entered her cabin. She probably has some hidden compartment for her daytime refuge. And your son has very potent magic. He had me bewitched long enough for my fog to burn off. I had to take him and flee before I was trapped."

Viktor blinked. His offspring must be powerful indeed to hold a siren in thrall for any length of time. Just the fact that Belladonna admitted that to him stunned him.

"Interesting. I wonder why an infant would do that."

Zeke broke in. "Boy wants a mama. Any female that comes in contact with him will fall prey to that trap until he finds what he wants."

"Do you still have him here?"

The old man nodded toward the hut. "He's in there. For now, Hell's Breath is providing for his physical needs, but he'll have to leave before long. He needs someone to nurture and protect him — and eventually train him."

Viktor stood and started toward the hut, but the old man stopped him. "You can't go in there. I can't go in there. He can come out on his own, or Belladonna can go in and get him."

"Do you really need to see him right now?" she asked.

He looked at her. It was plain she was afraid to come in contact with the child again. "Are you that afraid of him?"

"No, I'm afraid I won't be able to let him go if I pick him up again."

"Then no, I don't need to see him right away, although I would like to see him. Is he old enough to make it out on his own? How does he get about on land with a fish tail?" He was curious in spite of himself.

Belle sighed. "I know I'm going to hate myself for doing this." She entered the hut before she could think twice about it. Shortly, she emerged carrying an infant that was almost to the toddler stage. She balanced the boy on her hip as if she'd done so for years. Viktor could tell that she had her shields at their tightest, yet she exhibited an almost maternal tenderness towards the child.

The boy's human appearance surprised him. "How? Are you sure this is the right child? He looks human. Alyssa never lost her tail the whole time I had her."

"He's a new breed, boy." Zeke chuckled at his consternation. "Thanks to you, he can change back and forth. Dip him in the sea and you'll see his tail. Just one look at that shock of black hair and those green eyes says he's your whelp."

Viktor reached for the child and found he had to use his link with the siren to make her release him. Her venomous glare quickly changed to a look of gratitude.

"He's certainly well-formed." He held the child up to inspect him. "I agree. He's definitely my get. That's an impressive set he's got on him."

Viktor's masculine pride in what he had made was suddenly dampened. The baby picked that moment to relieve his bladder and shot a hot stream directly into his father's face.

"He has your aim, too," Belladonna giggled and took the child back.

He pulled a much-abused handkerchief from his pocket and dried off. "Indeed."

"He's grown. He was so tiny when I handed him over to you, Zeke."

"Aye, that's part of the reason why he can't remain on Hell's Breath much longer. Seems he grows faster than a human child. He'll be walking before long, and there're things I don't need a toddler getting' into."

"You sound like Mother Celie." Vik smirked.

"Hmph. I won't send him to you right now. Rosalia doesn't need to know about his existence. I don't trust her. But, once your business with her is done, we'll see how you like havin' him underfoot."

He pointed toward the hut. "Go on and put him back, girl. Time's runnin' short, and there's still business to attend to."

Once she took the child back into the shelter, Zeke pulled Viktor aside and spoke low. "When I do send the boy to you, it would be best to keep her away from him. She's already besotted with the whelp."

"So I've noticed. I've never seen her behave that way before."

"There's something else. Take extreme caution in any future dealings with other vampires, especially the ones you already know. This one that's hunting you, she's a powerful one. I suspect she has even more powerful backers."

"Why is that?"

"Because I did not foresee her, and something powerful prevents me from seeing her now. I don't know why she's looking for you or even what she looks like. The fact that she's hidden makes me think her purpose is not for your benefit."

The vampire nodded that he took the warning very seriously. He saw the siren emerge from the hut and asked,

"What about you, Belle? Did you get a look at this vampire you say is looking for me?"

"No. I had to stay hidden. I only caught a glimpse when she fought and killed Alyssa. All I can tell you is she has dark hair, but I would know her voice if I heard it again. And, unless she shields, there would be no mistaking the volume of her power."

"What about a name?"

"Odd thing about that. I never heard it mentioned. From the captain on down, all the humans seemed to make a point of avoiding saying it, and they spoke of her with near dread, except for the captain." Before he could ask, she added, "He's called Wormsloe. The ship is called the *Lorelei*."

Viktor wore an astonished expression. Although it had been many years since their paths had crossed, he recognized the name of the ship and knew her captain.

"Wormy. I thought he was dead. I haven't heard news of him for close to a decade."

"You were friends?"

"Hardly!" He laughed. "Our enmity goes back to childhood. Bartholomew Wormsloe would like nothing better than to see me hanged, I'd wager."

Zeke pursed his lips. "Mm-hmm, if this Wormsloe is working for vampires, it might explain why you haven't heard of him in a while."

He clapped his hands together and declared, "You have had warning of them now, something they are unaware of. Therefore, you have the advantage. Now you need to get on about your business with Rosalia. Just remember, she has her father's wiles."

☠

Once they were back aboard the *Incubus*, the fog lifted, and Hell's Breath Island was nowhere to be seen. They also were no longer in the same part of the ocean.

"Land ho!" cried the lookout. It was obviously not an island. They were about a half-day's sailing out of a good-sized bay with a port town.

Viktor sent Lazarus to scout it out and started to laugh at what he saw through the raven's eyes.

"What is it, Captain?" Grimm asked.

"Zeke dropped us at our destination. That's Juchitán we're approaching."

Chapter 32

Rosalia stood on the roof of her cantina and frowned. There had been an unnatural fog on the bay for most of the morning. It reeked of an ancient magic she had hoped never to encounter again.

As the fog gradually lifted, she thought she caught a glimpse of a rocky island where no island had been before, but it vanished with the fog. Anyone else that had seen it would merely think it a mirage.

She knew better. Hell's Breath Island had invaded her territory briefly and carried the Elder with it.

One thing new did not fade away as the weather cleared. A warship approached the harbor, but it flew no colors. As the Elder's magic faded, another, much younger, presence made itself known, along with a second, old but not ancient, magic that smelled strongly of brine.

Brandewyne had returned, and he had a sea witch with him. This made her both curious and apprehensive. The sea witch could interfere with her plan to snare the living vampire. She would have to proceed cautiously.

☠

Once again Viktor left Zach in charge of the ship and crew. This time, however, he gave strict orders to remain at anchor. The men were disappointed that they had to stay on board, but a fresh round of the blood-tainted liquor kept them in line.

Zeke wasn't the only one who didn't trust Rosalia. Viktor wasn't about to risk her taking his crew. The few who went ashore with him made sure to eat and drink before they left the ship. With a fresh supply of devil's hoof, she would be able to work her entrapment spells again.

Only Viktor, Grimm, Jon-Jon and Belladonna went ashore. As the only one of the group with absolutely no residual magic, Jon-Jon was chosen to tote the keg of peppers and honey for the exchange.

A wall of people stood before them when they reached the cantina. At first, they thought they would be blocked from entering, but the crowd parted just enough for them to pass single file. Grimm and Jon-Jon worried about how they would get back out.

Rosalia greeted them in the dining room. She sat in a chair on a dais at the end of the room. Flowers, terra cotta figurines and what appeared to be mummified hands lay scattered at her feet. A closer look revealed the "hands" to be some sort of roots.

Viktor and Belladonna felt the raw magic that filled the room. It was strong enough to make their skin crawl. Even Grimm looked uncomfortable.

"Welcome back, Captain Brandewyne. Did you find the devil's hoof?"

"I did. I have returned from the far side of the world to deliver it and complete our bargain."

"Let me see your hands." It seemed an odd request, but Viktor wasn't entirely surprised by it. He remembered the warning not to touch the flesh or seeds of the peppers that the Bengali village elder had given them.

She frowned. "I do not believe you found it. Your hands are unmarred."

"We cut the stems. Only one of my men got burned by the peppers. He remained aboard the ship to oversee the crew." He deliberately left out the fact that Belle had healed Zach and prevented him from losing his eyesight. He reasoned that she didn't need to know about the siren's healing powers.

"Why do I not sense the devil's hoof? I see the cask your man carries, but I feel no magic from it." The Sister continued to argue with him, obviously a further test.

Belled smiled knowingly and mentally communicated with the vampire through their blood bond. *"She knows damn well there is no magic in the peppers or the honey themselves. They are merely ingredients for spells or conduits for power."*

"The peppers have not been used, *Tia* Rosalia," Viktor stated aloud. "They await your magic to infuse them."

The Sister narrowed her eyes at Belladonna. "You are helping him, sea witch. I know it, but I do not know how or why."

"If you can't figure that out, perhaps you aren't as powerful as we thought." Belle shrugged.

"I am more powerful than you imagine. Why, this one was ready to bed me when my supply of devil's hoof was almost exhausted."

Before Viktor could add that she had rebuffed him, which would have strengthened her claim of power, Belladonna shrugged. "There have been days when I'd swear he'd fuck anything he could catch."

Jon-Jon and Grimm had to bite their lips to keep from chuckling at the remark. Viktor might permit the siren to speak about him like that, but he would take it as a sign of disrespect if either of them had uttered it, even if it was partially true.

It made Rosalia even more catty. She hissed and guessed, "And yet, I do not believe he has ever bedded you."

Viktor immediately placed himself between the two females. "Go outside and wait for us, Belle." He put just enough power into the command to ensure the irate siren's obedience.

"Hmm, perhaps I was wrong. You are very quick to defend her."

His reply as Belle left the cantina mollified the siren somewhat. "I wasn't protecting her. You can't help me and conclude our bargain if she kills you over petty jealousy."

"How can you be so sure the sea-witch would be victorious?" Rosalia remained irked.

"I'm not, but I do know you would have to answer to the Elder if you killed Belladonna. He assigned her to help me find the Sisters." He shrugged and smirked.

As he'd expected, the implied threat cooled her ire. "Very well, let me see what you have brought."

He nodded, and Jon-Jon set the cask down and popped the lid on it. When he stepped back, she stood and looked down into the keg. She stooped and dipped her bare hand into it and pulled out a small pepper.

Honey coated her hand. It was the only reason Viktor could think of for why she wasn't burned when she crushed it in her fist. She sniffed at the contents of her palm and stuck out her tongue. She touched the very tip of it to the pepper-infused honey. Her eyes fluttered shut, and she gave an almost sexual moan. When she opened her eyes, her pupils had dilated to the point that her eyes appear pure black.

"This is still fresh." She gave a throaty chuckle. "What I have received in the past was over a year old by the time it arrived and had nowhere near this much honey with it. You have exceeded my expectations, Viktor Brandewyne. Allow me to reward you."

She glided over to him and reached up in an attempt to dab some honey on his lips. The raw magic she wielded sent a wave of lust crashing over every male in the room. Not even Viktor was immune to it.

His reaction, however, wasn't what she expected. One thing he could not tolerate was someone trying to manipulate him. He grasped her wrist and stopped her hand a mere fraction from his mouth. He still remembered the strength of the enslaving spell she'd tried on him before. This felt much stronger, and he was having none of it.

"A reward is not necessary, *Tia* Rosalia." He smiled and his voice remained deceptively calm and civil. Both his crewmates recognized the signs of Bloody Vik Brandee at his deadliest. "My time is short. I have brought what you requested. Now I need you to deliver what you promised."

It irritated her that he'd thwarted her, but she didn't want to show it. She returned his smile. "As you wish."

He released her wrist, and she stepped away from him, damping her magic in the process.

She took a blue cloth and wiped the honey and pepper from her hand. Then, she retrieved an onyx mortar and pestle from the items scattered about her chair. She set them on the table and took a silver ladle to dip three honey-covered peppers out of the cask. Once she deposited them in the mortar dish, she placed the ladle back in the cask.

She pulled a small pair of silver scissors from the pocket of her skirts. She pulled a pin from her hair which allowed the braids coiled atop her head to drape down her back. She pulled one of the knee-length black braids around and snipped some tiny fragments from the end. She dropped the clippings into the mortar.

She crushed the peppers with the pestle and mixed it all into a thick paste. Once satisfied with the consistency, she looked back at the vampire.

"Give me the vial."

Viktor slipped the chain over his head and handed the vial to Jon-Jon who carried it to Rosalia. She frowned but took it and opened the cap. After she rolled the pestle around in the paste until it was well-coated, she held it over the open vial.

The paste was not as thick as Viktor had thought. It took a few minutes, but eventually a droplet formed and broke free to join the previous contents of the vial. A small flash shot up as it did.

Rosalia replaced the cap, and Jon-Jon held out his hand for it. She shook her head. "No, I must hand it directly to Viktor Brandewyne."

He grunted and motioned for his second mate to step back.

She handed him the vial with her right hand while she held his hand steady with her left.

He immediately felt the warmth and stickiness where she'd rubbed some of the pepper/honey paste on the back of his hand. His eyes flared emerald as his power reacted to the spell.

She stared up at him as she held onto him. Once again, her eyes dilated. Not only did they look black, but there seemed to be flames dancing in their depths. Awareness of anyone else in the room, or even the room itself, faded away.

The vampire and the Sister of Power stood alone in a dark space. Nothing but each other was visible. Viktor raised an eyebrow at the fact that their clothes seemed to have vanished along with everyone and everything else.

Rosalia smiled up at him. Her voice sounded just as spicy and sweet as he imagined the pepper honey tasted. "I know why you seek the Sisters, Viktor Brandewyne. Once you have visited all the others, return to me. Long have I sought a consort worthy of my heritage and power. You are the One, but you do not have to be a puppet of the Elder. He knows that once the curse is lifted, the final decision of who receives the power of the Sisters lies with you and you alone. Return to me, and I will see to it that you want for nothing."

She finally released his hand, and they were once again fully clothed and in the cantina. He suspected that they had never physically left.

He slipped the chain of the vial back over his head and tucked it into his shirt. In the process, his hand brushed against the Elder's crystal. In a flash, the spell shattered, but with no outward sign to alert the Sister.

He remembered Zeke warned him that Rosalia was very much her father's daughter. He also remembered that the old *brujo* in the mountains above Vera Cruz had told him she was once known by another name, Blancaflor, and that she was the devil's daughter.

He leaned down as if to kiss her but stopped just short of it. In a whisper only she could hear, he said, "I will remember your words, Blancaflor."

Gratified by her reaction to the use of her true name, he continued, "Yes, I know who and what you are, but I don't think you fully understand who or what I truly am. Know this, devil's daughter; I am no one's consort or puppet, nor will I be. I have what I need from you now. Pray that our paths never cross again. If you ever try to ensnare me with your magic again, it will not end well for you."

Then, he did kiss her, savagely, and cut his own lips on his fangs. He made sure some of the blood entered her mouth. She began to struggle, but he was too strong for her to escape. When he did release her, she fell back to the floor, sitting down hard and gracelessly. She even scrambled back from him some.

He smirked and turned his back on her and nodded to his mates. Together, they left the cantina. Grimm and Jon-Jon watched his back.

Rosalia sent all of her minions about their business and retreated to the small grotto hidden beneath her cantina.

She stayed there for days as she prepared the remainder of the devil's hoof and mulled over her plans. The small taste Viktor had given her of his power unnerved her.

The peppers he had brought her were the most potent she'd ever worked with, but she was unsure if any trace of her spell on the vampire remained. He truly was the One, the agent that would bring change to her world.

By the time she reemerged, she'd convinced herself that her spell had been prepared too hastily. When or if he returned, she would be ready for him.

She would have to be cautious, however. He was alert to her wiles now, and he was powerful enough to do serious damage to her and her magic. She thought it worth the gamble that he still wouldn't be fully aware of or in command of his true potential.

If he was, it could mean the end, not only of her hopes and plans, but her very existence.

Chapter 33

Viktor and his mates gathered in the captain's cabin. Charts lay spread all over the table as they discussed the next course of action.

"Unless we get news of a Sister elsewhere," Vik looked pointedly at the siren, "I say we head South and thread the Straits. Hunting is poor here, and it's quicker than going west, back across the Pacific."

"You know the price for my visions." Belle didn't even blink. "But you need to hunt first, and soon. All the supplies are low, and I prefer my meat healthy and well-fed."

Grimm laughed. "You had me worried for a minute there, lass. I almost thought you actually cared about us."

She bared her needle teeth at him in a mock smile. Zach was the only one present who wasn't accustomed to her occasional displays. The sight of dozens of sharp teeth in a mouth that could stretch ear-to-ear made him shudder.

His reaction caught her attention and spurred her predatory tendency to want to play with her food. "Does my smile bother you, Zach?" she purred and put a fraction of her seductive powers into her voice.

Grimm changed the subject to distract her. The young man had proven useful and valuable, and the first mate wanted to keep him intact. "What happened between you and Rosalia, Captain?"

"You were there, Hezekiah."

"Aye, but that doesn't mean I understood what I saw. For a full five minutes, the two of you seemed oblivious to the rest of the world. Then, there was that kiss. I don't think I've ever seen a woman react to you like that."

"Like what?" Belle's tone sounded more harpy than siren.

Viktor's glare at his first mate showed his gratitude for directing her ire at him, but it held no real threat. He sighed and faced the siren. "I scared the hell out of her."

"You frightened a Sister of Power?"

Jon-Jon nodded confirmation. "When he let her go, she fell down and crab-walked back from him. The look on her face said he would already have been back here on the ship, if she'd been capable of wishing him so."

Viktor had to laugh at his second mate's observation. "Trust you to recognize that look, Jon-Jon. I'm sure you've seen it often enough to memorize it, and you don't even have to kiss 'em to earn it."

"They just can't handle my manly beauty."

All the men laughed, although Zach's laughter was a bit bemused. He still hadn't been with them long enough to truly feel a part of the camaraderie.

Belladonna refused to be distracted. "How could a kiss frighten a Sister?"

"A drop of blood and a push of power to accompany it." The vampire smiled grimly and never dropped eye contact with the siren.

Belle's eyes dilated as her body prepared to flee. She felt his shields drop and his full power revealed as he made the statement. It served as a sobering reminder that he was just as much of a predator as she was. She had to fight herself to keep from reacting like prey. She wasn't entirely successful.

Her reaction coupled with her earlier mention of the need to hunt brought his predatory nature to the fore. His Hunger was not unmanageable yet. Rather, she fired a lower hunger. It had been months since he'd had a woman.

"Viktor?" Belle remained wary when he advanced on her.

When he didn't answer, she took his mood to mean he saw her as food at the moment. She knew she couldn't allow that. Her blood was toxic to him. A single drop could kill him.

He saw she intended to run. He didn't give her the chance. Faster than anyone could see, he pinned her against the wall. She gave a small grunt as the impact with the wood knocked the air out of her.

If they hadn't been more worried about their own safety, Zach's reaction would have amused Grimm and Jon-Jon. Even though he'd been disturbed by the glimpse of part of her true form, his first instinct was to worry about her safety.

"Miss Belladonna! Are you alright?"

Grimm knew his captain well enough to recognize the precarious situation their navigator was about to place himself in. "She can handle herself, boy."

Zach was about to protest, which could easily draw the vampire's ire.

Before he could speak or Grimm could stop him, Viktor ordered, "You three, out."

Grimm and Jon-Jon grabbed the young man and pulled him out of the cabin with them. Once they were out and the door closed, the first mate growled, "If you want to keep breathing, learn to not try to get between the Captain and what he wants, especially when he's in that mood."

"Aye," Jon-Jon confirmed. "Not even the Reaper here or I am safe from him killing us if he thinks we've crossed him in the smallest way. They don't call him Bloody Vik Brandee for nothing."

Zach Brumble visibly gulped as the full import of that revelation sank in.

Belle was pleasantly surprised by his kiss. She'd been tensed to keep him from biting her. She had to throw her own power at him to keep from drowning in the wash of his, however.

Viktor's power had grown considerably, and she sensed there was still a great untapped potential in him. Unlike Rosalia, however, it didn't frighten her. It excited her. The siren had begun to come to terms with the fact that the living vampire could master her. And she'd started to realize and appreciate the benefits that could come with that.

They were both nearly naked, when a knock came at the door.

"Go away, Hezekiah," Viktor growled as he recognized his first mate's scent through the door.

"Hell's Breath, Captain," Grimm called back. He knew he had taken a chance with his life. Nothing short of this could have impelled him to interrupt Viktor's sport.

Belle expressed her ire with a low growling scream and slammed her head against the wall in frustration.

"God. Damn. It!" Vik spat.

They both re-dressed and headed for the deck. Everyone gave them a wide berth.

Fog surrounded the ship. The island was barely visible. Jon-Jon already had some of the lads readying a boat for the captain.

They spotted movement in the water and heard a strange mewling, crying sound. A closer look showed what appeared to be a small child in the water.

Viktor quickly gave the order to use one of the cargo nets to scoop the boy up and lift him to the deck. Several of the men gaped at the revelation that the child was a mer. They were even more astonished when, about halfway to the deck, his tail split and reformed into legs.

The transformation seemed to frighten the child. He screamed and started to cry. Belle proved she was almost as fast as Viktor. She moved from beside him to next to where the crewmen were lowering the net faster than most could see.

As soon as the net was clear, she stepped in and scooped the child up. She cradled him to her side and made soothing noises. The boy hiccupped as his sobs subsided. He grabbed one of her braids and started to chew on it.

"Damn," Grimm said, shocked. "I thought she was going to eat him. I've never seen her move that fast out of the water."

"I know. Belladonna isn't exactly the maternal type, but I'm not surprised by her behavior."

"You've seen her do this before? Is that her child? He changed like she does."

Viktor shook his head. He wore a strange smile Grimm wasn't sure how to read. "No, he's my son. Remember that mermaid I caught when we were dealing with Dorada?"

"Then I'm really surprised she didn't eat him. I recall her saying mermaid was her favorite food."

"She knows better." His tone left no doubt about that. "Besides, the whelp has some very potent magic. Our Belle is bewitched."

The siren had finally gotten the child calmed and carried him over to the captain and first mate. He looked like he'd grown another inch since Viktor first saw him on Hell's Breath. He wondered if that was what he'd looked like at that age.

"Is the transformation that painful?"

"Not really," Belle answered. "It does itch a little the first few times, but I suspect it frightens him. He is the first of his kind, and the instincts he inherited from his mother didn't prepare him for it. Pure mers cannot change shape."

"What's that around his neck?" Grimm started to reach for what looked like a glass tube on a cord. He recoiled quickly at the siren's warning growl.

Viktor eased it off the child's neck. She watched him warily but seemed to accept that he meant no harm to the child.

He opened the vial and pulled out a scrap of parchment with a note scrawled on it. It read: *Boy's too big to stay here. He's too curious. If he's too much for you to handle, take him to Celie or Glory. They're the only two I'd trust him with and that can handle him.*

"What does it say?" Grimm asked.

"To deliver the boy to either Celie or Gloribeau."

"No!" Belle clutched the child to her.

Her reaction startled Grimm, but Vik had half-expected it. "It has to be done, pet. A ship is no place for the boy. There are too many ways for him to get hurt." His tone was amazingly tolerant and patient.

The first mate looked back and forth between his captain and the siren. Neither was behaving normally, in his opinion. He secretly agreed with Zeke's note. He saw the child as disruptive and a potential weakness for his captain. The one thing that had kept Viktor alive more than anything else was that nothing and no one was more important to Viktor than Viktor. It looked as if this mer-child could change that.

Belladonna continued to argue and plead to be allowed to keep the boy. "I'll take care of him, I promise. I can keep him safe."

Viktor shook his head and reached up to caress her cheek in an effort to comfort and calm her. "His magic is too strong, Belle, and it's only going to get stronger. The longer you're with him, the harder it's going to be to let him go. He needs to be with someone who can train him."

At that moment, the baby started to cry. The more she tried to shush him, the louder he got. "What's wrong with him? She asked in frustration as the child squirmed in her arms.

Viktor saw he was trying to reposition himself to get at her breast. He chuckled and said, "My guess would be that he's hungry."

The toddler screeched as she tried to keep him on her hip. He reached as far as he could. He slapped at the nearest breast until he finally caught a handful of it and shirt. He squeezed and tugged with an insistent whine.

"Ow!"

She thrust the child at his father, who took him a bit awkwardly. Grimm could barely suppress his grin at the sight. To keep Vik from seeing his smirk, he volunteered. "I'll go see if we've got any nanny goats or at least some buttermilk aboard."

"If not, we need to find a prize or a port soon," Viktor called after the obviously fleeing first mate. "It's going to be a long trip around and through the Straits."

"No, it isn't." Belle contradicted him.

"I know you can give us favorable winds, pet, but that is still a lot of ocean to cover."

"Look around, Captain. Hell's Breath has saved us the trip. We are in the Gulf of Mexico. I recognize the color of the water and the taste of the air. If my senses are right, we are close to land, as well. The breeze smells faintly like Havana."

He sniffed the air and realized she was right. Now that the fog had lifted and the island was gone, he could see that the water did look different.

He looked up at the sky to get his bearings then bellowed out, "Mr. Brumble, set us a course southeast. Full sail."

The navigator gave him an "aye" and relayed the order to the riggers.

The child settled down to a hiccupping whine at the sound of the shout. He gazed up at the man that held him with large eyes. Then, he spotted Viktor's goatee and reached for it with a burble.

"Ow," Vik grunted, momentarily caught off guard. He smiled. "You are a strong one, boy."

He glanced over at the siren. She looked like she wanted to take the toddler back. He thought about his options and made a decision.

"We'll lay in supplies in Havana then head for New Orleans."

"Why there?"

"Mother Celie has already had to deal with raising me. It wouldn't be fair to thrust this one on her, as well. Besides, New Orleans is closer, and if the lad's magic is similar to yours in any way, Glory's bayou magic will mute it and make him more manageable. Celie is surrounded by salt marsh."

Belle mulled it over then sighed in resignation. "You're right, but I still don't like it."

"You'll get over it, pet. Ah, Mr. Grimm, I see you found something to feed him."

The first mate nodded but looked puzzled over which one to hand the leather flask to. Viktor smirked and handed the child back to the siren. He nodded for Grimm to give her the flask.

The sight of her face as it lit up when she fed his son sent an odd sensation through the vampire. When Belle took the lad below, he muttered to Grimm, "The sooner the boy is off my ship, the better."

Grimm kept his silence, but he heartily agreed.

Tamara A. Lowery

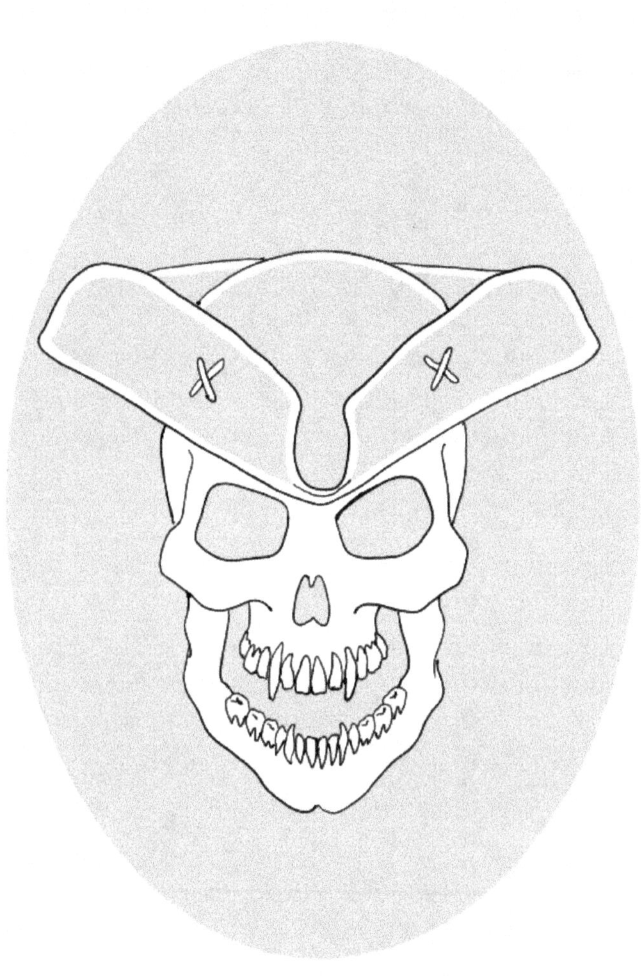

Tamara A. Lowery

Afterword / Bibliography

Thank you for reading this book and hopefully the rest of the series. I hope you have had as much fun reading it as I had writing it. This book, in particular, steered me to some interesting research and reading. Never underestimate the wealth of plot fodder to be found int the juvenile section of your local library.

To read the story of Blancaflor, check out the book *Fiesta Feminina, Celebrating Women in Mexican Folktale* by Mary-Joan Gerson, Barefoot Books, New York copyright 2001, p.34-45.

Or "Rosalie" in *The Monkey's Haircut* by John Bierhorst, William Morrow Co., New York Copyright 1986.

I paraphrased the story of Daskin Rey and Bonobibi from an account of the folktale given in *The Man-Eating Tigers of Sundarbans* by Sy Montgomery, Houghton Mifflin Co., Copyright 2001, p.37-38.

Tamara A. Lowery

Here be Spoilers

Blood Curse:

After being shipwrecked by a British Navy ship and a killer hurricane, Bloody Vik Brandee and the survivors of his crew make shore in the fishing village of Terra Beau on the north coast of Hispañola. While waiting for a suitable ship to steal, he kills a local boy over a tavern wench, incurring the wrath of Mamaan Juma.

Juma sends her zombies to fetch the pirate. She curses him to become a living vampire. The tavern wench, Carmella, becomes his first victim.

Vik returns to his home port, Savannah, and learns from his foster mother Celie, aka the Thunderbolt Witch, just what has happened to him and how to break the curse before it destroys him. While there, Jim Rigger, his first mate, becomes his second victim. Celie resurrects Jim as a black cat which can take the form of a raven.

Celie sets Vik to find the seven Sisters of Power and sends hum to Hell's Breath Island to Uncle Zeke, an ancient wizard of sorts. Zeke sends the siren/sea witch Belladonna with him to locate the Sisters using her visions.

She pinpoints Madre Dorada on the Isle of Youth. En route, Vik learns an old friend, Hezekiah Grimm aka the Grimm Reaper, has been taken by pirate hunters in Havana. He detours to rescue Grimm despite warnings from Zeke and Belladonna not to stray from his course

Manages to find and rescue Grimm but arrives at the Isle of Youth only to find Dorada fled. With the aid of Paella, a local girl, he manages to track the Sister down and brokers a deal with her: one of her golden tears in exchange for an opal pendant called the Mermaid's Tear.

After some misunderstanding of what the Tear actually is, he finds it, helps Dorada regain her magic, and makes the exchange.

Demon Bayou:

Viktor tracks the next Sister, Granny Glory, to the bayous north of New Orleans. When he finds her, she sets him to capture the demon Tulimanchulo, who possesses the body of a white alligator. He finds and captures the beast with a magic cast-net but is wounded in the process.

Glory slaughters the demon gator, collects its blood in a cauldron, and has Viktor remove all its teeth. She throws them in the blood and pulls them out as a necklace. Viktor must take it to Zeke. She warns him not to wear it at any time. She then has him toss her into the boiling blood. The hag emerges as a beautiful woman.

On Hell's Breath, Zeke burns the alligator teeth, releasing the demon's spirit. He fishes out a coal from his fire and puts it in a conch shell for Vik to return it to Glory with instructions no one else is to touch it and not to let it extinguish.

Vik returns to New Orleans and discovers a storm has altered the paths through the bayous.

While waiting for a guide back to Glory, he encounters true vampires for the first time. He ends up tangled in the local vampire politics because of attacks on two of his favorite brothels, one by agents of the Church, and the other by vampires curious about him. To get out of this predicament, he must kidnap the daughter of the Lord

Mayor and make her vampire. This gives Jeorge, king of the local vampires, a means to spy on him.

On his final return to Glory, Belladonna begins to grow weak as the Sister's black water magic wars with the siren's salt water magic. She falls unconscious into the swamp but does not change into her true form. Vik must remove the coal and place it in his mouth to protect it before he can dive in after Belladonna. He knows she'll drown if she remains in human form. When he surfaces with her, the boat with his other companions is no longer in the area. He climbs out onto a hammock of land and Glory appears to him. He passes the coal to her via a kiss, returning the powers the demon stole from her ages earlier. She adds her spit to the golden tear of Dorada in the silver vial Vik carries for that purpose.

He returns Belladonna to the sea and sacrifices several of his crew to her appetite to restore her. He then abducts a couple of unwary sailors from port to swap for Grimm and Jon-Jon, rescuing them from Glory's amorous clutches, as he's learned she now has the nature of a succubus.

Tamara A. Lowery

About the Author

Tamara A. Lowery, who once considered herself close to becoming a Crazy Cat Lady is now down to three cats. She lives with them and her husband in Tennessee and builds cars to pay the bills when not writing. She's been writing since the early 1980s but only published since 2011.

In addition to the Waves of Darkness series, she is the author of a steampunk episodic serial, The Adventures of Pigg & Woolfe.

She hopes to release a short story collection sometime in the near future, as well.

Website: talowery.wordpress.com

Facebook: facebook.com/Waves.of.Darkness

Instagram: Instagram.com/talowery_author

Plurk: plurk.com/Viksbelle

Smashwords author Page:
smashwords.com/profile/view/Viksbelle

Tamara A. Lowery
YouTube: youtube.com/user/Viksbelle

Waves of Darkness

Sisters of Power arc

Blood Curse

Demon Bayou

Silent Fathoms *November 2022*

Black Venom *May 2023*

Hell's Dodo *November 2023*

The Daedalus Enigma *May 2024*

Maelstrom of Fate *November 2024*

Daughters of the Dragon arc

Hunting the Dragon *(still in draft)*

The Adventures of Pigg & Woolfe

Season 1

The Girl Who Fell from the Sky (S.1 omnibus)

Episodes

A Chance Encounter

The Truce

In the Woolfe's Den

Chase the Lightning

Peril in the Philippines

Tamara A. Lowery

Rendezvous in Hong Kong

Double Jeopardy

Chance and Fortune

The Italian Connection

Rescue at Sea

Ghost Riders in the Sky

Castle in the Clouds

Season 2

S.2 Omnibus (Title TBD) *Coming January 2023*

Episodes

Airborne Alliance

Under the Mountain

Reversal of Fortune

Frustrations

Going Underground

Evade and Elude

Escape

Sanctuary

Message in a Bottle

Strange Bedfellows

Family Reunion

Berthing Assignments *December 2022*

Season 3 2023

S.3 Omnibus (Title TBD) *Coming January 2024*

Silent Fathoms

Episodes

The Canary Has Flown *January 2023*

Truth and Consequences *February 2023*

Detective Work *March 2023*

Family Secrets *April 2023*

Organizing a Fox Hunt *May 2023*

Divided Forces Part I *June 2023*

Divided Forces Part II *July 2023*

Queen of the Nile *August 2023*

Foiled Again *September 2023*

Doom in Khartoum *October 2023*

Fly Me Away *November 2023*

The Fall of Tunilia *December 2023*

Season 4 2024

Tamara A. Lowery